Trying to shut her mind to all that was going on around her, Molly went back to her bed, ready to sink her head into her pillow for a cat nap. Despite everything she had said, in a strange kind of a way she would miss this place with its peculiar mix of people, miss little walks in the grounds . . .

She decided to put it out of her mind. She had a lot of thinking to do – and a lot of planning. She was going to have to choose exactly the right day and the right time for her belongings to be moved from the house to the flat. But it would be worth it. At last she would be free of the abusive man she had married out of loneliness. Molly could hardly believe that it was not a dream and could hardly wait to begin her new life in Wanstead. She couldn't remember being this relaxed and happy in a very long time, if ever. All that she could hope was that it wouldn't go wide of the mark, and could hardly wait for her son to come and get her.

Sally Worboyes was born and grew up in Stepney with four brothers and a sister. She now lives in Norfolk with her family. The author of eighteen previous novels, she has also written plays for TV and radio, and adapted her own play and novel, *Wild Hops*, as a musical, *The Hop-Pickers*.

Also by Sally Worboyes

NOVELS

Wild Hops
Docker's Daughter
The Dinner Lady
Red Sequins
Keep on Dancing
Down Stepney Way
Over Bethnal Green
Whitechapel Mary
At the Mile End Gate
Banished from Bow
Girl from Brick Lane
Down by Tobacco Dock
Where Sparrows Nest
Time Will Tell
Jamaica Street
Room for a Lodger
Lipstick & Powder
Handbags & Gladrags
Valentine Moon

MEMOIR

East End Girl

Valentine Moon

Sally Worboyes

An Orion paperback

First published in Great Britain in 2009
by Orion
This paperback edition published in 2010
by Orion Books Ltd,
Orion House, 5 Upper St Martin's Lane,
London WC2H 9EA

An Hachette UK company

A CIP catalogue record for this book is available
from the British Library.

Typeset at The Spartan Press Ltd,
Lymington, Hants

Printed and bound in Great Britain by
Clays Ltd, St Ives plc

The Orion Publishing Group's policy is to use papers that
are natural, renewable and recyclable products and made
from wood grown in sustainable forests. The logging and
manufacturing processes are expected to conform to the
environmental regulations of the country of origin.

www.orionbooks.co.uk

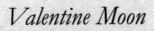

Valentine Moon

Chapter One

1960

On a warm and pleasant Saturday afternoon in July, seventeen-year-old Patsy Lamb, a natural blonde with pale green eyes, was standing on the wide and worn polished pine floorboards of Hobbins & Son Grocers carefully analysing her shopping list. Oblivious to the conversations going on around her, she was trying to fathom what her mother, Alice, had written on the back of a used envelope but could hardly make head nor tail of it.

The writing, a touch indecipherable to say the least, was the reason why Patsy was unaware of the blather of the other customers. The store was full of local people discussing what they had heard through the grapevine about the changes taking place in the area. Shops and characterful pubs in London's East End, which had stood there for half a century or more, were now on the list of timeworn buildings to be demolished. These friendly establishments were going to have to make way for new developments that were being planned.

The background banter made little difference to Patsy, who shopped for her mother every fourth

Saturday when she herself didn't have to go into the local hairdressing salon where she worked as a stylist. She was of course quite used to hearing gossip while she was busy snipping and cutting hair, so the present tittle-tattle simply floated above her head – after all, she had been shopping in this store for her mother since she was eight years old and there had always been gossip that the place, along with the other shops in this narrow back-turning of decrepit two-storey buildings, was going to be demolished. But now they were all but staring into the face of the bulldozer: a tiny shoe shop, a family-run tobacconist, a fish and chip establishment and a small doll-making factory; the time for their demise had finally come.

Nor was it just this street. It seemed the whole of this little corner in the heart of Tower Hamlets was changing fast. Several of the narrow backstreets and terraced almshouses were gone, as well as the local blacksmith, the ironmonger and a cobbler's shop. And it was the same all around the East End of London and its winding backstreets down by the river Thames, where old-fashioned terraces were giving way to low and high-rise blocks of flats and company offices.

The much talked about time of change had finally arrived and, on the whole, the locals were pleased with the promise of improvements that modernisation would bring. Most people were fed up with having to live in damp old houses and they now wanted a taste of luxury. They dreamt of wall-to-wall carpets for comfort and picture windows for light.

Patsy's parents, however, had been lucky. They had

rented the same house from the day they had married some twenty years since, and were just as happy now as they had been on the day they moved into their lovely home. They had been in the right place at the right time when they visited the housing association office a month after their wedding. Not only had they been allocated the house of their dreams, but one with a lovely spacious walled garden at the back, and they were more than content. Theirs was a two-bedroom solid Victorian terraced house that not only had gas at the turn of a switch but electricity as well, and even the luxury of an inside lavatory instead of the more usual one in the back yard.

So intent was Patsy on her mother's shopping list that she hadn't noticed Danny McDonald, the tall, blond and handsome young shop assistant, looking at her admiringly. But then, in his beige button-up shop-keeper's coat, he all but faded into the background. She had seen him before when shopping in there and had smiled shyly back when he had smiled at her, but what she didn't know was that the nineteen-year-old had been teased about how he went all soppy whenever she came into the shop, and had done from the day he first set eyes on her.

Two of Danny's colleagues, who served behind the cold meat and cheese counter, had enjoyed egging the lad on to ask the girl out on a date. Now even the manager of the store had encouraged him to make a move. He knew that Danny was smitten with the girl and had teased him on and off since he came to work there two months before. Today though, the lad had made up his own mind that he would ask her out. He was going to ask her if she would like to go with him to a dance, a Scottish Catholic do that was to be held in a hall just south of the river where his family lived. He had been building up to this moment for a week.

Patsy, still preoccupied with trying to fathom her mother's scribble, hadn't picked up on the joshing that was quietly going on around her. She finally managed to make sense of everything and, once her supplies had been wrapped, packed into her shopping bag and paid for, she smiled at the assistant who had served her, thanked him, and made for the door. On her way out she heard Danny call her name and assumed that the shop manager, who had known her since she was knee high to a grashopper, had told him who she was. She turned to face Danny, who was now almost by her side and smiling shyly at her. 'I'm Danny McDonald,' he said. 'Excuse me for calling out like that but I've got something to ask you,' he said, quickly adding, 'I just wondered if you'd like to come to a dance with me a week from today, next Saturday? If you're not doing anything, that is.'

Taken aback by his sudden approach, Patsy smiled tentatively and felt the blood rise in her cheeks. 'Well . . . on Saturdays . . . I usually go out with my friends to one of the local dance halls but—'

'Well, I would invite them as well,' Danny replied, 'but it's tickets only and they've all but sold out. And you're going out dancing tonight then, are you? With

4

your friends? If not we could maybe meet up for a coffee and I'll explain more about the dance I'm inviting you to.'

'I'm not going out tonight, no. The friend I was going with has got a sore throat . . . and anyway, I've got things at home to catch up on.'

'Fair enough, but if you can't go for a coffee tonight, would you like to go to the dance with me next week then?' He smiled, then glanced over his shoulder to see if the others he worked alongside were watching him and taking the mickey. The manager winked at him and gave him a supportive smile.

Patsy could hardly keep up with this lad whose smile was warming those parts of her that the sun didn't shine on. Apart from anything else he reminded her of Adam Faith – her heartthrob. The pop singer's picture cut out from a magazine took pride of place on her bedroom wall.

'I'm not sure. Is it all right if I let you know on Monday, on my way home from work? I finish early, so I could pop in here then.'

'That sounds good. Well, I'd better go, I don't want to upset any customers. I'm meant to be working.' He glanced over his shoulder again. 'I'll see you then. I'll keep a look out for you. See what your parents think about it in the meantime.'

'My parents?' She wondered what he could be thinking. 'I don't have to ask them. I don't have to get permission.'

'Well, you might when I tell you where it is. South of the river. And by the time the dance is over there won't

5

be any buses or trains running . . . it's being held in a hall and it won't end 'til after midnight.'

'Oh,' said Patsy, thrown by this little bit of information. It did change things. She shrugged. 'I'm not so sure . . . I don't think I'd want to come home that late at night by myself and my parents would be none too pleased about it either. And a taxi would cost the earth after midnight.'

'Well, I was going to say . . . you'd be more than welcome to stay at our house. It's a big old-fashioned place and there's plenty of room. Mum and Dad share it with a couple of aunts as well as my grandparents. And your mum knows me. She's always in and out on her way to work or coming back in the afternoons. Ask her and then ask your dad. Maybe she'll be able to sway him if he's a bit unsure.'

This was going a little bit too fast for Patsy. She hardly had time to think. 'You've only been working here for a few weeks,' she said, 'and yet you sound as if you know my family. How come?'

'I wouldn't say that I know them well, but . . . I saw you, and – er – then I asked questions. One of the guys pointed your mum out to me when she came in and we got chatting. The manager reckons that the way to a girl's heart is through her mother.' He offered a hopeful smile.

'Oh does he? Right . . . well, I'll see if Mum agrees to my staying out all night. I can't imagine my dad going for it though.' She glanced from him to the guys who were serving behind the counter and saw that they were deliberately politely looking the other way.

6

'I'll tell you what I'll do,' said Patsy, all thoughtful. 'I'll broach it to Mum and Dad later on today, and pop in on Monday like I said, and give you a yes or no. If that's all right . . . ?'

'Of course it is,' said Danny. 'And don't look so nervous. I don't bite.'

'I'm not nervous,' she said quickly. 'You've caught me on the hop, that's all. Anyway, you'd best get back behind the counter, that queue's growing.' She smiled back and left the store, her mind working overtime. Staying out all night and sleeping in a strange house with people she didn't know would be a first, but Danny seemed nice – easy to talk to – and handsome too.

Having left school at the age of fifteen to work full time as a junior trainee in a local hairdressing salon Patsy was a touch lonely. Her three best friends, who she had grown up with, going to youth clubs then, later, to dance halls in and around the area, were all now courting. She had been on dates but none of the lads had set her heart on fire. Now, today, Danny had sent a few sparks flying. Not only was he tall, blond and handsome, but not in the least bit pushy. If anything, he seemed a bit shy of her – nothing like the cocky Jack-the-lad types that she was used to – and that made a nice change.

On her walk home, smiling and wrapped in her thoughts, trying to imagine the dance and what it might be like, she strolled past the Charrington brewery and was brought back into the here and now by the soft jovial voice of Ritchie, her favourite cousin. 'Once a daydreamer always a daydreamer,' he said.

Snapping back into the real world, she smiled back at him. 'Sorry Ritch – I was miles away.'

'On a slow boat to China with Adam Faith no doubt?'

'No, as it so happens, I wasn't. But wouldn't chance be a fine thing. How's your mum?'

'A lot better now. She's still a bit under the weather but over the pleurisy. She's a bit miffed with you, though. Her favourite in the family and you never came to visit after work.'

'Well, you tell her that I'll be there soon. She still likes Milk Tray doesn't she?'

'I hope so. She's had four little boxes bought for 'er all in all. Buy her a bottle of Lucozade instead. That'll perk 'er up.' Ritchie winked and then showed a hand as he continued on his way. He and Patsy were very close even though there was eighteen months in age between them. As children, playing together in the streets, they had even sometimes pretended that they were brother and sister.

'I'll see you tomorrow!' Patsy called back, and had every intention of doing so: apart from visiting her aunt and uncle, she wanted to tell Ritchie about Danny McDonald and the dance invitation. She wanted his opinion on whether or not she should go.

Thinking about the next day, she made a mental note to visit Molly, her gran, as well as her aunt, so as to kill two birds with one stone. Her gran lived just one street away from her aunt and uncle in a terrace of two-up, two-downs. Patsy had always been close to her relatives and especially her grandma, whom she saw as a second mother. Molly's early Victorian terrace house was like a second home to Patsy even though she did not like Joe, her step-granddad. He seemed amiable enough in company, but at home with her gran he was not only a miserable sod but also aggressive, and critical of whatever Molly cooked or the way she ironed his shirts.

With thoughts of the good-looking shop assistant swimming in and out of her mind, Pasty arrived at the narrow white steps that led up to her home but stopped in her tracks to look across at the small groups of people gathering in front of the church on the opposite side of the street. Knowing her mother would hate to miss the wedding that was clearly about to happen and would want to see the bridesmaids and the bride arrive, she ran up the steps to the front door and let herself in. She called out to her mother, telling her what was going on outside. Both of them loved watching the weddings held in the church and had been sharing this treat since Patsy was a baby in a pushchair.

Alice came down from the tiny box room she used as an office for running her mail-order shopping business. She untied the strings of the apron she was wearing, slipped it off, and then brushed herself down before checking her face and hair in the hall mirror. Like most of the local women, Alice wore pretty pinafores to protect her clothes but she hardly ever wore them in the street – though she was one of those people who looked lovely in any old thing. Her hair was a dark wavy auburn, her eyes were pale green, and she had a smile that could warm the cockles of anyone's heart. She was a good and friendly person who had always loved children and had wanted four of her own, ideally two boys and two girls. This was not meant to be, but she had her Patsy and was now quite content. The two of them were very close, and in Alice's eyes this made up for everything.

Mother and daughter stepped outside where, raising an eyebrow, Alice shrugged and said, 'It must be someone that we don't know, sweetheart, or I would have heard about it.' Looking across at the people milling around in the church grounds, she then murmured, 'Oh Patsy . . . look at the hats and outfits, babe . . . don't the women look lovely?'

Patsy smiled. 'You always say that.'

'Do I? Well, I'm really pleased that you got back in time to see what was going on because I would 'ave missed it all. I was right into the swing with my new vacuum cleaner up in the office. You should see the way it sucks up the dust.'

'Oh Mums . . . stop talking about housework. Come on, let's make our way to the front of the onlookers and sneak in the back.'

'Sneak? I live closer to that church than any of this lot. I've got a right to a seat.'

Manoeuvring their way through the onlookers as if they themselves were guests of the bride or groom, mother and daughter went into the church and joined a few other women who were there for the show. Once seated in a pew, Alice looked along the aisle at the others and then turned her attention to Rose, the woman she had sat next to and whispered, 'If it hadn't been for my Patsy I would have missed this. Why didn't you knock for me?'

'I didn't think that I would have to. You never bloody well miss a wedding or a funeral and you live opposite the church. How could you miss anything that's going on?'

Alice smiled. 'Don't swear in God's house or he'll be cross with you.'

'You should read the Bible,' said her friend. 'Bloody is in there, so it can't be swearing can it? Ask God if I'm right the next time you're down on your knees praying.'

'The word *is* in the Bible I grant you that, but not in the same sense as you use it.'

'All right, enough said. Do you know who the bride is?'

'No, I don't. Do you?'

'No. What about the groom?'

'Well, if I don't think I know the bride I'm hardly gonna know the groom am I? Talk sense.'

'*Will you two be quiet!*' hissed Patsy. '*We're in a church not down the market.*'

'Ooh . . . forgive me for breathing,' said Alice, and turned to give her friend a sly wink and a smile.

'*Stop it!*' whispered Patsy. '*Remember where you are!*'

'Sorry darling,' said Rose as she trapped laughter. 'You're right. We are guests in His house after all.'

'If you two keep this up I'm leaving.'

Pushing her shoulders back, Rose smiled all saintly and said, 'We won't say another word. I promise.'

'Good. Because the last of the guests are coming in and the bridegroom's stopped looking over his shoulder. The bride must have arrived.'

'Unless she's gonna stand him up, as I should 'ave done with my old man,' said the friend. 'I still can't believe how ugly he's grown with age.'

'I'm not listening to this. I can tell that you two are going to get worse.' With that Patsy eased her way along the aisle and slipped out of the side entrance, leaving them to their fun.

Once outside she had to smile because there in full view were the beautiful bride and the lovely bridesmaids – and she had seen them before the congregation had. She slipped behind the groups of onlookers in the grounds and crossed the narrow road to her house. She was happy. She had seen all she wanted to and now all she needed was to be by herself with a cup of Camp coffee and to think about Danny.

Alone in the silent house, Patsy went into the kitchen to make her drink and imagined herself one day walking down the aisle in a beautiful white wedding dress. It seemed that weddings were going on all over the East End with local churches enjoying a heyday. But amid all the happiness and celebrations, there were darker events too. There had been masses of coverage in the newspapers, on television and on the radio of a huge police clean-up operation. The previous spring the BBC had announced that some of the most vicious gangsters that Britain had ever seen had been taken into custody: a local East End protection racket led by the King brothers had been smashed. According to the press they had been responsible for acts of unthinkable savagery, including torture and murder. It had been shocking – and exciting, too – to follow the ongoing drama via the news, like watching a real-life crime thriller. The local papers had certainly enjoyed boom sales over the weeks when detectives raided homes in and around the East End. According to the grapevine no less than seventeen members of the criminal gang, led by notorious brothers Johnny and Ronnie King, had been arrested.

Still, most of the headlines were taken with a pinch of salt. There had always been trouble in the East End of London between various gangs, some of them small time and some bigger players. It was almost expected, as if it was part and parcel of local life. And the human race being what it was meant that some people thrived on the gossip and fear and danger that the gangs were creating. Ordinary locals took it with a shrug of the shoulder for most of the time and few gave a toss whether or not the villains slept with a gun or a bag of jelly babies under their pillows. They might rule the underworld now but they were ordinary kids on the streets once upon a time, kids who had been born and bred in the area and were still there, even though they moved in a different world to the ordinary folk for most of the time.

As far as Patsy's family were concerned, they, like most other East Enders, were pleased that there was a major clean-up going on. No Londoner, whether from south, west, north or east, wanted their birthplace to go down as one of the worst areas in which to live, and their East Enders' sense of pride was evident in the packed church and the immaculately kept church gardens.

At around six-thirty that evening, while Alice was having a nap, Patsy curled up in one of the two matching red and black patterned armchairs in the sitting room and listened to the latest chart records playing on the radio, but her thoughts were still on Danny. She wasn't sure as to which way her dad was going to go with the idea of her staying out all night. She had broached the subject with her mother earlier on and she had seemed fine about her going, but warned her that her father was going to be a problem. He was over protective when it came to his girl and always had been, so getting it past him was not going to be easy. Even though Patsy knew that she could usually twist him round her little finger whenever she wanted something badly enough, she was also clued into the fact that she was going to have to be a step ahead of him in her thinking. Sleeping in a family home in South London under the same roof with a boy that Andy hadn't even met? She very much doubted that he would go for it, unless of course there was a good enough reason.

She was so caught up in her thoughts while a new single by The Drifters was filling the room that she didn't hear the street door open and close again. Her dad's voice filtered through the lyrics of the song, asking where her mother was. 'She's having a nap,' said Patsy, then murmured, 'I've got something to ask you, Dad.'

'Sorry babe, but I can't find my wallet,' he joked.

'No, I'm not after a treat.'

'Good. I take it there was another wedding? The pavement outside the church is covered in confetti.'

'There was, Dad. The bride looked beautiful and there were four bridesmaids. They were all dressed in different shades and—'

'Yeah, all right babe, I don't need to know the ins and outs, I could do with a cup of coffee though.'

Immediately up and out of her armchair Patsy told him to sit down and relax while she made them both a cup of their favourite drink. This wasn't just coming from a sense of duty but from a desire to get on the right side of her dad, who could be a bit dictatorial when the mood took him. She felt sure he would baulk at the idea of her going to the dance if she didn't handle it properly, but he was in an easy mood and seemed happy enough to let Patsy mother-hen him, so things looked okay. He slumped down on the sofa and kicked off his shoes and she went into the kitchen with a hopeful smile on her face. Yes, he was definitely in his nice and easy mood . . . from what she could tell.

Amused at the way his daughter was making an effort to fill Alice's role, Andy leaned back and closed his eyes, relaxed and content now that he was home from the furniture-making company in Shoreditch where he worked. Since the day he had been promoted from manager of the factory floor to sales manager he had had to go in every other Saturday to oversee the smooth running of the business. It wasn't something that he relished but neither did he complain because his wages had almost doubled with the promotion and new responsibilities. Closing his eyes, he laid his head back and briefly wondered what Patsy might be after since she had been up and ready to wait on him within seconds of him coming in the front door. He thought that it might be a pair of shoes that she had seen in a shop window that she'd say were absolutely made for her if she could but afford them. He knew that she knew how to get round him. In truth, his girl could have anything in the world. Whatever she asked for.

Coming back into the room with the coffee, Patsy handed a cup to her dad and then settled herself on the settee. She drew a deep breath, trying to ignore the way her heart was beating nineteen to the dozen and attempted to look relaxed. The room was quiet now, the radio switched off, and the only sound was the ticking of the clock on the bookshelf. Making the most of this opportunity she said, 'I've got something special to ask you. It's to do with something that I would really *not* like to miss out on, and – once I ask you – promise me you'll take a little bit of time to think about it before you answer.'

Andy slowly nodded, contained a smile and did his best to take his daughter seriously as he leaned back, folded his arms, and gazed down at the floor as if he was all ears. 'Off you go then babe. Fire away.'

'Well, I'd rather explain a little of it before I ask – if that's all right.'

Again Andy managed to look studious as well as interested. 'That's fine by me, Patsy darling. All in your own time sweetheart.'

'It's nothing bad or that . . . it's just that . . . well, I'm not sure how you're going to react to something that I would really like to do.'

'Oh get on with it Patsy, I'm tired babe. What can be so grave that you need to talk to me as if I'm gonna baulk at whatever it is?'

'It's a date.'

'What d'you mean – a date? Are we talking about history or you going out with a lad?'

'Don't try and be funny Dad. You know what I mean. I've been asked to go to a dance next Saturday.'

'And?'

'It's south of the river so I'll need to stop overnight.'

'Why? Why will you 'ave to stop out all night?'

'Because by the time it finishes the buses and trains will have stopped running and the boy who's asked me doesn't have a car.'

'Boy? What boy? I don't recall you telling me that you had a boyfriend other than the lads that I know, the local ones you see at the dance halls. Did you meet someone at work? A drippy hairdresser?'

'No,' said Patsy, 'it's Danny McDonald, the boy who serves in the corner shop. In Hobbins. Mum knows him and likes him.'

'Oh, right.' Andy sighed, inwardly relieved. This was easy to deal with. 'Well I don't see why you can't go. If it's only across the river sweetheart I'll pick you up around about eleven o'clock.'

'But that's the point. I don't really want you to do that. It's a family and friends do. It's being held in a church hall and then possibly carrying on at Danny's house . . . I'm not sure. His family's home is a shared house. His parents and a couple of old aunts and an uncle or something.'

'All right, so I'll pick you up at midnight. How's that sound?'

'But I don't want you to do that Dad! For one thing it's not fair on you, and for another it's not fair on me! I want to accept the invitation to stay overnight.'

'And where did this invitation come from?' said Andy getting a touch hot under the collar.

'I just told you! From Danny! When I went in to get some errands for Mum. The older shop assistants know about it and they seemed pleased that he's finally plucked up the courage to ask me out.'

'Well, what would they care? It's not *their* daughter what's being lured into staying at a fellow's house all night is it? If you want to stop out, the answer's no. And that's an end to it.'

Miffed at the way this was going, Patsy stood her ground. 'What do you mean no? Why not? He's from a good family. What do you think he's going to do? Rape me in the night while his parents and aunts look on?'

Andy pointed a finger at her. 'Stop right there Patsy, I won't have that kind of talk under my roof. I'll give him "all night dance". And he'll get it straight from the shoulder on Monday morning because I'll be in that shop first thing.'

'Don't you dare do that! I would leave home if you did something so horrible!' Upset and angry at her dad's response she was determined not to back down. 'I'm seventeen! And I've got every right to stay out overnight if I want to. And I've also got every right to leave home and live in a bed-sit if I want to. A girl my age at work lives in one and so do quite a few of her friends. I could move to another part of London and flat-share. I could live in the West End and afford to pay for a room in a shared house.'

Andy slowly shook his head and chuckled. 'Live in the West End in a room. You wouldn't last five minutes, babe. You'd soon find out where your bread's best buttered.'

'Well at least I would 'ave given it a try!' Thankfully, Patsy could now hear footsteps in the passage and knew that her mother was on the way. 'And anyway, stop changing the subject. This isn't about whether or not I move out.'

'I never brought it up, you did. So it must be at the back of your mind.'

'Move out?' said Alice, coming into the room. 'I shouldn't think you would want to sweetheart. What's brought all this on?'

'She wants to go to a dance over in South London which means stopping out all night and I've said no. Done and dusted.'

Alice looked from her husband to her daughter. She knew how to play this. 'Am I missing something here Patsy? Because I was under the impression that it was a charity do in a church hall and you've been invited as a guest to stay overnight in Danny's family home.'

Picking up on the way her mother had chosen to play it, Patsy shrugged all innocent. 'You're not missing anything Mum. I s'pose I didn't explain it properly to Dad.'

'Yes you did,' said Andy, quite used to his wife and daughter ganging up on him like this. 'She wants to stop overnight with strangers and I said that I would pick her up after the dance and fetch her home.' With that, he stood up and left the room.

Alice winked at Patsy raised her voice a little and said, 'I think your dad's right, sweetheart. I mean, we hardly know the lad other than what Mr Ridley who works in Hobbins told me.'

'Oh? And what was that?'

'That he's a good lad who'll do well for himself when he goes it alone. That was only a passing comment really, while he was slicing ham on the bone for me. And thinking about it, I have only seen his father just the once. He was there to pick up his son because they were going to the People's Palace together to listen to a speaker. I don't know what the talk was but I've a feeling it had something to do with the history of old London, I can't remember, but the one thing I do recall was the car that was parked up outside the shop. A very nice dark blue Jaguar saloon that looked brand new. According to one of the lads it belonged to Danny's father, so his family can't be short of a few bob . . . I wouldn't have thought.'

Coming back into the room Andy tried to hide a smile because he knew full well what his wife was up to. He looked her in the eye and said, 'If the boy's dad does have a Jag and the blokes in the shop tell me that they know his father then I'll concede. She can stay with the family overnight and I'll be there ten o'clock sharp the next morning to pick 'er up. And that's an end to it. No more discussion.'

Patsy looked from Alice to her father and smiled. 'Thanks Dad. For letting me go *and* for offering to collect me. But please don't go in the shop to check up. I would die of embarrassment.'

'Whatever,' he said, and swaggered out of the room calling over his shoulder, 'I'm going into the garden to sit in the sunshine. Fetch me a fresh cup of coffee, out!' He knew that he had been swayed but, more importantly, he knew that he was still very much at the top of the tree in this small household. From the passage he called out. 'And a slice of chocolate cake would be nice!'

That night when the family of three was tucked up in bed and the house was quiet, Alice lay on her back thinking about her daughter. Her Patsy. Looking up at the shadow pattern on the ceiling, created by shafts of light from a full moon that was coming in through a gap in the curtains, she tried to force back tears that were welling in the back of her eyes. She could tell that Andy was drifting off to sleep and yet she knew that she was going to be lying awake and worrying. Patsy's talk of Danny and the dance had made her realise that her little girl was now a young woman. That maybe now was finally the time to tell her the secret that she and Andy had guarded closely all Patsy's life. Their daughter was now of an age when she should be told the truth about her real parents. It was something that neither she nor her husband had wanted to think about, let alone sit down and explain to Patsy – that she had been adopted by them when she was a new born tiny baby. It had been a well-kept secret between themselves and their families ever since.

When Andy's brother Tom and his sister-in-law Eileen had first found out that there was a third child on the way – one they could not afford and had not planned – the couple had been beside themselves with worry. By then Andy had been diagnosed at the London hospital as sterile: the consequence of having been seriously ill with mumps as a child. It seemed the obvious thing was for him and Alice to adopt Tom and Eileen's baby, and that baby had grown up to be their Patsy.

Judging by the sound of her husband's relaxed breathing, Alice guessed that he hadn't quite gone off to sleep but might be on the verge of it. Nudging him gently with her hand she whispered, 'Are you awake sweetheart?'

The slow and mumbled response was, 'Not quite.'

She turned to face him and murmured, 'We need to talk, babe.'

Yawning he sighed, 'About what?'

'About Patsy. I think that it's time . . . whether we want it to be or not.'

'Oh don't start that again. Leave well alone.'

'I can't. She'll need her birth certificate one day, and that day could be any time and for any reason. I don't think we can put it off any longer. We've got to tell her before she finds out, Andy. It would be horrible for her if she does and not all that nice for us.'

Andy eased himself into a sitting position and sighed. 'You've gone on every so often about bringing it out into the open before she finds out from someone else. And has she? In all of her seventeen years? No. So what's all this about?' He turned away and gazed up at the ceiling so as not to have to look at her sorry face. He wasn't quite ready for this. He couldn't bear the thought of telling his daughter that he wasn't her father. 'Let's talk about it in the morning,' he murmured. 'I'm tired.'

'But I'm wide awake and worrying. I can't sleep. I think that we might have left it too long already. We should have taken the advice given by the authorities and told her when she was younger, but old enough to understand.'

'Spilt milk, Alice. Spilt milk. No use crying over it. What's brought this on then?'

'A gut feeling. She's almost all grown up now. She deserves to know. Like I said, we've got to sit her down and tell her before it comes out, before she hears it from someone else.'

'And what makes you think it'll come out?' he said, a touch more tetchy this time.

'I don't know! Her age maybe? I'm not saying that she's going to suddenly ask questions, I just don't think that we should put if off any more that's all. Call it instinct. Call it what you like. We'd be gutted if she found out from someone else, and please don't tell me that you haven't thought about that too because I know you have. I know you're just as concerned as I am so stop pretending that you're not. We've put if off for as long as we can afford to and we both know it.'

Silence filled the bedroom until Andy sighed and then quietly said, 'I know you're right Ali . . . of course you are. But it's not gonna be easy. I've got a knot in my stomach just thinking about it.'

'So have I. But she might resent us for not telling her now, never mind much earlier on. We always knew that it wouldn't be easy for any one of us but she's seventeen . . .'

'I said all right! We'll talk about it first thing and decide when and where we should tell her. We'll have to think on it.'

'What do you mean – *where* we should tell her? Here surely? In her familiar home surroundings?'

'We'll see. To be fair all round it might be better if we're at my Tom's place and when Ritchie's there. You know how close those two are. It might help us – and her.'

'That's true,' murmured Alice. 'Maybe we'll do that. In a few weeks time.'

'That's the ticket,' whispered Andy as he turned over and yawned. 'That's more like it. In a few weeks time. No rush.'

Chapter Two

With a horrible sense of worry in his gut Andy was up earlier than usual the next morning. He liked to cook a full breakfast for the three of them but today, while the girls were still sleeping, he wanted to have the silence of the house to himself to sit down with a cup of tea and think things through. He wanted to think about his Patsy, who had grown into a lovely young lady and who meant the world to him . . . his daughter . . . who was going to have to be told that he wasn't her dad. His stomach churned for the umpteenth time at the thought of it. He loved her so much and had always thought of her as his very own flesh and blood. His girl.

Filling the kettle, he did his best to get a grip on his emotions because if Patsy were to come down from her bedroom and give him his usual kiss on the cheek he couldn't guarantee that he wouldn't shed a tear. And he knew that if there was ever a time that he had to be strong, it was now. He spooned three measures of tea into the pot and thought that he could hear soft shuffling on the staircase. Patsy was sometimes up early on a Sunday and if this was her approaching he wasn't sure he could talk about anything other than what was on his mind. Luckily, it was Alice.

'I didn't sleep very well either,' she murmured as she stood in the doorway.

Pinching his lips together, Andy swallowed against the lump in his throat and then held his arms out to her. 'Come here you old worry guts. Come and give me a cuddle.'

On the verge of tears Alice fell into his arms and whispered, 'I mustn't cry. She'll know by my red puffy eyes if I do and she won't be satisfied until I tell her what the matter is. And I can't do that yet. I just can't.'

'Nor can I sweetheart,' he whispered back.

'I'm sorry I brought it up. It was stupid. Maybe we don't have to tell her yet. Perhaps we don't really have to tell her at all. The surname on the birth certificate is the same as ours so she won't know any different, will she? If she ever needs to see it that is. I mean that was why we only put the surname down, wasn't it.'

Pausing for breath, Andy looked into her face. 'Of course the name's the same. She's my brother's child. We need never say anything. We fooled the neighbours by you pretending to be pregnant and my sister-in-law fooled hers by saying that her baby never made it after a difficult birth in the hospital, so, why should it have to come out now?'

'I just panicked I suppose . . . but I've always wondered what we would do come the day she'd need proof of who she is. But, no, we don't have to do anything. So none of it matters.'

'Yes it does matter babe, and we both know that. And one day we will sit down and explain what Tom and Eileen did for us. *And* what we did for them. It's not as if it's a nasty story, is it? We're family and we all love each other. And Ritchie is like a brother towards her in any case even though she thinks he's her cousin.'

'I know. And she feels the same about him.'

Andy smiled and gave his wife a little kiss on the lips. 'We'll say it all one day, just not today. You take a cup of tea back to bed with you and read the Sunday paper. It's on the doormat already.'

'Yeah . . . I think I might just do that. I must admit I do need to be in that little Sunday sanctuary world.' She kissed him lightly and left the kitchen. Breathing a sigh of relief, Andy told himself that they had been worrying all night over nothing. His family was all right. More than all right. Everything boded well.

But Alice, as well as worrying about the secret, had something else on her mind. She wasn't as relaxed about the dance as she made out. She had heard through the grapevine that Danny had been in the doldrums because his engagement had been broken by his fiancée. And to her mind, if the lad had been engaged to be married, he most likely would have been dipping his cornet into the ice-cream and she worried he might expect more from Patsy than a goodnight kiss and cuddle. She knew full well that had she mentioned this to Andy it would have put the kibosh on their daughter staying at Danny's home overnight. But all of this aside, she liked the lad and, in her heart, felt sure he wouldn't take advantage – not after having gone to such lengths to get their approval for Patsy to stay over. Surely he wouldn't want to push his luck . . .

*

27

Later on that morning, having thoroughly enjoyed her breakfast in bed fetched by her dad the way it always had been on a Sunday, Patsy placed the tray with the empty plate and cutlery on her side table and sank her head back into her big feather pillow. The night before, she had drifted off to sleep with Danny on her mind. She could hardly wait to see him again. She couldn't wait to tell Ritchie about him and, as she had many times before, she quietly wished she had a sister that she could talk to.

She was still smiling when her dad poked his head around the door. 'Someone looks happy,' he said.

'I am, Dad. I'm happy because you think that it's all right for me to go to the dance and stop overnight.'

'Oh, right . . . I should 'ave known you'd be thinking about that. Are you going to visit your nan today? I thought I remembered you saying something yesterday . . .'

'I did and yes I am. And Auntie Eileen as well. I saw Ritchie and he said that she was a bit disappointed that I've not been round there while she's been poorly.'

Seeing this as a good opportunity to test the water, he said, 'Well, he was right to tell you, babe. Your Aunt Eileen thinks the world of you . . . as does your Uncle Tom. You know they do. You're the apple of your nan and your aunt and uncle's eye.'

Patsy smiled. 'That's because I'm the only girl within the little group of cousins. I'm spoilt because of it. Anyway, I wanted to say thanks again for giving me permission to go to the dance and stop at Danny's.' She was double-checking that he really hadn't changed his mind.

'No problem, babe.' With that he winked at her and went back downstairs, feeling all right about himself and all right about the way he had raised Tom's child. As far as he was concerned, Patsy was a shining example of a well-bred girl, unselfish and not in the least bit spoilt. All in all, everything in the garden was rosy on this Sunday morning and he was pleased that Patsy was going to see her nan. He knew that his mother, Molly, thought the world of Patsy and vice versa. Like Patsy, though, he always found it difficult when visiting the old couple because he couldn't stand Joe, his mother's second husband. As far as Andy was concerned, Joe was a bar-leaning pub-drinking thick-skinned selfish bastard who nearly always had a heavy smell of cheap gin on his breath. And the worse of it was that Andy knew his dad would have hated the thought of such a man wheedling his way into Molly's life. Into her home and into his dad's armchair by the fireplace. Deep down, he knew that his mother had realised that she had made a big mistake in marrying the man.

Then, with his own dad's gentle smiling face coming into his thoughts, he cursed himself for not giving his stepfather a good talking to, not telling him to mend his ways and treat his mother with a bit of respect. But there was still time. He promised himself that soon he would start to make regular visits to the house – if for nothing else but to gauge whether his mother wanted to be with the man or not. After all, bad company might, for her, be better than loneliness.

Pasty strolled along to Molly's house via a cobbled back turning which had an old-fashioned cul-de-sac coming off it where her grandma lived. She could see a group of youths further along the narrow street. She knew them from the nearby council estate but with the sun on her face she felt as if she were in a world of her own, and it was only when she heard one of the lads cry out in pain that she stopped in her tracks. Peering under her hand she recognised a youth with ginger hair who was known to be a vicious little bastard. He was rounding on Nathan, a polite and friendly boy she knew because he delivered the Sunday papers. Stepping up her pace Patsy decided to help him and to stop him being pushed around and sneered at.

Arriving at Nathan's side she pointed a finger at the gang leader's face and said, 'If I see you bullying those more polite than yourself again, Kenny, I'll go straight round to the Bethnal Green police station and report you.'

'Listen to it. Anyone'd fink you were seventeen going on sixty,' he sneered.

'Hardly. But I am old enough to have seen you stark naked when I was with my friend who was your babysitter. What a puny little scrap you were, so nothing's changed has it?'

'If you weren't a fucking girl I'd kick your teeth in.'

'I'm sure you would, too. Now . . . on your way, the lot of you. Go and find something useful to do.'

'Hark at it,' Kenny said, as he turned to his mates. 'Come on, she's boring the shit out of me.' With that he pushed his hands into his trouser pockets and sloped off with a sneer on his face and with his little gang following behind.

Patsy turned around to face Nathan. 'Why don't you go the other way, Nathan, when you're heading for Cambridgeheath Road? Go through the council estate and out onto the corner of Hobbins store. Little bullies like Kenny don't hang around with their mates there.

'I suppose I should but it makes my blood boil to think that I have to.'

'I know, but it's best not to walk in their footsteps. Have you heard from your mate Charlotte since she left for Norfolk?'

'Oh sure. We're pen friends now.'

'I expect you miss 'er?'

'Not really, he said, blushing. 'I'm usually too busy. I help my grandparents out at the shop and stuff like that. But I'll give Charlotte your regards when I next write her a letter. Your mum and her aunt were good friends weren't they?'

'For a while. They worked at the cinema together.'

'That's right. I miss the complimentary tickets now that Charlotte's gone. Still, too many films can damage your eyes, or so they say.'

She smiled at the way Nathan was trying to be grown up. The lad pushed his loose, round national health glasses up onto the bridge of his nose and did his best to show a brave face. 'Thank you very much, Patsy, for telling those boys off. I appreciate what you did.' He then showed a hand and retraced his steps to leave the way he had come, via the old railway arch.

Patsy turned into the cul-de-sac and saw somebody she knew from schooldays. Maggie Baroncini was older than her and had been a prefect. She had always been considerate and kind to the beginners at the school and Patsy had been very shy at that time so she'd clung onto her during the lesson breaks in the playground. Maggie was now married to her London-born and bred Italian sweetheart, and had her six-year-old son, Peppito, with her.

Patsy gave a little wave and quickened her pace until she was at her side. 'I thought that was you, Mags. How are things?'

'Not too bad. And you?'

'I'm okay. I'm just on my way to see my nan.'

'Good for you. Today's a special day you know,' Maggie smiled and winked before glancing down at her son. 'It's Peppie's birthday. We're just on our way to visit Auntie Rita who just might have a present all wrapped up.'

'I'm sure she will.' Patsy laughed. 'That girl thinks the world of this boy. And who can blame her, eh, Peppie?'

'Dunno,' said Peppito. 'She's mum's best friend so she has to put up with me. But she does love me though and I like her. Even if she is a torment. But she's always got a toffee apple put by for me so I must be'er favourite, mustn't I?'

Patsy laughed at his funny old-fashioned expression. 'I'm sure you are her favourite person in the world.

And what about your great-aunt, Naomi? Is she still a torment?'

'She's not right in the head but she's all right. She bought me this wristwatch.' He lifted his arm to show her. 'It's a Roy Rogers watch. Roy Rogers on his horse, Trigger.'

'I like the watch but I don't think that you should say that your great-aunt is not right in the head.' Patsy did her best to keep a serious face and not laugh as she fumbled in her pocket for some change that she knew was in there.

'Well, that's what my dad says. And he knows everything.'

'I'm sure he does.' She gave the boy a two-shilling bit and wished him a happy birthday. The girls then went their separate ways, promising to get together soon for a coffee and a catch-up.

'Say hello to your nan for me!' Maggie called after her.

'Will do,' said Patsy with a wave, and cheerfully continued on her way. She could hardly wait to tell her gran about Danny and the dance. Molly was someone that she had always seen as the best grandma in the world. She had looked after Patsy before she had started school while Alice was working, and now she couldn't imagine life without her nan being in the centre of it. She not only brought colour into people's lives but love and warmth too, even though she could swear for England when the mood took her. Molly had a heart of gold and had always helped friends and neighbours in their hour of need.

The only fault that Patsy could find was her choice of her second husband. As it turned out, Joe Spinks had been drinking heavily since he had been in his late twenties and this had only worsened over the years. It wasn't until Patsy had heard the word 'alcoholic' whispered that she realised just how bad things were for her beloved grandmother. But because Joe was her gran's husband she had always behaved as if she didn't know about his habit. She and him had never hugged because he wasn't the hugging kind, but still Patsy had been able to smell the fumes on his breath, which sometimes made her feel sick. As a child she hadn't known why he smelt the way he did. Now of course she knew better.

Apart from this she, like most people, had at first just thought of Joe as an agreeable old boy who wouldn't harm a fly. He had always been a bit of a joker and always ready to put the kettle on when visitors popped in. But gradually Patsy realised that the face that Molly saw was not the face that smiled at all and sundry. He was not only a disagreeable man but could also be a tyrant and quite cruel at times, so when he sneaked money out of Molly's purse and helped himself to several shillings from a tin where coins for the gas and electric meters were kept, Molly pretended not to notice, fearing his violent anger. At times – more often than not – when he had been at the bottle non-stop, an ugly mood and short temper came to the surface. Not long after they were married, when Molly, who was his third wife, had dared to answer him back, it had resulted in him shoving her, gripping her arm overly tightly or even punching her where he knew the bruises would not be seen by others.

When he had moved into her house after their registry office marriage he had behaved like a true gentleman for the first couple of months and, because of this, Molly had been able to close her eyes to any short spells of sulking and silence during those early days. Sadly though, as time went on Joe showed his true colours. He was a dour man who drank himself to sleep most evenings with cheap cider on top of a few pints at the local pub.

Arriving at her gran's front door Patsy bent down and called through the letterbox, something that she had done as a child and which had become a habit. Within minutes the door opened and there stood the woman she loved. 'Well, look what the wind's blown in,' said Molly, a big smile breaking out on her face as she leaned forward and kissed her granddaughter on the cheek. 'I've got a bread pudding in the oven,' she announced, hardly able to contain her joy at the visit.

'Good,' said Patsy as they went into the passage. 'That and a cup of coffee are just what I fancy. Is the old man about?'

Molly closed the street door. 'No. He's probably in one of his regular pubs with a few of his cronies, drinking out of hours.'

Relieved, Patsy went into the kitchen-cum-dining room. She sat down at the old-fashioned oak table and eased off her shoes. 'Do you think that Joe will ever give up the booze, Nan? Or just carry on drinking as much as ever?'

'Of course he'll carry on. But don't you dare mention it to anyone.'

'Oh Gran . . . how many times have I told you that your secret's safe with me. But you realise that everyone knows he's a boozer in any case. The old bastard's inebriated most days so how can it be as much of a secret as you think? People are not daft. And don't forget that just because he's a good old boy in company it doesn't always wash. You know what people are like. They keep schtum because they've heard the old saying: *Confront the drunk and the devil will drive him.* That might well be the reason why people smile at him in the street or wherever. And anyway, why should you give a toss what people think, one way or another?'

'Well I do. I give a toss what they think about me for marrying him in the first place. Of course I had only seen one side of the man when he courted me. I should have known better than to rush in but I was lonely after your grandfather passed away. Now . . . do you want your coffee with all milk or just a dash today?'

'Just a dash,' whispered Patsy, a touch choked by her nan's confession and doing her best not to let it show.

But Molly was no fool, she had picked up on the sad look on her treasured granddaughter's face. With her back to her she spoke in a whisper. 'The thing to remember, Patsy sweetheart, is what we can't cure we must endure. It's the way of things.' She then busied herself at the stove and pushed Joe from her thoughts as she had done so many times before. 'So what's put the glow in *your* cheeks then?' she said.

Quietly laughing at the canny old woman who missed nothing, Patsy said, 'I'm in love.'

'Oh, are you now?' Smiling wickedly, Molly glanced sideways at her. 'Who is he then?'

'I was only joking Nan, but I have met someone that I like. His name's Danny McDonald And he's invited me to go to a dance with him next Saturday. His family and some friends are arranging it to raise funds for the poor people of Glasgow.' Patsy then told her all about Danny and more about the dance.

Molly was all ears. 'Scottish eh? I would never 'ave thought it. I was in the store only a few days ago. I know the lad by sight and I've heard him talking to the other customers and I would never have said he was Scottish. I certainly didn't detect any accent.'

'That's because he was born and bred in London.'

'So where does he live now then?'

'Over the river.'

'A South Londoner? Well I suppose it could be worse.'

'I'll be stopping at his family home overnight. After the dance.' Patsy waited with a smile on her face for her nan's reaction.

'Oh will you now?' said Molly. 'Well, you make sure you keep both legs in one stocking.'

Patsy laughed out loud. 'I knew you'd say that! I just knew it!'

'Well then I wasn't far out was I? Not if it had

lodged in your mind as well. Has he tried anything so far?'

'I've not been out with him yet!'

'I mean when you've been in the shop. Has he got you out the back in the storeroom?'

Laughing at her gran, Patsy slowly shook her head. 'Our generation's not like yours. We're not promiscuous.'

'I should hope not. We had every good reason to be, what with two bloody wars! We never knew when we might be bombed out of our beds and blown to bits. I should think we did make the most of life. Your generation 'ave got no excuse not to behave yourselves though. You've never 'ad it so good.' Molly turned to point a finger at her granddaughter, ready to give a lecture on horny young men but as she did a pain shot through her rib cage and the look of agony on her face spoke volumes.

Patsy was up from her chair and by her side in a flash. 'Nan! What is it Nan? What's wrong?'

'Just leave me be for a minute sweetheart,' whispered Molly. 'I'll be all right. I've pulled a muscle that's all. Just under the shoulder blade.' She was fibbing, but was by now used to covering up for her bullying husband. Three days earlier, in one of his nasty moods after a drinking bout with his cronies in a pub, Joe had provoked an argument with her – one that had resulted in Molly receiving a right-hander that had sent her flying. And while she had lain crumpled on the floor, cursing him aloud, he had finished what he had started with a kick to her ribs. It wasn't the first time she had

had to cover up what she thought of as minor injuries, but she was now of the mind that it was going to be the last. She had had enough. More than enough.

Knowing her nan's acting ability, Patsy wasn't in the least bit convinced by the excuse of a pulled muscle. She carefully helped her onto a chair and said, 'You have a rest and I'll make our hot drinks. And I'll do the—'

'No you won't, I'll be fine in a minute. Don't make a fuss. You know that fussing around me puts my back up. And don't go telling your mum or dad or they'll be poking their noses in.'

'I wasn't going to make a fuss. I was just going to say that I'll do the vacuuming if it needs doing or that I'll do a bit of ironing while I'm here.'

'Vacuuming? I hope you're not saying that my floors are dirty,' said Molly, steering the conversation away from her state of being.

'Oh shut up Nan. You know I'm not saying that.'

'Of course I know. Don't be so touchy. Now pour me a cup of tea, that's all I need. And don't look so worried. And anyway I'd rather wear out than go rusty. A bit of housework never did me any harm. All I need is a nice cup of tea and then a little chat about the birds and the bees and this boyfriend you've come to tell me about.'

Patsy laughed. 'That's not the only reason I'm here. And as for the birds and the bees, you've been telling me since I was knee high about boys and what dirty little sods they can be. It's a wonder you've not put me off for life. Danny's really nice though, you'll like him.

But I don't want you going into the shop and starting to fire questions at him. And don't you dare give him the evil eye.'

'Evil eye? Me? Far be it for me to do such a thing, sweetheart. All I want is a peaceful life. For my grandchildren to stay innocent until they're engaged to be married.'

'Is that what you did then?'

'Of course not. But that was due to the wars like I said, whereas you lot were born and bred in peacetime. So there's no excuse for hanky panky and a bit of the other under the arches.'

Patsy smiled. 'Anyway, don't you dare go in the shop and tell Danny to keep the buttons on 'is flies done up!'

Molly sniffed and raised one eyebrow. 'Buttons? A quick zip more like.'

'You *know* what I mean.'

Leaning back in her chair Molly winced in pain. 'Stop being so touchy and pour that tea out. I'm gasping. It's thinking about the war and those lovely young soldiers . . .'

Laughing at her nan as she attended to the tea-making Patsy said, 'You're a filthy cow on the quiet.'

'But you can't help but love me.'

'No, Nan, I can't.'

'And you'll keep schtum about me and that little turn?'

'Of course I will if that's how you want to play it. But don't ask me to *forget* because I won't. I'm not as green as I make out you know.'

Molly raised her eyes to study her granddaughter's face. 'What's that supposed to mean?'

'Never you mind,' said Patsy. 'But I will say this and then I'll leave it be. You don't 'ave to stay living with *him*. Kick him out. And before you say that I don't know what I'm talking about, I do.'

'I don't know what you're talking about,' Molly sniffed.

'See? I knew you'd say that.' Patsy handed her nan a cup of tea. 'Sugar it yourself because I never do get it right do I?'

'No you don't.'

Back in her chair Patsy sipped her coffee and glanced at Molly's pale face. 'I'm not poking my nose in Nan I promise, but—'

'Good job an' all,' Molly interrupted, getting up from her chair and going to the larder. 'I've got the last of a nice bit of fruitcake in the tin if you want a slice. I'm having a bit, if for nothing else but to keep the wolf away from the door.' Then, as she turned to Patsy she dropped the tin and gripped her rib cage as her legs buckled under her and she crumpled to the floor.

Quickly on her knees by Molly's side, Patsy pulled a cushion off an old-fashioned high-back chair close by and placed it under Molly's head. Seeing how pale the woman's face was, her stomach churned but she managed to put on a brave smile and said, 'Can you manage to sip some water, Nan?'

Molly slowly shook her head and raised a trembling hand to give the message that a drink wasn't what she wanted. That she just needed a few minutes to collect herself. Knowing her nan inside out Patsy went quiet and waited. She knew that this fall had come from sudden pain. Pain that no doubt her gran had been having on and off and covering. And it was more than just instinct that was telling her who was at the bottom of it. Joe. The anger was now rising from the pit of Patsy's stomach but she managed to quell it. This wasn't the time to sound off about the bastard that her nan was married to, but from the colour of Molly's face, which looked as if all the blood had drained down to her feet, she knew that she had to do something even though it would go against the grain where this independent lady was concerned. Steeling herself she said, 'I'm phoning for an ambulance, Nan. And nothing you can say will stop me.'

'Go on then,' Molly just managed to whisper. 'Tell them that I'm in hellish pain.'

Now she was not only scared by the way Molly looked, but also by her showing no resistance to getting help. Patsy was taken aback to see that she was actually giving in without a fuss and admitting that she couldn't carry on, but she kept her cool and pulled another feather cushion off a chair to gently ease it beneath her nan's bony knees. 'Don't move a muscle,' she whispered. 'Just lay still and breathe easy and we'll have you in safe hands soon.'

In the hallway Patsy reached for the phone and saw that her own hands were trembling. She forced herself to get a grip and dialled 999. Once she had given the information needed she replaced the receiver and was back by the old lady's side to see that her eyes were now closed and her face was a ghastly colour. With fear coursing through her, she tried to remember what she had learned during a First Aid lesson at school but nothing came. She relaxed her shoulders and drew long slow breaths of air, waiting a few seconds for the shooting stars in her own head to ebb away, then went to pour herself a glass of water. A lovely smell now wafted through the air and she remembered that Nan had a bread pudding cooking, so she went back to the kitchen and turned off the oven.

Once Patsy was feeling steadier, she asked Molly if she was comfortable and a slow nod was her answer. She knelt down beside her and whispered that an ambulance was on its way and she was going to phone home to let her mother know what was going on. Molly nodded again, her eyes still closed and her body limp. Before she pulled herself away from her beloved grandma, Patsy kissed her on the cheek and then went to the street door to watch out for the ambulance. She could hardly believe her ears when she heard in the distance the sound of the emergency bells of the vehicle that was on its way. But then the Bethnal Green hospital was only a short distance and, in a clearer frame of mind, Patsy would have realised that they hadn't to wait many minutes before help came. To her at that moment, the sight of the familiar white ambulance coming along the turning with its lights flashing was better than being given all the tea in China. Her nan would soon be in safe hands. She would be taken to hospital and cared for in the same way that she had always cared for others when they were in need. It was now Molly's turn to be looked after by nurses and made better by doctors and fussed over by the family.

Back inside the house, having left the street door open for the ambulance men, Patsy again kneeled at Molly's side and stroked her face. 'The ambulance is here Nan. You'll soon be in a nice comfortable bed, all tucked up and cozy.'

Molly looked into her granddaughter's tender face and managed a weak smile. 'Good girl, sweetheart. Well done.' And that was it. That was all she could manage. She closed her eyes and was only too ready to let the people who were now coming into the house get on with it. She was all done in.

Chapter Three

Two days later in the day room of the Bethnal Green hospital Molly was wearing a treasured pale green and pink mock satin nightdress and matching housecoat. This had been a gift from Alice and Andy, which she'd saved since the previous Christmas, when she had unwrapped the parcel. Content to do little else other than thumb through a woman's magazine in search of the agony aunt page, she was quite enjoying her little break. Apart from bruising to her body, X-rays had shown that two of her ribs had a hairline crack and that a bandage brace and bed rest was what she needed. Secretly, bed rest was exactly what she wanted. Even Molly, if asked, would have to admit that the fall had been the last straw. She had been coping with aches and pains for too long. While the collapse from the cracked ribs had only caused Molly local bruising, there were other marks on her body from previous knocks and bangs that had not slipped past the eyes of the consultant doctor. Until now, Molly hadn't wanted any conversation to do with any of her injuries because she was ashamed of Joe and of what he could do when he lost control of his temper.

Having had hours while in hospital to think about her life, Molly had now come to a firm conclusion that

45

it was time that she and Joe went their separate ways. Apart from everything else, she suspected that he was seeing another woman, a drinking partner who wore cheap perfume. She had not only picked up the scent from his shirts but also his body. But all the same, she didn't think he would agree to leave the comfortable nest in which he enjoyed a comfortable life without a fight. The only consolation was that their little terraced house had been her home long before he arrived so the rent book was in her name. Having the courage to tell him to go once she was back home was mostly what niggled at her while she lay in her bed. She knew from experience that his temper could rise within seconds. However, on the day that she was admitted, she had bumped into a patient called Gwen, an old friend of hers from way back. Gwen had not only gone to the same school as Molly but had been her close friend right up until they were married. Eventually, each had children, which had kept them too busy for leisurely visits to each other, but seeing Gwen again on the day that she was admitted into hospital had been just the tonic that Molly needed. Once reunited, the friends had immediately picked up the rapport they had once shared, and it had given Molly a much-needed boost of confidence: she was determined to move on.

But for now, comfortably propped against two big pillows with her magazine, Molly was quite content to wait for her granddaughter who was due to visit. Checking her wristwatch, she guessed that Patsy wouldn't be in for another ten minutes or so. With a wry smile, she glanced at the girl who was there on a trainee's placement, an eighteen-year-old student who was poring over some papers nearby. She was wearing a baggy orange blouse, tight black pedal-pushers, and what looked to Molly like school plimsoles on her feet.

Her eyes back on her magazine, Molly spoke quietly, but just loudly enough so that the student could hear her. 'My mother would turn in her grave if she could see what you've slung on today.' Receiving no response from the girl, who was quite used to her by now, she said, 'Shall I read you a letter from the agony aunt page? You do look a bit bored, sweetheart. Either that or you're hung over.'

'No thanks Molly.' The girl laughed. 'I'm not bored, but I might be hung over. I went out with a gorgeous medical student last night.'

'Oh did you now.' Molly grinned. 'So that's a love letter you're reading then, is it? One that he's slipped down your drawers on the quiet? Not that I for one minute blame yer. I wouldn't stop any of the doctors from trying it on. Handsome bastards most of 'em.'

'Chance would be a fine thing!' Gwen, who was sitting up in her bed reading a book, couldn't resist joining in the banter. 'I shouldn't take too much notice of her, nurse. She's winding you up and reeling you in sweetheart. She's a married woman.'

'Worse luck,' Molly murmured. 'The selfish so and so spends all his earnings on booze then free-rides back home when it comes to meals and bills.'

'Come on Molly,' said the student nurse, 'Don't get yourself agitated. Why don't you go and help poor old

Agnes in the corner bed with that puzzle she's working on?'

'No, ta.' Molly raised an eyebrow. 'Now, had it have been a puzzle of England or Ireland or Scotland or Wales, I might well have helped out with it by now. But a ship on the ruddy Danube in Germany? I don't think so. Either someone's taking the rise or don't know their geography. We might be a charity ward where people can dump books and rubbish they don't want but we're not brain dead. The war wasn't all that many years ago. Whoever accepted that into the ward can't have much upstairs. Germany? I do wonder about you students at times.'

The young nurse, restraining laughter, wagged a finger at Molly and said, 'You might think that we're still wet behind the ears but don't forget that we've passed all our first exams. You never know . . . next time you're in for a stay one of those who you have a go about might well be here as a matron. A matron in a crisp uniform and keeping an eye on mischievous patients to play tricks on . . . Such as prescribing a bit of chocolate ex-lax to slip into hot cocoa.'

'A matron? Any one of you lot? I don't think so darlin'. No, I shall be dead and buried by the time any of you've got a proper job in this place. I'm not saying I blame you though. All you have to do is prance about for two or three years, reading books and filling in your forms. But there you go – I expect you get a nice allowance to keep you out of full-time work.'

'Don't mind her. She's in a tormenting mood!' professed Gwen. 'She likes to pretend that she's tough as old boots but beneath it all she's as soft as butter. You shed a tear and she'll be all over yer.'

'Me? Soft? I don't think so.' Molly raised an eyebrow. 'My old chum's read me wrong again, nurse.' She raised her magazine to hide a smile. 'Now then . . . listen to this letter that some silly cow 'as written to the agony aunt . . .'

Taking the opportunity to sidetrack her friend and stop her from winding up the student, Gwen raised her voice. 'Look who's arrived! It's your lovely granddaughter Molly and I've just this minute finished what I've been knitting for her.'

'She doesn't wear gloves. How many more times have I got to tell yer?'

'Only because she hasn't got any,' said Gwen. 'I shall knit her a scarf to match as well. Ready for the winter. Bless her heart, she's a treasure she is. You don't know how lucky you are.'

Smiling at Gwen as she approached, Patsy pulled a packet of sweets out of her pocket and tossed them to her. 'There you go. Cough candy. I told you I wouldn't forget.'

Giving the woman a knowing wink, Patsy followed protocol and went straight over to her nan's bed and kissed her on the cheek. 'You all right Nan?'

'In this place? With most of the women a penny short of a shilling? Pigs might fly. Did you remember the chocolate raisins and the clean knickers and vest?'

'Of course.'

'And did your mother manage to keep 'em white this

time? Or are they all pink and patchy just like my last wash load she did when I had the flu?'

'That wasn't Mum's fault Nan. I already told you that. It was mine. A pair of my new knickers had found its way in by mistake. And before you ask, yes, your underwear is sparkling white. I only had to throw away one vest, a woollen one that shrunk.'

'Well, I suppose that's better than me wearing grubby underwear. And what's with the sexy red knickers? You've not known this new chap ten minutes.' She glanced at the magazine that Patsy was holding. 'Is that glossy journal for me or for a complete and utter stranger you've taken pity on?'

'You know it's for you. It's your *Family Circle*. And I bought the red panties long before I met Danny.'

Molly raised an eyebrow and smiled at her grand-daughter – the most treasured person in her world. 'Good. That's put my mind at rest. Everyone out there all right are they? All weeping buckets over my being in here as well as buying me presents for when I come out?'

Pulling up a chair, Patsy sat close up to her nan's bed. 'Everyone's fine. But I might leave my job at the hairdresser's for more pay elsewhere. One of the stylists is doing just that.'

'More pay? They give you four pounds ten shillings a week plus tips just to cut and wave womens' hair. What more do you want?'

'A decent wage. Plenty of other salons up West pay more than that. A mate of mine gets six pounds ten shillings a week. She works in Holborn, which isn't even the West End really, is it, so there you go.'

Molly leaned back into her pillow all thoughtful. 'When I hear how much money you young people earn it makes my blood boil. When I think how much I got for slaving long hours when I was your age . . . it doesn't bear thinking about.' She shrugged, and mumbled, 'You wouldn't believe how little I earned. Mind you . . . it is 1960 after all and not the 1940s, when I was out there working for governors who treated their staff like slave-whippers would. We had to clock in and clock out and have pay docked from our packet if we were caught leaving five minutes early or getting in five minutes late. Tight bastards.'

'Don't swear in here Nan. Remember where you are,' said Patsy.

'Where I am? This is a hospital love, not a church. Anyway, you had better make sure you've definitely got another job to go to before you start blabbing at work that you're going to hand in your notice.'

'Of course I will. God . . . I wish I hadn't mentioned it now. It was only an idle thought. The fares into the West End would probably take up the extra pay.

Molly sniffed, then reached for a box of Licorice Allsorts from the bedside table. 'All that money just to bloody well snip a bit of hair off. That's a small fortune Patsy.'

'Nan . . . *please* don't swear in here unless you whisper it.'

'I *was* whispering . . . wasn't I?'

'No! You shout. You know you do. And it's a bit

embarrassing at times. Ladies don't swear Nan. Not as a rule. And especially not women of your age.'

Molly couldn't help laughing. 'Women don't *what*? You should 'ave paid me a visit when I worked in the soap-making factory. We never stopped swearing and laughing. When the boss was about we turned it around a bit . . .'

'I know. You've told me. And *bucking fastard* was the best one.'

'That's what we called the supervisors! Well what could they say? We weren't really swearing were we?' She looked sideways at her granddaughter. 'How comes you know that?'

Pasty sighed and raised an eyebrow. 'I've no idea.'

'I must 'ave told you already.'

'Possibly.'

'I did. See? My memory's better than yours is. It came right back to me in a flash, my telling you about that. Anyway, we never saw it as swearing. We were just playing around with words.' She laughed at the memory. 'Snooty bastards, they was, giving it all the airs and graces and yet most of 'em would 'ave eaten sh—'

'Nan, please!' Patsy looked around and lowered her voice to a whisper. 'That is so disgusting.'

'The truth often is, sweetheart.' She sank back into her pillow and took Patsy's hand in hers. 'So . . . 'ave you got any gossip to tell me? I didn't see you yesterday so something must 'ave happened out there.' She smiled and winked. 'Is your secret admirer still gagging for yer?'

Blushing, Patsy lowered her eyes and sighed. 'I wish

I never told you about him now. And don't be crude. You're supposed to set me a good example.'

'Well I do! Always have done. I might be set in me ways but I can't help that, can I? But I will say this: I don't reckon he's the best you can find. He's got the looks – so you say – but slow? He's worse than a snail on crutches. He should 'ave asked you out weeks ago. He should've been all over yer!' A faraway look was now showing on Molly's face and in her eyes. 'Now your grandfather – not this one I'm with now – your *real* grandfather who passed away while we were—'

Patsy held up a hand to stop her. 'You've told me already Nan . . . and I don't want to hear it. You're sharing a ward with other patients. Show a bit of respect.'

'That's one of my sayings. Good God, how the tables do turn on you when you get old. *Show a bit of respect*. That's what I used to say to you when you were a cheeky little cow. Anyway, I wasn't going to shout at the top of my voice. I wasn't going to let this lot know that your proper grandfather was a better lover than any one of them movie stars. He had the best pride in the local fire brigade. And probably England for that matter.'

Slyly looking around to see if she had an audience Molly kept a straight face. Of course the others had heard and some were quietly laughing while others were trying not to because they had post-operation stitches to consider. But there was no denying the woman her spectators who loved her crude sense of humour. This was why she was playing up today. Molly was happy and in an entertaining mood, and Patsy knew that she wasn't ready to come out of the limelight just yet. It was as if she was on centre stage, and she was going to make the most of it.

'And there I was. An innocent until I married your grandfather. The rumour about his pride and joy had spread around the dance floor well before I waltzed up close to the man. At that time, when I finally agreed to go out walking with him – I was a regular church-goer . . . a sanctimonious virgin.'

'You lying cow!' came the voice and laughter of Gwen. 'More men had dipped their cornet into your ice-cream than they had hot dinners, Molly. And I should know 'cause I was out there with you dar-ling . . . having just as much fun!'

'That's partly true I suppose, but I think that we had more hot dinners than we had men . . . well, the majority of the time, I think . . .'

In spite of stitches or plaster of Paris the women in the ward were chuckling more than was good for them and so too were a nurse and a doctor. And Molly relished this more than anything else in the world. She was the centre of attention and was having a lovely time. She looked from Gwen to Patsy and said, 'I couldn't half do with a ciggy sweetheart. Help me out of this bed and onto the veranda before I pass out from low nicotine levels.'

'I will Nan . . .' whispered Patsy, 'but first answer me one question.'

'Go on then. Fire away.'

'Are you gonna let me tell Mum and Dad about the other bangs and knocks?'

Molly looked Patsy in the face and lowered her voice. 'No. That's between you and me and no one else. I will do something about it though. I've got a plan, but you don't say a word. Not one word. I'll get rid of him in my own sweet way, don't you worry.'

'What if he won't go?'

'I just told you – I've got a plan.'

'And what's that?'

'*I'll* go. I'll organise a removal van and clear the house out, lock, stock and barrel. And I'll let the landlord know the date that I'm going. It'll all be above board. *He* won't pick up on it because he's mostly too pissed to think straight.'

Patsy could hardly believe what she was hearing. She looked into her nan's face and then broke into a warm smile. 'You really mean it this time?'

Molly lowered her voice to almost a whisper. 'Yes I do. And I'll tell you something else – I've got somewhere to go. A very nice one-bedroom apartment in Wanstead. It's in a house next door to where Gwen lives, my friend who you fetched sweets in for, so you can't tell me you don't know her.'

Instead of letting Molly's rambling go above her head as she usually did, Patsy looked at her as if she had lost the plot. 'What are you talking about? Wanstead? That's miles away from the East End.'

'No it's not. You're gonna get on a bus and go to South London to jig about with a load of Scottish folks aren't yer? Wanstead is closer to where you live than

South London is. But if you don't want to bother yourself . . .'

'All right. Point taken. And you're sure it's Wanstead and not Wapping?'

'Of course I am! It's a rib that's cracked, not my brain!' She then pushed her face closer to Patsy's. 'Now, mind that you mind your own business until it's done and dusted. I'm fairly certain I am gonna go down that road but I don't want that old bastard to get wind of it.'

'No, of course you don't. I won't say a word. I'm a bit speechless that's all. I don't know what to say.'

'Good. That's how it should be. And remember. Not a word to *anyone*.'

'Of course not! I'm gonna have to go now, Nan, because I want to pop round to see Auntie Eileen. I promised cousin Richard that I would pay her a visit on the day you had your fall but I didn't get there, what with everything happening.'

Whenever Patsy mentioned Eileen, a surge of unease swept through the old woman who, of course, knew the family secret. In fact she had been the one for telling Patsy much earlier in life about the adoption. But that was water under the bridge and it was too late now for her to interfere. Still, it concerned her more than she let on. 'Well you say hello to her for me and tell her not to worry, that I'm all right. She's a lovely woman is that daughter-in-law of mine. Generous to the core.'

'I know that, Nan. You don't have to tell me. I'm as close to Auntie Eileen as I am to you.'

'Good. That's how it should be. Now off you go,

and thanks again sweetheart for coming in. And for keeping quiet about you know what.'

'The secret's safe with me Nan. And it gets my thumbs-up any day of the week. Get yourself away from the old tyrant.'

'All right. Enough said. Now then . . . if I've not been chucked out by tomorrow make sure you fetch *me* in some barley-sugar sweets to suck when you next come in.'

'Will do.' With that Patsy kissed her on the cheek and left her to it. She was pleased that her nan had found her best friend after all these years, as well as making other friends to chat to in the ward. Molly had been leading a bit of a lonely life one way and another and it was time for a change. A change for the better.

Once Patsy had left the ward Molly looked across to Gwen and beckoned her over. Gwen eased herself off her bed, slipped her feet into her fluffy slippers and shuffled across the ward to Molly's bedside. 'She's a lovely girl, your granddaughter,' she said. 'I was watching from over there and you can see she thinks the world of you.'

'She's a good kid, *and* she's got a sensible head on those young shoulders. She knew what my old man was like before her mother and father cottoned on. I told her that I might be moving into my own little flat next door to a good friend of mine. You should have seen the smile on her face. It spoke volumes.'

'So you think you'll do it then?' said Gwen, a look of hope shining out from her eyes.

'Only once *you've* had plenty of time to think it through. After all, do you really want me for a next-door neighbour?'

'Of course I do! You've made me all cheerful while I've been in here, and having you live that close by will be fun. You remember how we used to have fun? Well, you're never too old Molly. I don't want to be lonely any more. And it's not as if we'll be under each other's feet. Mrs Clark who'll be your landlady is a lovely woman too. The flat that's vacant is in the basement but there's plenty of light. Nice big windows and your own little bit of garden as well. It's separated from the main garden that Mrs Clark keeps for herself. The flats above don't have use of either of the gardens.'

'It sounds ideal . . . So long as the rent's not more than I'm paying now. Although, to be honest, with my bit of savings from the insurance endowment I got when my first husband died, I could pay a bit more.'

'Haven't you spent that yet? On little treats for yerself?'

'No. I put it where it's making a little bit of interest for me.'

'Well done you. And in any case, Mrs Clark wouldn't charge you much. She's not short of a few bob but she could do with someone like you to cheer her up a bit. She's canny enough but she's a bit lonely if you were to ask me. But you should see her apartment – as she likes to call it. It's got two bedrooms and it's beautiful . . . really spacious and it's filled with lovely antiques. She comes from good stock.'

'Well, I'm gonna try and not get my hopes up just in case she's found someone else.'

'I'm telling you she won't have done! I'll be out of here tomorrow and I'll have a word.'

'Thanks,' said Molly. 'You always were a good friend. We should have kept in touch.'

'Yes we should have. But never mind. We've found each other again, and of all places, in a bloody hospital ward.' She gave a little laugh. 'We might not have been in touch but I never forgot our time as kids on the street. Life was more colourful then, wasn't it?'

'I should say it was Gwen; growing up surrounded by street gamblers 'n' hard drinkers and prostitutes and scoundrels. We children were sharp though, and mischievous little sods if we're honest. We behaved like little princesses on a Friday night when our parents got paid and little sods on a Monday, didn't we?'

'That we did. And didn't we make a little packet during the build up to Guy Fawkes night! Mind you, we did always make a good Guy and not just shove old newspapers into an old jacket and pin a cardboard mask to it.'

Molly laughed. 'Do you remember that old woman who lived above the corner sweet shop? She used to tell us kids that if we begged for pennies we'd be locked in a coal shed.'

She shook her head slowly and smiled wickedly. 'The streets were more exciting in those days weren't they? By the time we were six years old we were playing on the railways tracks, in alleyways and arches and narrow backstreets, with only those old lamplights to see by.

And all the while our parents were working hard for a living and hoping that we kids would have more of a decent life. But then we're no different when it comes to our offspring are we? And I wouldn't have wanted it any other way. The East End was never a bad place to live and nor is it now. We've got our museums, haven't we, and art galleries and theatres, and the picture palaces of course.'

'As well as the thieves,' Gwen smiled.

'But', said Molly, 'the mix of people is what makes it special. People even come from abroad now to go on tours around Whitechapel so as to see where Jack killed the prostitutes. I've seen them. It'll be a pity if they do go and knock all of the old terraces down and build rows and rows of skyscraper flats.'

'I don't think that'll happen. And anyway, it will always be the friendly old East End with a mix of religion and race. No-one can change that, can they?'

'We'll see, Gwen. We'll see. Don't forget that lot what are looking to stir up trouble, saying that if we're not careful all of London will be filled with people from overseas and there will hardly be a true blue English face in town. I think it's a load of nonsense. People are just taking the chance to move out. It's no wonder that East Enders are moving out into the countryside to new towns. If I was younger I'd be gone on the fast train to Suffolk or Norfolk to live. I was taken to a seaside resort up there once. When I was little. I loved it.'

'I don't think you would settle,' Gwen said. 'London's in our blood. And don't forget, it's much cleaner than it used to be. The air I mean. You remember the way we always dreaded the fog? And not to mention the bad street lighting in winter when we had to leave the house not long after the crack of dawn and go to work in the dark. I was so scared sometimes, walking through those back turnings with me own footsteps echoing when the heels of me boots hit the pavement.'

'That's true enough. It might have been nice I suppose . . . once upon a time . . . to move out into the country. Meet different people.' Molly shrugged. 'But not now. I've got my memories and that suits me.' She yawned and said, 'That's me done. It's time for my little nap.' With that Gwen wandered back to her bed and her pillow.

Two days later, sitting in a small armchair in the same ward, Molly was waiting to be collected by Andy who had taken the afternoon off to fetch her. The original plan had been for him to take her to his house, where she would stay in the spare bedroom until she felt ready to look after herself at home. But of course things had changed now that Molly had decided she was going to do a moonlight flit and leave Joe. She had made up her mind that she would go even if the plans for her to move into the flat next door to Gwen went pear-shaped. She knew that she could always put in for an exchange on the quiet and make the arrangements she needed to while in her old house. She had no intention of telling anyone else about any of it. Not until it was in the can.

Of course Molly hoped that once Gwen had been discharged she would pop back in with a positive answer, because plan A was what she wanted. What she needed. But she needn't have worried, for Gwen did indeed come with good news. The flat was Molly's to rent, and Gwen could even arrange for a cousin who had his own small removal company to go in to Molly's house as soon as she was out of hospital and Joe was out at the pub. Molly had already decided to decline Alice and Andy's offer of being a guest in their house. She knew that, in any case, both her son and daughter-in-law, deep down, would prefer not to have her move in with them for a while because both of them had to work every day to keep up their standard of living. So she hadn't worried that she would hurt their feelings by having a change of heart. She wanted to get on with arrangements for her new life.

Browsing through an old magazine she had picked up from a pile on a round table close by her bed, Molly looked around the ward and slowly shook her head. 'Not one of these poor old cows get sufficient visits,' she murmured softly to herself. 'They've all got families that 'ave all got the same old excuse, that they're too busy looking after themselves or working five days a week, eight hours a day.'

'Talking to yourself again, Molly?' said Steven, the male nurse, as he steered a trolley loaded with medications between the table and an old-fashioned high-backed armchair. 'Don't forget that you've had a head injury. You'll end up in Ward Seven if you're not careful.' He smiled.

'My head's fine thank you. It was me rib cage that took the brunt of me fall.'

'Ah, but you did have a bump on the head as well.' This nurse loved to tease Molly now and then just to get a reaction. And of course Molly knew this and loved to oblige.

'Had I 'ave slipped arse over head and not just crumbled with pain from a cracked rib I would agree with you. The bruise that you're talking about as a matter of fact is one that came about prior to my fall. And as for Ward Seven . . . those poor sods have been dumped in there because of age. And I'm not on my last legs yet. Far from it. You look as if you might be though, Steven.'

'You're not far out, Molly. I'm dog tired. And why aren't you miles of smiles? You're going home today.'

'It's the waiting to be collected. This is hardly a cheerful place is it? It should 'ave been pulled down and rebuilt years ago. It puts me in mind of a Victorian workhouse.'

Steven wheeled his trolley towards the next bed and checked his list. 'I won't say I don't agree that it's out of date Molly, but a workhouse? It's not that bad.' He then glanced across to another patient who was sitting in an upright chair gazing out of a window, and checked her list as to what medication she was due for.

'Well it's too bloody gloomy for my liking,' mumbled Molly.

'It would be to a live wire like you. I'm going to miss you. We all will. Especially that gift you've got of prompting a singalong.' He raised his voice a little to speak to another elderly woman who was gazing out at nothing.

'We'll all miss Molly once she's gone, won't we Gladys?'

'Eh?' The woman cupped one ear. 'What you saying?'

'We'll miss Molly! She's going home today!'

'Molly? Milly Molly Mandy? She's going home today? I didn't know she had been admitted. Shouldn't she be in the children's ward?'

'Oh leave it be for heaven's sake,' murmured Molly 'She'll go on about that non-stop now.' She glanced at her wristwatch for the umpteenth time. 'My son's always late. He'll be late for 'is own funeral.'

Steven chuckled. 'Perhaps you'll sign up as a voluntary visitor. Patients could do with cheering up no matter what ward they're on.'

'Well, it looks like we're in for a bit of entertainment now,' said Molly, glancing through a glass partition to the corridor. 'We are about to have company, ladies! Lilly, who's as mad as a March hare is on 'er way!'

'You're very wicked Molly.' The nurse hid a smile.

'At least she brightens a dull day,' said Molly. 'Which is more than I can say for you lot. I don't think I've ever heard one of you crack a joke.'

'That's not why we're here.'

'I know. I'm only teasing.' Molly then craned her neck to look out of the window at the lovely gardens below. She could see some of the patients strolling around, some in a world of their own, others in small groups, chatting. Then, as expected, Lilly, who was not all the ticket, rushed through the ward piercing the quiet.

'*Someone* has stolen *my* wedding dress,' wailed the forty-year-old, close to tears.

'Here we go again!' said Molly as she picked up her magazine again and buried her head in it.

'You're not supposed to shout, Lilly, or even be in this ward,' said another of the patients from the safety of her bed. 'You don't want to go and get yourself into trouble now do you?'

Ignoring the advice, the woman who was a long-term in-patient continued. 'Has any of you seen a white organza wedding dress? It was in my room hanging on the door!' The poor soul, who was wearing a faded but spotlessly clean blue dressing gown that covered a matching nightdress, was distraught.

'I saw a nurse wearing it earlier as a matter of fact,' said an elderly patient with a smirk. 'The black nurse as a matter of fact. I shouldn't think she'd give it back.'

'That's not a very nice thing to say!' said Molly to the woman. 'You wouldn't like it if someone said something like that to you.'

'Well, I shouldn't think that anyone one would. I'm white!'

'No you're not. You're a mixture of grey and yellow. Your skin's a terrible colour as a matter of fact.'

'Well, that's because I haven't been abroad on a holiday for a while. But I shall once I'm out of this dreary place. My son is going to take me to Spain as a matter of fact. He has a second home out there.'

'Then let's hope he leaves you there!' Molly said, keeping the rest of her thoughts to herself where this racist woman was concerned.

'My fiancé will be here any minute!' moaned Lilly. 'He'll go away again if I'm not ready! The cake's been iced and everything!' She then sank down into a faded armchair and covered her face with her hands. When she heard the reassuring voice of the male nurse she turned around, looking to him for comfort. Steven was quite used to her and knew that a bit of kindness was all that she needed. He squeezed her arm and told her that it was time for her to go back to her own ward, and also time for everyone to have a nap before doctors came on their rounds.

Trying to shut her mind to all that was going on around her, Molly went back to her bed, ready to sink her head into her pillow for a cat nap. Despite everything she had said, in a strange kind of a way she would miss this place with its peculiar mix of people, miss little walks in the grounds . . .

She decided to put it out of her mind. She had a lot of thinking to do – and a lot of planning. She was going to have to choose exactly the right day and the right time for her belongings to be moved from the house to the flat. But it would be worth it. At last she would be free of the abusive man she had married out of loneliness. Molly could hardly believe that it was not a dream and could hardly wait to begin her new life in Wanstead. She couldn't remember being this relaxed and happy in a very long time, if ever. All that she could hope was that it wouldn't go wide of the mark, and could hardly wait for her son to come and get her.

Chapter Four

With everything that had been going on Patsy could hardly believe that the day of the dance had come round. The time had simply flown by. And now, having taken this Saturday as one of her days off, she was sitting on the edge of her bed, in her dressing gown, wondering what she should wear. It was, after all, a family do held in a dance hall and not a young people's party that she had been invited to, but then again, she wanted to look her best so as to not disappoint the very handsome Danny. And of course she wanted to make a good impression on his family.

With this in mind she hauled herself off the bed to go through her wardrobe. She picked out different garments, mixing and matching until she finally decided to wear what she had first imagined herself in – an up-to-the-minute Prince of Wales check skirt and jacket with a plain red top beneath. She knew her much-loved top would set off her gold St Christopher and chain, a gift from her parents one Christmas. She then carefully removed the large rollers from her head and pushed a hand through her hair, telling herself that she looked all right and that with her make-up on the picture would be complete. She took everything off again and hung it up ready for later then, pulling on her dressing gown again and hungry for an early lunch of Welsh rarebit topped with sliced ham, she went downstairs.

With her parents out the house was quiet, which suited her down to the ground. Her dad had gone to pick up her gran from hospital and Alice, having filled in her forms for goods that her regular customers had chosen that week from her mail-order catalogue, was now out shopping. This little business that Alice had been running from home for years gave her a sense of pride in being able to buy treats for herself instead of having to rely on Andy to have to put his hand in his pocket. This apart, she had always been a bit on the independent side and she enjoyed the work. She liked seeing her customers now and then when they popped in to borrow her thick catalogue to browse through for goods they needed to purchase on the weekly payment plan.

In the kitchen preparing her light meal, Patsy wondered whether Molly was all right to be taken home or whether she should have spent a little more time in the recuperation ward. Of course she knew why the old girl wanted to be in her own house and not in this one. For one thing she didn't want to be looked after by anyone. She was far too independent and wouldn't want to be an encumbrance, not even to her own family even for a few days, as had been Andy's thoughtful suggestion. And besides this, Patsy knew that her gran was bursting with secret joy at the thought of doing a moonlight flit, and she herself couldn't help but smile at the pensioner's pluck. Even so, she was going to have to keep her feelings to herself because she, just like Gwen, had been sworn to secrecy.

She was so carried away with her thoughts that she didn't hear her dad come in. 'Your gran can be so stubborn at times, Patsy,' he said. 'She's back in her house insisting that she can look after herself and won't be talked out of it.'

'Well she's old enough to know her own mind, Dad – that's for sure.'

'Tell me something that I don't know.' He smiled. 'So, have you found something suitable to wear for this dance? Or am I gonna have to treat you to an outfit?'

Patsy laughed affectionately. 'No, of course you're not. I did find something but, if it's all right with you, I might take you up on that new outfit another time.'

Andy couldn't help but smile at his daughter who was a chip off the old block. 'Cheeky cow. So what time are you meeting up with the boy? The shop closes at half past five on Saturdays, I believe.'

'It does but the staff don't leave until six, after they've cleaned the ham-cutting machine and the cheese—'

'Yeah all right, babe. I don't need to know all the ins and outs. So you'll meet him there then? Instead of him coming here to pick you up?'

'Of course. Hobbins is on the way to the bus stop. You wouldn't expect him to come and collect me, surely?'

Andy splayed his hands. 'I was only asking. Don't get aerated.'

'I'm not, but you asked me that yesterday. It's only a

date. I'm not running off with him for a dirty weekend in Clacton by the sea.'

'Perish the thought,' said Andy as he left the room, a bit thrown by the way his girl was beginning to answer him back. It reminded him that his daughter was now a beautiful young woman who deserved to know the truth about herself. The familiar feeling of dread began snaking its way back into the pit of his stomach. He knew that it was time for him to call on his brother and Eileen to ask if they also thought that Patsy should be told what was what, now that she was no longer a kid. He hated the idea, and once again tried to convince himself that there was no rush. He went out into the back garden to prune his prize rose bushes to take his mind off of things. 'Better to go at a snail's pace than to rush in like a whippet,' he murmured to himself. 'What she doesn't know can't hurt. And my girl's none the wiser and quite content. In fact she's more than that right now. She's happy.'

By the time Patsy was dressed and made up she was a bit panicky because she had only ten minutes to walk from her house to the corner store before it closed. Had she been more relaxed she would have realised that Danny would wait outside after the shop had closed if she was late. By the time she arrived at the meeting place her face was flushed and she was a touch out of breath, but was relieved to see him on the corner looking out for her. She broke into a warm smile and so did he. His was from relief because he hadn't been certain whether she would stand him up or not and,

71

apart from the disappointment, he would have had to face the chaps at work who were bound to ask how he had got on.

Once Patsy had apologised for being late they each felt relaxed in the other's company. Then, as naturally as if they had been going out together for weeks, Patsy casually slipped her arm into his and they walked along quietly. From that moment on everything seemed to go smoothly. A bus just happened to come along as they reached the stop and they found two empty seats next to each other on the upper deck. Once they were seated and on their way, with no trace of inhibition from either of them, Patsy confessed to Danny that she had been a bit nervous the night before because she wouldn't know anybody – never mind that she was going to stay in his home as a guest. Danny not only smiled fondly at her but also kissed her lightly on the cheek and told her that she had nothing to worry about.

During the bus ride to his neck of the woods he explained that they would go to his family home first so that he could have a wash and brush-up and don the suit he kept for special occasions. Patsy asked if the dance had been arranged as a one-off or if it was a regular thing. 'Yes and no,' he said. 'It's just something that the club puts on now and then to raise money and this time it's for the very poor Catholics in Glasgow, people who are living below the breadline, so an organised dance suits two purposes. Everyone involved gets to have a bit of fun and a bit of dancing now and then, and at the same time they feel as if they're doing their bit for the cause. The ticket money goes into a bank account that was set up for the charity decades ago. The women bake and cook for days beforehand and the men sort out the booze.'

'Sounds good,' said Patsy. 'Does your family know that I'm not a Catholic, never mind not having a drop of Scottish blood in me?'

Quietly laughing at her, Danny shook his head. 'No, but they won't send you to Coventry over it. We have all kinds of friends of different race and religion and we all bumble along nicely together . . . and at the same time raise a decent amount of funds.'

'It sounds great. So I won't be seen as an outsider then? That's good.'

Again Danny shook his head. 'Hardly.' He then looked earnestly at her and said, 'My family can't wait to meet you. They've been laughing at me if you want to know the truth. Laughing and saying that I've been walking around like love's lost dream.'

'Well, I'm not sure what that means but it sounds nice. I hope I'm not a disappointment.' She blushed.

He looked into her face, into those lovely light green eyes. 'You won't be. Just don't go breaking my heart or they might hunt you down.' He smiled. 'We'll have a nice time – you'll see.' Then, after a short pause he said, 'You look fabulous.'

'Thank you,' said Patsy. 'Now . . . I want to know everything. Why don't you tell me about yourself and any hobbies that you've got.'

'Fair enough.' Danny smiled. 'I'm a member of a dominoes club. I swim in our local baths every Thursday evening. I enjoy a good film. I hate the circus and

73

pantomimes and always have done. I like going out for a Chinese supper now and then but I don't like Indian food. Your turn.'

'I'm a hairdresser and want to run my own salon. I enjoy going to Ilford Palais and the Tottenham Royal dance hall with my friends now and then. I'm an only child and spoilt. And . . . I'm on the game.'

Danny took the joke in good spirit. 'Oh really? I won't ask what you charge, in case I can't afford you.'

'You wouldn't be able to.' Patsy laughed in the moment's silence that followed, and suddenly feeling sure she could trust Danny, she added, 'Oh and I adore my nan but hate Joe, her second husband, who's not my real grandfather.'

'Why do you hate him?' said Danny.

'Because he's a secret bully and my nan is a lovely person and she doesn't deserve to be treated like a dish-cloth.' She then turned her face so that she was looking directly into his and said, 'Can you keep a secret? And I do mean *keep* it.'

'Depends what it is.' His expression changed to one of apprehension.

'It's about the way he treats her and what she's going to do about it on the quiet.'

'You said he's a bully . . .' said Danny.

'Yes. In every sense of the word and he's also a drunk.'

'Does he knock her about then?'

'He has done but nobody knows apart from me. I worked it out for myself. Too many bruises for one thing and too many excuses as to how they came about. And anyway I can read my nan like a book.'

Drawing breath, Danny raised his eyebrows. 'She must love the man if she's prepared to put up with that and tell no-one.'

'No, she hates him. And deservedly so. But she's gonna be all right. She's going to do a moonlight. And before you ask, yes she's got somewhere to go.'

Danny broke into a smile. 'Your nan is going to do a moonlight? How old is the old girl?'

'She's not an "old girl" and at heart she's as young as she feels. I think she's in her sixties. Sixty-five, I think.'

'Well all I can say is good for her. As long as the place that she's going to is all right. You don't want her to jump out of the frying pan into the fire.'

'No. I would never let that happen. She's going to move into a flat in Wanstead that's part of a big house and is next door to a good friend of hers. They met up again in hospital of all places.'

Danny sank back into his seat. 'I hope she knows what she's doing. It's quite a thing to do for a woman of her age. She is an old-aged pensioner after all. But if you think that she's up to it she must be. And you say that no-one else knows she's going to do it? Not even your parents?'

'That's right. But she'll be miles better off for it. And her old mate Gwen is a social person so gran will start mixing with people of her age who, from what I hear, like to have a bit of fun. They go to see a show up west twice a year, for instance. My parents don't know about any of this but they'll be so pleased once it's done. She might be a pensioner but she's young at heart.'

All thoughtful, Danny then said, 'Why can't you tell them now? Before she goes?'

'It's the way my nan wants to play it and I think she's right. No fuss. No debates. No anger. If my dad knew how that old bastard has been treating her I think he would kill him. But he'll handle it better once she's in her new place and happy and that Joe's out of the picture. That's when she'll fill him in on the details. Although Nan's favourite saying is let bygones be bygones and Dad has always said that he goes along with that sentiment as well. So if he finds out he'll have to practice what he preaches won't he?' She smiled.

Danny raised an eyebrow. 'And you're part of the secret. Did you encourage her when she told you about it?'

'Too right I did.'

'And I thought that you were a quiet shy girl that wouldn't say boo to a goose.'

'I am. Unless someone gets up the goat in me.'

'Right. I had better watch my step then, hadn't I?'

'Yep,' said Patsy keeping a straight face.

Danny looked a touch bemused and couldn't work out whether she was play-acting or not. But it didn't matter. He was comfortable in her company and this was more than enough for him. He liked this girl. He liked her a lot.

With mixed emotions now that she was out of hospital Molly was trying to make a real effort to make it look like she had settled back into her little house so that Joe wouldn't suspect anything. Now that she knew she wasn't going to be stuck there forever, she was feeling better about life in general. She glanced at the clock on the mantel shelf to see that it had just turned three o'clock and this suited her fine. She would watch some afternoon television, then have a nice warm sudsy bath and a snack, then go to bed early. So with the rest of the day mapped out she went into the kitchen to make herself a cup of tea. She so appreciated the quiet and guessed that Joe would, as on most Saturdays, stay at the local to play cards with his cronies into the evening.

As Molly made her drink, Patsy came into her mind. She wondered how she was getting on with the lad from the corner shop and the dance that he was taking her to. She smiled at the thought of her granddaughter behaving all grown up. She hoped Patsy would still come and visit her in her new flat. As she thought about the future and all that might lie ahead of her once she moved out, she felt tears in the back of her eyes but they were from relief and not sadness at leaving her birthplace. At last she could see a light at the end of the tunnel. So wrapped in her thoughts was she that the sound of the doorbell startled her.

Wondering who it might be calling on her out of the blue like this, she went to the door and was pleased to see the cheerful face of her young neighbour who lived a few houses along. This was Rita – a very good friend of Patsy's – who always lifted her spirits.

'What a little ray of sunshine you are Rita. How are you darling?'

'I'm fine,' said the young woman who, to Molly, seemed barely old enough to be married. She and Patsy had pretty much grown up together, and now Rita was married to the lovely West Indian lad, Errol. 'It's you who's not been well, and I've come to see how you're doing. And if you want me to get any errands for you or that.'

'That's a lovely thought, sweetheart. But I feel a lot better now and my daughter-in-law's been in while I was in hospital and stocked up the cupboard and the old fridge.'

Having closed the door behind her, Rita followed Molly into the sitting room, talking as she went. 'I wanted to make sure that you were all right after that fall and being in hospital an' all.'

'Oh bless your heart. I'm fine darling, and you're a sight for sore eyes any time . . . but I will say that I'm glad you knocked today. And yes, I'm better than I've been in a very long while.'

In the sitting room Rita lowered herself into one of the old fireside chairs and smiled. 'Why's that? Why are you glad that I knocked?'

'Why? Because my life is about to turn around.' Molly in her chair leaned forward towards her young friend. 'I know I can trust you to keep a secret, so I'll tell you what I've got to say and then I can catch up on how your family is. After all, your mother was a good mate of mine when we worked in them offices at Charrington's brewery.'

'I know that Molly. What's with all the nostalgia?' Rita asked.

'Nostalgia? Yes. You could say that's on my mind. While I was in hospital I met up with a good friend that I hadn't seen in years. And . . . consequently . . . this is a tight secret, sweetheart . . .'

'Go on then. You know you can trust me. I'm all ears and longing to know.'

'My friend is arranging for me to move out of here and into a lovely little flat in Wanstead next door to where she lives.' Molly then sat back in her chair and smiled. 'What d'you think of that then?'

'Brilliant.' Rita broke into a smile. 'But what about the old man?'

'He doesn't know. I'm going to do a moonlight. Take all of my furniture and belongs in one clean sweep. My friend, Gwen, is arranging it all. The removal men and van – everything.'

'Jesus,' said Rita, smiling. 'I can't believe it. Not that it's not about time. It is. Does your Patsy know?'

'Yes. And she's the only one in the family who does. So you've got to keep it close to your chest my girl.'

'Oh I will, don't you worry. I think it's great. I'll miss us having our little tea breaks together but I can always visit you can't I?'

'Of course you can. I shall be glad of it.'

'The miserable old bastard doesn't deserve you in any case. But then I've been saying that for ages haven't I.'

'Yes, I know you have. And it all went in, don't you fret. I might 'ave looked as if I wasn't taking no notice darling, but I was. And now, what with my old mate Gwen chivvying me, I've made up my mind and I can't wait to go. I shall give our Patsy the address to pass on to you and you can come and see me whenever you feel like it. And let your mate Maggie know where I am once I've gone. She's a lovely girl as well. And I'll have my own little back garden so Peppie will be all right if he gets bored. And your husband is welcome as well should he want a few hours out of Bethnal Green. And I shouldn't worry about 'im being black. The woman who owns the house that's split into flats sounds like a freethinking person, so she won't have colour prejudice.'

Rita smiled. 'Well, that's just as well then. So your cracked ribs are healing nicely then, are they?'

'Yes. I've had a good rest and I'm taking it easy. I don't ever want to feel pain like that again. Which is why I'm leaving.' Molly gave a sigh that spoke volumes. Then, after a pause, she all but whispered, 'You know . . . Bill, my first husband, was a very smart man. You should have seen the way that the neighbours used to look at him when he strode along the pavement. His black hair was thick and always slicked back and he had two suits. They were a touch old-fashioned but they weren't threadbare and in those days that was something to be proud of. You don't get suits like that now. A lovely wide lapel; a waistcoat as part of the package and his father's silver fob watch and chain in the waistcoat pocket. He had an aura of someone that came from a family that once had money. Strangers weren't sure whether he was from posh or poor lineage. I knew though.' She slowly shook her head and smiled wistfully. 'He was a lovely man whichever way you looked at it. I can't believe that after all those years with such a lovely man I went and married such a scoundrel, just because I was blinded by loneliness when I was widowed.'

Rita spoke in a quiet voice. 'Does the rest of your family know now that Joe is such a tyrant?'

'Only my Patsy as far as I can tell. But you knew that she knew in any case. Now – I would offer you a cup of tea sweetheart, but I've got some secret packing to do. Clothes and that. I shan't be taking the stuff I've had for years on end, only what I've bought in the last few years or so. Patsy told me that that's what I had to do and she's right. The rest can go to the Red Cross. They put a pamphlet through this door now and then and I've kept one of them. The phone number is on there so all I have to do is give them a call and they collect.'

'I know. Errol gave them some of his clothes that had gone out of fashion.' Rita slowly shook her head, adding, 'I'll miss you so much, but I'm really pleased for you, and I will definitely tell Maggie and we'll bring Peppie to see you. Errol's not one for making visits—'

'Well, I thought as much. Why would he want to visit an old woman that he hardly knows? But you and I go way back. I fed you your bottle more than once when you were a baby and your mother helped me out when I went down with the flu, and of course you're pals with Patsy. Now then, off you go. And not a word to anyone. Promise?'

'God's honour.' Rita smiled and winked and then took her leave.

Once Molly heard the door close behind the girl she

glanced around the room as if it was for the last tim and saw an empty milk bottle that she had left on th small dining table was still there. She had forgotten t put it out that morning and Joe hadn't bothered to do when he left the house. Walking slowly to the fron door she asked herself why it hadn't crossed the laz man's mind to do that one small thing when he left fo his pub crawl. It *was* only a small thing it was true an not something to nag about . . . but it was the sma things that got her down. Even when he was sober h did very little around the house other than potter in hi shed at the end of the garden where he kept his bee crates.

Opening the front door she instinctively looke along the narrow turning that faced the public garden and saw Joe staggering out of the entrance of the old fashioned corner pub. She placed the milk bottle on th side of the doorstep and then looked around to see i any neighbours were about. She was ashamed to se him in this state at this time of day, and in the summe too, when it was still light. He was good fodder fo the gossips that lived in the turning. She had long sinc picked up that he had become something of a spectacl for those with little to do with their time other tha people-watch and gossip.

Arriving at the door, red in the face and grinning, Jo spoke to her in a slurred voice. 'Wait 'til you hear th joke I heard in the pub. It's crude so you'll like it.'

Nodding at him and keeping her thoughts to hersel Molly went back inside. She was sick of his silly slurre prattle and sick of him staggering through the passag to the small sitting room. And now, his joke already forgotten, he was swaying and saying, 'I'm going for a little nap.' This was not out of the ordinary and she knew that in the bedroom he would pull off his top clothes and leave them crumpled on the floor then roll into bed and out for the count. It was at least one blessing that years ago he'd taken to sleeping in the spare room so she didn't have to put up with sharing a bed with him. But it didn't matter any more. She no longer cared what he did so long as he was not in her way. And soon she wouldn't have to look at him ever again.

She thought back to all those times when, in a bad mood brought on by drink, he had deliberately grabbed her arm – the one she'd broken which had never entirely gone back to normal. It hadn't quite reset properly and caused excruciating pain. When he did this she felt nothing but hatred towards him; hatred, and fear of what he might do to her next. At first she hadn't been sure if he had done these little things on purpose, testing to see if she really did have a bad arm or not. But she knew better now.

Even worse than Joe's spiteful streak was when he would go silent on her for days on end and walk about the house as if she didn't exist. He would get up in the mornings and not say one word before, during, or after his breakfast; ignore her when she tried to make con- versation, then leave the house and loudly slam the door behind him. In fact he nearly always walked about the house as if she was invisible unless he wanted to say something mean.

The most important thing now was that she no longer cared. And, if truth be told, she had stopped caring a good few years back and tried to give as good as she got where the silent act was concerned. All that she wanted now was a happier life as far away from him as possible. She didn't need him – she had found her old friend and she had her family who all knew her inside out.

Molly knew she wouldn't have lasted as long as she had without her family. In fact the biggest blessing of all was when her son Andy had arranged and paid for a telephone to be put in for her because this meant that there was always someone that she could dial up and talk to during those lonely times. Times when Joe had been in the house and she had tried to make conversation, just to hear another voice, and he had behaved as if he hadn't heard. He would simply deliver a silent, detestable look when she tried to find something of common interest to talk to him about. For years now they had been sharing the same house and eating at the same table and that was all. But now, instead of it bringing her down, she actually relished the peace and quiet – especially when he wasn't in the room and she could enjoy watching afternoon television or listening to the radio without his dour presence.

Now, as she sat in her comfortable armchair, she recalled other past incidents that she had put to the back of her mind. Once she had looked through the gap between the hinges of the door into this very room and had seen Joe sitting at the table gazing into his teacup, sad and sorry for himself. Taking pity on him,

she had gone into the room pretending to check something such as whether the paraffin heater in the corner
of the room needed fuel, just so as to fill the silence. To
give him a sense of someone being about just in case he
was feeling lonely, but he hadn't even acknowledged
her presence. And she had so often wanted to sit at the
table with him and ask why he disliked her so much,
why he hardly spoke a word to her, why he was so
moody. But she soon learned not to ask questions
because he would only tell her to get on with her own
life and mind her own business . . . or simply ignore
her. She had often questioned why they hadn't gone
their separate ways before now and had always told
herself that she had been too lacking in confidence to
let go. But now of course it was different and all of this
was about to change.

Feeling a touch on the lonesome side after the
friendly company in the hospital, Molly switched on
the television set to bring some folk and sound into the
room. She was ready to relax back into her armchair
and watch whatever was on when she heard the floorboards creaking in Joe's bedroom and then on the stairs
and wondered why he hadn't been able to settle. He
came into the room in a slightly more awake state than
when he had left no more than ten minutes since,
wearing what she recognized as a sour expression. He
glanced at her with a disdainful look and said, 'You had
to put that on with the sound up, didn't yer? You knew
I was going for a doze so you put the telly on and the
sound up.'

This was utter rubbish but she had no inclination to

rise to his bait and kick off a row, which he was clearly spoiling for. She nestled further into her chair instead but, suddenly feeling bolder than usual, looked back at him and said, 'One of these days I'm going to leave you, then you'll know what a good woman you had. They say that a man doesn't know how lucky he is 'til his luck runs out. But at least you'll be free to come and go as drunk as you like.'

'Come and go as I like? I already do. And I'll have you know that there's a lovely woman in a pub where I sometimes drink that's taken a fancy to me. A divorcee. Glenda. She lives by herself now. I've grown quite fond of her as a matter of fact. She's a bit coy as well as sexy and that makes her all the more attractive. She's nothing like you.'

'Well, there you are then. Why don't you clear off and move in with her,' said Molly, feeling the old hatred towards him rise from the pit of her stomach.

'Well I might just do that – if I can be bothered to pack all my stuff up. One of these days I might just do it.'

'Let me know when and I'll go out for the afternoon. You can take what you want.' Molly said this knowing that she had every intention of clearing the house of everything when she left. 'I don't care what you do any more. I can't stand the sight of you – if you want the truth spelt out.'

'What're you talking about? You never *did* care. What 'ave I been to you? Eh? A bloody slave? Someone to get the coal in; light the fire; dig the garden; run errands. And I'll tell you something else . . . My Glen's not tough as old boots neither. No. *She's* soft and tender-hearted. She's been let down by her old man who's gone off with another woman. I don't know yet if she'll be able to put her trust in me or not.'

'And she knows that you're a married man, does she?' said Molly, not giving a toss either way.

'Of course the woman knows that! D'yer think it would bother her? Her husband was a married man as well, wasn't he? But she's all right. She's a nice bit of old. And she's got a few bob tucked away. We're the same age give or take a couple of years, but she thinks that I've seen more and done more than she has. That's why she's interested. That, and the money she imagines I've got put by.' He started to chuckle in a drunken leering kind of way. 'But she's a right little goer between the sheets so who's complaining?'

Molly looked at Joe and felt physically sick. 'Well all I can say,' she sighed, 'is that she must lead a solitary life and be desperate if she's ready to take on a drunk who's work-shy. The government dishing out dole money to people like you every so often has done more harm than good. It's created lazy alcoholics.'

'What are you talking about? I do work. Cash in hand. No tax. I do all right, don't you worry.'

'I know you do. And if you dig into my savings, should you find them again, or go down my purse to filch any of my money I'll shop you as a fraud. So help me I will. A bit of prison life would do you the world of good. It might even get you off the booze.'

'Dig into your savings? Ha! Chance would be a fine thing. You've found a clever hiding place this time. A man could search high and fucking low for your money and never find it. You crafty old clapped-out cow.' He then turned and stumbled out of the room again – back to his bedroom and his bed – leaving Molly in peace.

Patsy, with no idea as to the scenes with Joe that were happening under Molly's roof, was feeling a touch apprehensive now that the bus ride from East to South London was at an end. If asked, she would have to admit that she was feeling out of her depth and wasn't sure why. She was hardly miles away from home but she hadn't been into this part of the capital before and it did seem different to what she was used to. The roads were wider and the buildings grander than where she lived in East London, and of course the air wasn't tainted with smoke coming from the trains on the railway close by or from the brewery so close to Patsy's home. She had heard Blackheath mentioned in passing but knew nothing about it. One thing she noticed straight away was that here where Danny lived there didn't seem to be as many children out and about playing rounders or Tin Tan Tommy noisily in the streets. Instead there were several couples, old and young, walking hand-in-hand or with arms linked, and the pace of life seemed tranquil and the locals a touch calmer as they strolled along.

Once off the bus and being guided by Danny into a wide street, she noticed that not only was this quieter than she was used to but the streets round here were tree-lined, giving a sense of being in the leafy suburbs of London which she liked. She slipped her arm into

Danny's and felt very much at ease as they walked along, talking quietly about the area and the difference between where he worked and where he lived. It didn't occur to Patsy to ask why he chose to travel from South London to East London every day just to serve in a grocery store.

The fact was that his father and uncle owned bits of land here and there around London and were at the point of signing a contract to purchase the ground on which stood all of Patsy's local shops, including Hobbins & Son where Danny was working. His father had thought it sensible for Danny to get to know the area and find out if it was a safe bet for investing in land. But it had all been done very quietly. Secrecy was vital because there was fierce competition for land like this which, once cleared, would be perfect for building a shopping precinct or a grand supermarket. There were several other property developers around who would be serious rivals were they to get wind of the fact that land was up for grabs in this promising part of London. And even though the deal was almost sealed it was not done and dusted.

Having done all the research, once the contracts were signed it was Danny who was going to be in charge of running the new development. Of course it was going to take time for the sale to go through and the land to be cleared, never mind the re-build, but Danny had been excited about the project from the start. Until now, that is. Suddenly it felt like a skeleton in the cupboard that he had to keep from Patsy. He had no idea how Patsy might react if she knew he was one of the people behind the demolition of her local area. Though he knew the shopkeepers were getting a fair deal, and that the buildings themselves were long past the point of repair, he realised they nonetheless held a lot of sentimental value for some people. He hoped Patsy was part of the modern generation – but all the same he wanted her to get to know him first for who he was, not for what his family did, so he had decided not to tell her until after the dance.

Guiding Patsy into another wide tree-lined avenue, Danny nodded towards a tall, detached early-Victorian house, its walled front garden filled with shrubs and a few trees. Smiling, he shrugged as if a touch embarrassed and said, 'That's where I live.'

Presuming that this was a joke Patsy laughed and said, 'You wish.'

Enjoying the little surprise that was in store for this lovely girl holding his arm, he spoke without any sign of boasting even though he was proud of his family achievements. 'It's in need of updating,' he said, in a matter-of-fact tone, 'but my family can't agree on whether they should keep it in the style of the period or go modern.'

Patsy glanced sideways at him and wondered if he was going too far with his fantasising 'Oh . . . I would knock it down and build a block of council flats if I was in on it,' she joked. And then, as they arrived at the gate leading into the lovely front garden she added, 'Is this what you want then? To one day live in a house like this? A house fit for a prince?'

'Oh, I wouldn't say that. Not a prince, just one that

belongs to a long-standing old Scottish family.' He pushed the wide entrance gate open and stood aside to allow her to go in first.

'Very amusing,' said Patsy, still believing that he was pulling her leg. 'Now close the gate or the owners won't be too pleased – should they be in and watching through the window. I don't want to get arrested thanks. It wouldn't go down too well with my parents.'

Danny shrugged almost apologetically as he took her by the arm and guided her through the open gateway and up the wide path towards the polished oak door. Then as he took out a door key from his jacket pocket Patsy stopped smiling. 'This isn't funny . . .' she said, now worried that he was taking his fantasy a bit too far. 'Whoever lives here won't be too pleased that we're trespassing.'

'Stop worrying,' said Danny as he pushed the key into the lock and opened the door. He smiled at her and shrugged again. 'It's a bit old-fashioned but this is my home sweet home.'

Still she could hardly believe that this was for real. Narrowing her eyes she looked into his face almost lost for words. 'You mean . . . this really is your house?'

'That's right – but it doesn't bite. Come on. Don't be shy.' He then showed her into the spacious entrance hall from which several doors led off into various rooms. There was also a wide curving staircase, traditional rugs on the oak wood floor, and heavily framed paintings and family portraits on the walls.

A touch in awe of the house and shy of it all, Patsy was at a loss as to what to say. She had never been in a private grand house such as this before. 'Why didn't you warn me?' She whispered. 'I wasn't expecting this Danny.'

'What difference does it make?' He smiled affectionately at her. 'This is a family house and like I said, we share it with a couple of aunts and my grandparents. Stop worrying.'

'I'm not worried,' said Patsy, a touch defensively. 'I just wasn't expecting this. That's all. I had no idea that you lived in a house like this. It's beautiful.'

'And so are you.' He smiled, then took her hand and led her through one of the doors leading into a large family kitchen – the heart of the home with the centre-piece being a long waxed and polished old pine table surrounded by eight mismatched period dining chairs. At the butler sink with her back to them was Danny's grandmother, who had her sleeves rolled up and looked a touch hot and bothered. She was the eldest of the family and by now a little hard of hearing. His voice raised, Danny said, 'I've brought someone to meet you Gran!'

Glancing over her shoulder, the woman wiped her forehead with the back of her hand as she peered at Danny who was the apple of her eye. Then, speaking in a quiet warm voice she said, 'You are most welcome Patsy. We've heard so much about you.' She smiled. 'But my grandson's timing is not that perfect. We still have things to do even after a rather busy day already, so you will forgive us for being all over the place. I've got buns in the oven and sausage rolls in the larder waiting to be baked. My grandson will make a fresh pot of tea for all three of us.' She smiled warmly. 'Unless of course you prefer coffee. In which case I'll make it myself because he's not very good at percolating. So which would you prefer my dear?'

'Tea would be lovely . . . thank you,' said Patsy, who liked this woman who told it straight from the shoulder. She reminded her a little bit of her own gran.

'Tea it shall be. Good.' The old woman then turned to Danny. 'I don't think that the kettle has grown legs as yet, sonny boy.'

'Yeah all right, Gran. I've only just walked in the door.'

Turning back to her chore of washing some dishes the feisty old lady continued to rattle on. 'There's no need to waste time telling me what I already know. I've still so much to do that I can't think straight. Make a nice pot of tea now, there's good boy. Your mother and your aunts are stripping the beds. Why they couldn't leave us all to sleep for just one night extra between the same sheets as they've slept in this week I'll never know. When I was a girl I was lucky if I had a sheet to lie on at all.' She glanced sideways at Patsy and winked at her.

Enjoying the old woman's sense of humour, Patsy smiled and then spoke in a quiet voice, saying, 'I'm used to helping out in the kitchen at home. Can I do anything?'

The head of the household then turned slowly around to face her and once again a lovely warm smile spread across her face. 'Och now, if that isn't music to my ears. But give yourself ten minutes to settle in Patsy.

And then if you wouldn't mind drying these dishes that would indeed be helpful. I've been at it all day, and that's the truth.'

Glancing at Patsy and mouthing the words, 'Are you all right about this?' Danny seemed a touch embarrassed, but once her reply came with a smile and a nod he relaxed. Then, after putting the kettle on, he turned to his grandmother and said, 'If it's all right with you Gran, I'll have a quick bath and get changed and then do whatever's necessary to help out.'

'Of course it's all right by me you silly boy. But try not to take too long.' That said his grandmother turned to smile at him. 'You don't want to keep this lovely girl of yours waiting while we all run around like chickens without heads.'

Satisfied, relieved and pleased that the head of the household had taken to Patsy, Danny left them to themselves. He took the stairs two at a time and was gone, to get himself ready for the dance of the season. Once in the big old bathroom he found himself smiling. 'So far so good,' he murmured, and then prayed that his old aunts wouldn't show him up once they had had a fill of Scotch whisky. He knew that his parents would be fine because they were as patient as saints when it came to the relatives that they shared this house with.

His grandfather as ever was keeping out of the way, pretending to be busy in his study. But Danny knew that this would be the case and that he could catch up with him later.

Soaking in the bath Danny closed his eyes and sighed with a smile. Now he could relax. He could hardly believe that the girl he had fallen head over heels for was down below in the kitchen with his lovely old grandma. He was so happy he didn't care about anything other than hoping he wasn't too obviously wearing his heart on his sleeve. All that he wanted now to make it perfect was a quiet cigarette behind this locked door while soaking in his bath. His family did not approve of smoking to the point of banning it in the house, but he knew he could get away with it in here.

Having enjoyed his secret smoke, and had a good soak, Danny was soon out of the bath, dried, and dressed in his best shirt and suit trousers. He wanted to show the garden to his very special guest and, while doing so, give Patsy the opportunity to have a sly cigarette too. He knew that she liked a smoke now and then because she had told him so during the bus journey. She had also told him that, just like his parents, hers were dead against the habit. To Danny it seemed ridiculous that even though he was thought old enough to be put up for the position of heading the family enterprise in the East End he wasn't considered mature enough to smoke if this was his choice. But now he had a partner in crime in Patsy and soon he would have her company in the grounds, out of sight in his favourite secret retreat behind an old oak tree.

Stretched out on his messy bed, Joe looked up at the ceiling, his mind working overtime. He had been planning to leave Molly for a couple of years now . . . ever since he first kissed Glenda. But he wasn't prepared to go away empty handed. No. He knew that Molly had money tucked away from an insurance payoff when her first husband died, never mind the savings she had told him about back in the early days – when he had got her to trust him. He learned then that she and her late husband had been saving up for a deposit to buy their own little house. He had never been able to fathom why they would have wanted to do that when they had this lovely little terrace at dirt-cheap rent. No, he hadn't swallowed that old tale. To his way of thinking, the way he saw it was that the woman he had married was a miser and that her first husband was just like her, most likely a Scrooge who saved for the sake of it. The one thing that he was determined about was that he would find her stash of cash. This was what was keeping him there. And once he had found it he would be away. He would slip out of the house and be gone for good. He grinned at the thought of it and then took a drink from the hip flask that he kept under his pillow.

Joe had searched the place from top to bottom but with no luck. And all the while his tart, Glenda, had been waiting for him in the little cosy house down by the river in Wapping that she rented. If nothing else he could satisfy her constant lust between the sheets. It was because of this – their mutual appetite for sex – that he had missed the opportunity of a lifetime to search high and low for Molly's money while she was in hospital. But he thought that in a way it had been worth it. His Glen had said that he was the best in bed that she had ever had. Over the years he'd used his prowess to win over a few ladies who had a bit of cash to spare, and Glenda looked to be no different to all the others. Ready to fall for his charm and empty promises.

With his mind flitting from one thought to another, he tried to conjure up a plan. It was crossing his mind that the easiest thing for him might be to stage an accident that his wife could not possibly survive. He felt sure there had to be a foolproof way that he just hadn't found yet. But he didn't have to wait many seconds for inspiration: as he was wondering what his next step might be, he heard the sound of tiny pattering in the loft and guessed that mice had come in again, or possibly even a rat.

Thinking about getting rid of the little blighters, it occurred to him that should he get his hands on some rat poison containing arsenic or cyanide, he could use it to suit his other purpose. He could slip some into Molly's food perhaps. After a while of conjecture and intoxicated thinking he came up with a plan that he thought was ingenious. The park-keeper in charge of the Bethnal Green gardens that backed onto the wall of Molly's back yard was a touch simple but very chummy. He was always ready to chat about his passion to win the cup for being the best keeper of public gardens in the area, and because of this the lawns and flowerbeds looked beautiful and tidy in all seasons. Lately, the proud gentleman had been a bit long-winded when telling him about pest control and the worst pests of all that had arrived in the ground beneath his immaculate lawns. The dreaded mole. He had said that he thought that the mole had learned not to eat the packaged pest poison that he had been using. So, to get round this, he had soaked live worms in cyanide and then carefully dropped one in the heart of as many molehills as had appeared in his lawns. And this had done the trick. The lethal substance had worked like lightning. He had got rid of every mole.

At the time, Joe had not been in the least bit interested in these long drawn-out stories to do with the bloody gardens. But now it was different. Now his mind was running on the fast track where poison was concerned. What if he was to get the man to give him some? What if he was to slip a little of the lethal substance into Molly's food? Some leftovers from a dinner for instance. Steak and kidney pudding came to mind. She always tended to over-salt it and go too heavy with the Bisto and she loved it cold the next day. So a bit of cyanide might well go undetected. And should it be discovered at postmortem he would say that she was always trying new ways to kill off the rats, and the moles that sometimes found their way into her beloved garden. He smiled at the thought of his ingenious plan. A plan that to his way of seeing it was infallible, and he felt very pleased with himself.

He felt sure that he had at last come up with a way of getting rid of Molly. With her out of the way, dead and buried, he would be able to search for her savings, and he and Glenda could live happy ever after, either in his little house or in a little country village somewhere up north where it was cheap to rent. But only after a respectable bit of time had passed by of course. Naturally, he would play the deeply grieving widower who would be pitied by all.

Smiling to himself, he slipped a hand under his pillow, pulled out his old chrome hip flask again and, with a contented smile, congratulated himself for coming up with a plan for the perfect murder of the old cow downstairs. He had never really liked her that much and had certainly never loved her. He turned on his wireless as a matter of habit and was satisfied enough with the way of things to try and drink himself into a nice doze. But so excited was he by his brilliant idea that he couldn't fall asleep. The cheap gin was making him alert rather than comatose. He couldn't stop himself from smiling. Soon the old hag would be dead and buried and he would be free and the richer for it. He could hardly wait to carry out the execution.

Chapter Five

A little later, with Joe upstairs snoring, Molly switched off the television – she was in no mood to watch a cookery programme with Fanny Craddock giving her husband black looks. She wanted to think about pleasant things and a more pleasant way of life. Coming across her friend Gwen again had been the miracle that she would have asked for should she have prayed for one. She couldn't wait to move into the flat. Her life was about to turn around and she was so ready for it. She wanted to wake up in the mornings with a smile on her face the way she had done before she had let Joe into her life.

In a more relaxed mood now, Molly believed Joe to be out for the count and allowed herself to drift off into a light doze. But this didn't last long because he was soon back in the doorway again talking gibberish. She guessed that he would probably have had a top-up from his flask that he kept under his pillow. In his slurred voice and with a strange kind of a grin on his face he said, 'I was talking to my Glen about when I was young. Before I met you. When I was in the army and stationed abroad during the First World War . . .'

Too fed up with him to listen to any drivel Molly told him to go away. She kept her eyes closed while talking because she couldn't stand the sight of him when he was like this. 'Leave me alone. I've had enough of you. More than enough.'

'Oh really? Well that's a coincidence because I've had enough of you as well. I'm going away soon. Leaving. Not yet though. Next month perhaps, or the month after. Who knows? I like this little house so there's no rush. And I'm not drunk before you say I am. I've fell in love that's all. She's a lovely woman is my new bedding partner and a good little worker as well. She cleans for a photographic company over in EC1. And she's a good listener. I said to her, I said, I'm like a fly trapped in a closed jam jar . . . and you've prised the lid off.'

'I bet she wept buckets listening to poetry like that,' said Molly. 'Did you meet her at work? Did she keep on walking past you and wiggling 'er arse? I can just see you being the kindly old caretaker who watches the tarts who come on all innocent and then spill out a life story of tragedy. Or did you fall for the whore in a pub? I should think that would be closer to the truth.'

'Well *you would* think that wouldn't you?' Joe, his face a high colour, was now swaying and hardly able to focus. 'I'm taking the dog out for a walk while you stew on it. She said that I could move into 'er place. It's plenty big enough for the two of us.'

'Oh?' said Molly, egging him on to tell her more. 'So you've already been inside her house then?'

'Of course I've been inside, you silly old mare. And I've been getting my leg over. She loves it and so do I.' Joe was boasting a little too much and he wasn't going to stop his drunken spiel. 'I've had her hundreds of times as a matter of fact.'

He then started to chuckle and Molly felt sick looking at him. His face was puffy and red, his eyes were glassy and narrow and he looked as if the alcohol was oozing out through his pores. Grinning at her, he then said, 'All I had to do when we first knew we fancied each other was to buy the tart some flowers on Valentine's Day. I'll go for a nice stroll now while you get used to the idea. You don't want my company and I don't want yours. There's nothing between us except silence.'

In a state of confusion, Molly wasn't sure if he was telling lies or not. His behaviour had got worse of late, so maybe he *had* found someone who was actually daft enough to take him in. All kinds of things were now floating through her mind – how she should have picked up on his hints sooner. He had been sleeping with another woman for God knows how long. She had had her suspicions but now it was confirmed she felt as if she was waking up from a horrible nightmare. At least she didn't have to feel guilty about leaving him . . . she couldn't wait to go. Knowing that the waster was in the passage by the street door putting the lead on Scamp, Molly hauled herself out of her chair and then winced from a pain on the heel of her left foot. It had begun to swell, and she had a feeling that there was a splinter of glass still embedded there, from a small tumbler she had dropped a day or two before she went into hospital. She had gone into the kitchen to fetch a drink of water when Joe had stumbled in from the shed in the garden where he had been listening to a boxing match on his old-fashioned wireless. Clumsy and staggering from drink he had come into the kitchen and knocked the glass out of her hand. She had quickly cleared the mess while listening to an angry outburst about her carelessness.

She knew that the splinter had embedded itself in her heel but had hoped that a few warm baths would soften the skin adequately for her to remove it with her tweezers. She knew from experience to keep quiet about such things because Joe would, as he had done before, insist on slitting the skin with a sharp razor blade to try and force the sliver of glass out with his thumbnails. She had been there before and he had caused her to suffer excruciating pain. The last time that she had let him get near her with a razor blade was a year or so ago when a thorn from a rose bush had embedded itself into the fleshy part of her thumb.

Coming back into the room in search of his tobacco tin, Joe started up again, saying, 'I was telling my Glenda about that stuck-up granddaughter of yours, and what a comedown she'll get when she finds out that her own mother gave her away to her sister-in-law. My girlfriend thought that was a disgrace and I agreed with her. I don't know what made me marry into your family.' He then staggered back out again and into the passage to put the mongrel on its lead. Molly couldn't wait to hear the front door open and shut again so that she could shed a few bottled-up tears in private.

But the sudden sound of the dog yelping, followed by loud bangs and thumps and Joe crying out in pain brought her to her feet and out into the narrow passage. And there he was, crumpled on the floor, wedged between the two walls and out for the count. At first it looked as if he might be dead, but then she saw that he was still breathing. His mouth was open and he was unusually pale, especially compared to the blotchy high colour that the drink usually brought to his face. Whether he had broken bones, hit his head or was simply comatose from booze Molly had no idea and at that precise moment, she didn't care. All she saw was an opportunity to rid herself of the ogre for a few days. She picked up the receiver of the phone in the hall and dialled 999. Now, hopefully, it was going to be his turn to be hospitalised. The sense of relief that swept over her was like a gift from God. This was her chance to pack up the house without risking him coming in. After all her years of suffering, now it would be his turn because without his daily intake of booze in hospital, it would not be too long before he'd drop the nice old boy act, as he always did when he went any length of time without drink. And she was sure the hospital would be none too pleased when they saw his nasty side.

Going back into the passage to check on Joe she felt a fleeting sense of pity for him. She glanced at Scamp, who was looking up at her with an expression in his eyes that she had not seen before. She was so used to seeing the dog cowering, it took her aback to see him looking so calm. She signalled for him to come to her and pulled a small handful of dog biscuits from her apron pocket, where she kept them to give him a little treat when the master wasn't looking. The dog was by her side in a tick. She and Scamp had a special relationship, probably because they were both treated with the same contempt by Joe for most of the time.

Molly sat down in the hall and Scamp jumped onto her lap, ready for a stroke and a bit of kindness. Together they waited for the sound of the ambulance. She didn't feel in the least bit sorry for Joe. She felt nothing. Nothing at all except for a comforting calm that seemed to be spreading through the house. All that she hoped now was that he would be taken away quickly. And to her joy, as soon as the ambulance men saw his condition and checked him over, they carried him out on a stretcher.

Just ten minutes later Molly was sitting in her armchair, smiling as she basked in the late afternoon sunshine that was coming in through the window. Then, thankful at the way that fate had played its hand, she went to phone Gwen to ask if it would be possible for her to move in straight away. The answer was a resounding yes. Keen to make sure Molly wouldn't have time for her courage to falter, Gwen told her that she would phone that cousin of hers who ran a removal company so as to get her out of the house immediately – if possible that very afternoon just in case Joe was discharged after only one night. Gwen told Molly to start packing her suitcases and that she would be there within the hour to help her. Hardly having any time to think, Molly responded with trepidation.

'But Gwen . . .' she all but whispered, 'what if they

fetch him home while I'm packing things up or moving out? He'll go berserk . . . because I intend to leave not one stick of furniture behind.'

'That's not on the cards. Even if he's not concussed or there are no bones broken they'll still have to keep him overnight because he was so blind drunk by the sound of things. Stop worrying and get going if you want to be out of there by tonight.'

'What about Scamp?'

'Leave him there with food and water.'

'I can't do that. I love the mongrel and he relies on me. He only takes him for a walk when it suits him and that's not nearly enough.'

'Oh, well then, bring him with you. We'll sort something out. Just get packing so we can get you out of that wretched house.'

'What about the rent? The man comes each week and he's due on Monday.'

'We'll phone the rent office and tell them that you've moved. They won't give a toss. Those houses are probably due to be knocked down in any case. You'll be doing the landlord a favour by going.'

'That's right. There has been a rumour about the bulldozer demolishing the lot.'

'Well there you go then. Now get packing and I'll be there as soon as I can.' With her mind in turmoil and feeling a touch light-headed, Molly went back into her sitting room and slumped down onto her favourite armchair by the fireplace where no flames burned. She knew she should be getting on with the packing – but she needed the dizziness to pass first. As she laid her head back she quietly thanked God for the turnaround. When she felt better, she sprang into action with a renewed sense of urgency. She had an almighty lot of packing up to do.

Wasting no more time, Molly went upstairs to her bedroom where there was a hatch into the loft. She quickly had the hatch open and the ladder down. She carefully climbed the ladder and went into the loft to throw down some large suitcases. Then she cautiously edged an empty tea chest through the opening and carried everything downstairs.

Working at a steady speed she began packing her china, saucepans, cutlery and crockery, using bundles of old newspapers to wrap them. Molly had plenty saved as she normally took them to the paper-making factory just off Cambridgeheath Road where she was rewarded to the tune of sixpence a bundle.

With no time for sentiment she worked methodically, making sure that all her precious things were wrapped properly so that they wouldn't get broken en route to the flat in Wanstead. She was determined not to leave one solitary belonging behind. Then, as she was wrapping her favourite china she went ice-cold as she heard the sound of the doorbell. Surely Joe hadn't suddenly recovered and insisted on being taken home? Going cautiously to the front door she put on the safety chain and then opened it to peer through the narrow gap into the outside world. To her relief it was young Rita standing there. Standing there and smiling.

'I saw the ambulance, Molly, and after what you told me earlier I thought you might be making your move while that old devil is out of your way. I reckoned you might need a hand with your packing.'

'Oh Rita,' said Molly, unhooking the safety chain so as to open the door wide. 'You are an angel. You really are. Come on in sweetheart. I can't tell you how happy I am to see you. I want to be out of this house as soon as possible just in case that bastard makes his way back here.'

'He won't be back today silly,' Rita said. 'But I think we should work at speed in any case. Before you go and have a change of heart. It can't be easy leaving your home where you were once so happy.'

'Oh yes it can sweetheart. I can't wait to get out.' She closed the door behind Rita and had to keep her emotions in check. 'I thought it was him at the door.'

Rita laughed. 'God forbid. Now then, we've got a race on our hands.'

'We have indeed,' agreed Molly. 'And to be honest I don't know if I would have carried on with this plan had you not called. Going through my possessions brought back all those memories of before I was made a widow. I do so want to take everything with me. Every last bundle of old Christmas cards, and of course every letter my beloved first husband sent me all those years ago when he was out there in Dunkirk fighting for Britain.'

'You can stop right there,' said Rita as she went through to the sitting room. 'I don't want to hear about the war, rations, or anything other than the future. Now let's get stuck in. The van will be here shortly.'

'And thank God for it. I can't wait to go. And nor

can Scamp. I'm sure he knows that we're leaving. He's in the garden watching my every move through the back door.'

'I bet,' said Rita. 'Come on, let's get you packed up and away. You've got a new life to lead Molly. A wonderful new life.'

The church hall in which the party was to take place was already decorated with streamers and balloons by the time that Danny and Patsy and his family arrived. It was buzzing with people and the band that had set up on the stage was clearly enjoying its little warm-up session. The hall was not all that dissimilar to the church hall opposite Patsy's home, just slightly larger. It seemed to her that it would be difficult to fill with enough guests to have it feeling anywhere near cosy.

As the evening progressed and people got into the swing of things it was clear that she was wrong. People came in their droves, and before she knew it she was being introduced to yet more of Danny's family and some of their neighbours. It was almost too much to take in but it didn't matter because everyone seemed to know each other, and the sound of talking and laughter accompanied the soft taped music playing in the background while the band had a break. In no time at all, everyone helped themselves from the copious cold buffet that had been laid out beautifully on large trestle tables, covered with white linen cloths, along one side of the room. All in all it smacked of being a very successful evening. Keeping one eye on Danny while she chatted to other people, Patsy could see that he was the centre of attention with the girls in the same way that she was with the lads – although the few times when she caught his eye he looked as if he wasn't sure that she was enjoying herself.

But their worries soon dissipated once Danny's grandmother arrived at his side and gave him what were clearly his marching orders. 'If you're not careful my lad you'll lose that wee girl. It's like bees to the honey pot where your cousins are concerned.' And this, without a shadow of doubt, meant that the head of the family liked Patsy and had not only accepted her into the fold but wanted to keep her under a safe wing.

Knowing that this was his gran's cue for him to relax because Patsy had her seal of approval, Danny gave his grandma a kiss on the cheek as he squeezed her arm and said, 'You're a diamond. I don't know what we'd all do without you.'

'Neither do I,' said his grandmother, smiling fondly at him. 'Now you just make sure that the girl has a wonderful time.'

'Don't worry – I will,' he said, and winked before leaving her to go over to Patsy and stay by her side. Taking her arm, he excused the pair of them from his cousins and walked her to a quiet corner close to the bar. 'I'm sorry I left you but I had to do the family bit,' he said.

'Of course you did. I was all right. I was fine.' She smiled. 'Nice cousins. But what about the girls? Where are they?'

'Can't you guess?'

'Ah. In the powder room touching up lipstick and swapping boyfriend stories.'

'That just about sums it up.' He looked into her eyes and at that very moment the band started up again and the lead singer was at the microphone, kicking it all off with a song from the hit parade, 'Blue Moon'.

Looking at Patsy's lovely face Danny said, apologetically, 'It's a bit of a tradition for us so-called youngsters to get on the floor for the first dance in the second half.'

'Well we'd best do it then, hadn't we,' she said, all inhibitions now gone.

'A slow jive all right with you?'

'Perfect.'

Within minutes they were dancing as if they had been partners for years, instinctively picking up on a style which they were both in tune with. Patsy couldn't have wished for more and, as the evening wore on with everyone in high spirits she, like most of the others, was singing along to the band and having a wonderful time. But as with all good things the hours simply flew by. Before she knew it the clock struck midnight and everyone had linked arms and were in a circle singing 'Auld Lang Syne'.

Declining a lift with the family in their highly polished dark blue Jaguar saloon, Danny and Patsy strolled back to his house, chatting quietly about their families. Patsy told Danny how she wished she wasn't an only child. He looked at her for a moment, then quietly told her the saddest thing that had ever happened to him –

something that he had not talked about in a very long while. He once had a sister, two years younger than himself, to whom he had been very close. Her name was Margaret, but when she was eleven she had been run over by a car in the High Street and had died in hospital that same night without ever coming round. Saddened by this brief but moving account of a tragedy that Danny had clearly wanted to get off his chest before any of his family might mention it, Patsy was silent, but her expression said it all.

'I still find it hard to talk about it,' murmured Danny. 'But my aunts insist that it's better not to bottle things up – never mind that it happened all those years ago – and then spill it out when someone new comes into our realm. Now I can put their minds at rest and tell them that I've told you.'

Knowing that there was little she could or should say to comfort him, Patsy slipped her arm into his and squeezed his hand. He responded to her silent sympathy with a warm smile and a look that spoke volumes: that it was the luck of the draw and there was nothing that anyone could do to change it. With no sense of having to fill the quiet spell that followed the couple strolled along, each with their own thoughts. Danny wasn't sure whether he should have told Patsy about his sister, but he wanted to prepare her in case one of the aunts would have a whisky too many and go all sentimental, spilling out tears and family sorrow.

Once back at the house, even though everyone was a little inebriated, tired and ready for bed, they all gathered in the big kitchen for a mug of warm milk spiked with a little brandy or rum. Chatting about the dance, they sat around the table relating funny stories of who had got up to what during the evening and Patsy felt very much at home even though it was a completely different scene from what she was used to. And as tired as she was after a very long and exhausting day, she wasn't quite ready for bed. She really didn't want this evening to end. She had had such a lovely time and just wanted it to go on and on.

Then, while the others were talking over the various incidents of the evening, she felt Danny's eyes on her and smiled at him. This was picked up by his dad who, in a firm but friendly voice said, 'Well . . . I like your company but I don't particularly like your hours. I'm of the opinion that it's time we elders turned in.' He gave his son a clandestine wink and turned to the rest of the gathering. 'I think that the young ones might enjoy a little confab between themselves about the way the dance went and the people that were there – including those who share this humble abode.'

'I don't think you could call it humble,' Patsy said. 'It's more like a mini-mansion house compared to ours.'

'Well, home is home no matter how many rooms there are,' said Aunt Vi. 'And it's off to bed with me.'

Yawning, Aunt Ada agreed. 'It's way past bedtime.' She then looked at Patsy and smiled, saying, 'Young company excluded, my dear girl.' In her own way, she was also letting the others know that they should leave the sweethearts to themselves.

'Well I for one am very tired indeed,' said Mrs

McDonald, who smiled at Patsy and said, 'I hope you enjoyed the evening as much as we all did.'

'I really did. Thank you for having me,' Patsy replied.

Then, with the head of the family leading the way, the others quietly left them to themselves. Once alone in the kitchen, Patsy at one end of the table and Danny at the other, Danny whispered, 'They won't all have gone to bed. The women will congregate in the snug at the back of the house that has the best view to the garden. Not that they'll be looking out at this time of night but it's the family meeting place when something has to be discussed.'

Danny then changed chairs to sit close to Patsy, and spoke in a quiet voice. 'They've been discussing for days as to where they should put you tonight. They think it's wrong for your room to be too close to mine because your parents might not think it right. But that's where the spare room is . . . although in any case it's filled with everybody's old junk.'

'That sounds like my gran all over. She's a hoarder too.' Then lowering her eyes she said, 'So where *am* I going to sleep?'

'Well, you can either snuggle down in a big double bed with one of my aunts, or in one of the attic rooms which are a bit isolated. Or they'll decide to put me in the attic and you in my bed.' He smiled and shrugged. 'Anyway, shall we have a little drink and slip out into the garden for a sneaky cigarette?'

'Sneaky? I didn't know that the one we had before going to the dance was a secret smoke.'

'Afraid so. The only one of them who knows that I

puff is Aunt Vi, who you might be sharing a room with. She puffs as well on the sly. The rest do know but pretend not to.'

Smiling, but a touch bemused, Patsy slowly shook her head and said, 'I'm not gonna break the rules and I don't honestly mind where I sleep. To be honest I'm really tired. Don't ask me why, but I *have* been awake since the crack of dawn.'

Danny, with his elbows on the table that would not usually be allowed, leaned forward and looked into her face. 'Why?'

'I said don't ask me.'

'I know you did, but why?'

'Because I don't know why, silly thing.' Laughing at him and the soppy smile on his face she reached out and cupped his hand. 'I think that your family are great. Thanks for a really lovely evening. And for looking after me the way you have.'

'I've enjoyed every minute, Patsy,' he said. 'In fact, it's because I've had such a lovely time that I want to tell you something.' With that he told her everything about his family owning her local tumbledown shops, and all their plans for redevelopment – with him at the helm.

After he'd finished, Danny looked at her. 'I hope you don't think any differently now of me you know. I know some people think we're tearing the heart out of the East End, but I really think it could be a wonderful thing.'

Patsy was silent for a moment. Then said, 'I believe you, Danny. I know you think you're doing the right thing – and do you know what, I think so too. It's about time us East Enders had a few mod cons of our own. I bet my mum would love a fancy new supermarket. Yes, I've grown up with those old shops, but they've had their day.'

Relief flooded through Danny, but before he could say anything else, he heard footsteps on the oak floorboards in the passageway and some deliberate coughing from one of his aunts to let the young couple know they were on their way back in – just in case they were having a cuddle in the kitchen.

With Danny's elder aunt leading the way the four women, almost in a line, came into the kitchen, talking between themselves and trying to act natural. Smiling first at Patsy and then at her son, his mother said, 'You'll be pleased to know that we've finally come to an agreement, but we'd like to run it past both of you.'

'Go on then,' said Danny, trying his best not to chuckle.

'Well . . .' she said, as she gazed thoughtfully out at nothing. 'We feel that it would be far more comfortable for Patsy if she were to sleep in the lovely bedroom at the front of the house on the second floor.'

Danny smiled affectionately at her. 'Mum, I know where Aunt Violet's bedroom is. Just get to the point because I'm dog tired and so is Patsy. It's been a long day for all of us, and don't forget I did do a day's work before helping out at the hall. I think we'd both fall asleep on a plank if that's all we had.'

'Oh well, here we are then,' said Mrs McDonald relieved. 'I'm so pleased that Patsy feels at home and is ready for a good night's sleep. I've been worrying myself thinking this and thinking that. That we might not have made her feel at home, or that she might have felt out of place.' She turned to Patsy. 'So – you won't mind sharing a bed with an old woman then?'

'Old woman?' The aunt in question sniffed haughtily. 'I'm only just in my sixties. That's not old . . . is it Patsy?'

'Of course it's not.'

Quietly chuckling at the way the three of them were standing together as if they were holding court and about to deliver a sentence, Danny said, 'I honestly don't think she'll mind where she sleeps.

'That's right,' said Patsy. 'And if it's in a bed and not on a put-u-up, what more could I ask for?'

'A Put-u-up?' said one of the aunts as she clasped her chest with a delicate hand. 'We have *never* had to use one of those in this house . . . and let's thank the Lord and our Lady Immaculate for it.'

'It was just a passing comment, Aunt,' said Danny. 'Now you've told us where she can lay her head we can all get some shut-eye. I don't know about you old ones but I'm all done in.'

'I think we all agree,' said the other aunt, a touch haughtily, 'Except of course for calling us the *Old Ones*.'

Danny's mother then took charge and, with a firm straight-from-the-shoulder tone, said, 'Patsy will sleep in the bed with Auntie Violet.'

'Great.' Danny smiled. 'Now we're getting somewhere. Aunt Vi will be the chaperone.' He then turned to look at Patsy. 'Is that okay with you?'

'Of course it is,' said Patsy, wondering why they had had to have a debate over it.

Danny was just glad that his mother hadn't gone into the whys and wherefores of her decision. Aunt Vi had in fact been chosen because the other one, Ada, snored like a trooper. On top of that, although it was never expressly mentioned, Ada was rumoured to be a lesbian. The word lesbian of course had never been voiced aloud in this house, even though Ada had had a best friend sharing her big double bed for decades – until the best friend had skulked off and left her for another best friend. But this was considered personal business and never mentioned.

With a sigh of relief Danny's mother, one hand pressed against her chest, said, 'Well that's settled then. Good. Now then Patsy, would you like to join us for a mug of cocoa? Or are you too sleepy?'

'That's very kind of you,' she said, 'but I really would like to go to bed now, if that's all right?'

Resounding agreement from the three women that it was perfectly all right for her to turn in ended it there and then. Mrs McDonald and the aunts left the room so that the young couple could say goodnight in private. Once they had gone Danny turned to Patsy, held out his arms and then hugged her. 'I'm sorry you had to go through all of that,' he said.

'Don't worry about it.' Patsy shrugged. 'I think they're lovely. And so what if they like to do the right and proper thing. It's old-fashioned but it's nice.'

Looking into her soft green eyes Danny murmured, 'You are so lovely . . . I've been longing to hold you close since the moment I saw you in the shop. I can't believe that you're here – in my home. I hope this assortment of relatives won't scare you off. They're all right once you get used to them.'

'Stop worrying.' Patsy smiled. 'It is a bit of a bizarre household and not something I'm used to, but I think it's great. And I do mean that.'

'That's because you're an angel in disguise.' His voice low and sincere he then murmured, 'I'm nuts about you and have been since the day you breezed in to the shop. That was weeks ago when you popped in for two pound of sugar because your mum had run out without realising and your dad takes four spoonfuls in his tea.'

Patsy blushed. 'Well, you do have a good memory,' she said then eased herself off the kitchen chair ready to go to bed. Danny took both her hands in his and then kissed her on the lips, longing for more, but keeping his passion at bay. He simply whispered the words 'Good night Patsy. Sleep tight.'

Upstairs in the old-fashioned en-suite bathroom, Patsy brushed her teeth and had a quick wash of her hands and face before undressing and getting into her pink and white polka dot pyjamas. She then went into the large bedroom with the big quaint bed that was its grand centrepiece and slipped in between the fresh and beautifully ironed white cotton sheets. The bed was not only deliciously comfortable but it had hand-painted birds on the headboard and little flowers at the foot end. She had had a lot to drink at the party and it had been a long day, so she knew that once her head sank into her feather pillow she would drift off into a lovely and very welcome sleep. Just then the two aunts came into the bedroom. Aunt Ada's single bedroom was next door to theirs and she was carrying a long bolster in a sparkling white pillowcase. It looked like a long white sausage.

'Here we are my dear,' said Ada. 'I completely forgot to place this down the centre of the bed earlier on. What with the dance and so on it quite slipped my mind. This will give you and Violet each of a bit of private space to sleep in.'

Patsy couldn't help smiling at the caring ways of this family. Ada said goodnight and took her leave while Violet went to change in the bathroom. The free-flowing drinks that had been supplied to her all evening and into the night were now taking effect on Patsy. She could hardly keep her eyes open and drifted off within minutes, with no thoughts of anything other than Danny's handsome smiling face.

Chapter Six

That night after leaving her home for pastures new, Molly – and Gwen – were exhausted by the move. But now, with the disappearing sun leaving a red glow on the horizon, Patsy's beloved gran was quietly comfortable in an armchair in Gwen's living room, sipping a hot milky drink. She was relaxing more and more as she listened to her friend giving her a pep talk to make sure Molly felt no guilt about doing a flit. These two old comrades had been parted for more than a decade or two and yet they were chatting away as if time had stood still. And tonight they would be sleeping under the same roof, as it was too late to settle Molly in her new flat.

Molly could hardly believe that she had made this, the biggest leap of her life. She had left her cruel and selfish husband and taken everything, lock, stock and barrel, except of course for his few belongings and the single bed that he slept in. And the best of it was that when Joe discovered she'd gone, he would have no idea where she might be.

All of her belongings were in situ next door, waiting for her to place them wherever she wanted when she unpacked. She and Gwen were going to sort out what would go where the next day when they were fresh. It was a lovely spacious one-bedroom apartment, just as Gwen had described. Molly had been nervous about moving into somewhere she had never seen, but she couldn't have hoped for a nicer place.

To top it all, she had felt an instant rapport with the woman who was going to be her landlady, Mrs Clark. She had met and spoken to her while her furniture was being taken into the flat by the removal men and had immediately felt at home with her.

Satisfied that it had been a good day's work, Molly and Gwen were exchanging stories of what each of them had had to put up with during the past twenty years or so, for it turned out that Gwen's story was not that dissimilar to Molly's. The women then chatted about the area and how nice it was and what a lovely person Mrs Clark was. Molly was now filled in about the grief that her landlady had had to endure in the early days of her life. The woman's sad story almost brought tears to Molly's eyes, but she at least found comfort in the fact that things could and did get better for people who had suffered in one way or another. And from what Gwen told her, it sounded like Grace Clark had certainly suffered . . .

Newly married at twenty, Grace's mother had been gloriously happy and very much in love with her husband. When baby Grace had come along they'd moved here to what was in those days a somewhat grand period house. But everything changed for Grace when she was still just a little girl . . . She hadn't got to know her father because he had run off with a secret mistress when she was barely more than a toddler. Apart from the rogue's sordid affair, it had turned out that he had not only been leading a double life where women were concerned but had also been moving dodgy funds, stocks and shares, and depositing them in his mistress's bank account offshore. Naturally, it had come as a terrible shock all round when this was discovered, especially since all that Grace's mother had been left by way of an explanation was a short note telling her that she would never see her husband again – that he would not be returning to England. Soon after this Grace's broken-hearted mother had been told by a friend that her husband had sailed off to South Africa to begin a new life.

At that time Grace had been just four years old. She had adored her father and had missed him badly until time erased him from her memory. Luckily she had had a kind and gentle doting mother, who had not only to cope with the heartache of losing her husband to another woman, but also the shame of the scandal that had spread within their circle by the gossips. Grace, even though just a small child at that time, had been the light that had pulled her mother through it all.

And if being abandoned by her father hadn't been hard enough for her and her mother to cope with, it turned out that the funds left in the family bank account were insufficient to carry on the lifestyle to which they had been accustomed. Far from it. And it was for this reason that an architect had been called in to draw up plans to convert the spacious house into three self-contained flats – one for mother and child to live in and two that could be let to create an income.

The house had seemed forlorn and quiet during the first year after her father's departure and, even though Grace had been so very young, she had had to hold back her tears for the sake of her mother. Of course she had cried into her pillow at first, begging God to send her daddy back home. She had simply adored the man who had always said that she was his little ray of sunshine. And yet all the while he had been making those secret plans to run off and take the family fortune with him. Sadly, the once elegant house, lit by brilliant cut-glass chandeliers, that had so often been filled with the sound of laughter and friends took on a jaded and forsaken ambience. Apart from anything else, the wall above the ornate fireplace in the glorious sitting room bore a huge oblong mark where a portrait of Grace's father had once hung. This had been taken down soon after he had gone and thrown onto a bonfire that had been built in the spacious walled garden at the back of the house.

When asked by her mother what she would most like to do with her life Grace had said, 'I want to be a dancer, Mummy. A singer. Or an actress. I want to go on the stage.' And so, once the money from the rented flats started to come in, she began piano lessons, voice training and then drama classes. By the time she was eighteen she not only enjoyed being seen as a gifted young lady but also had fallen deeply in love with a handsome aspiring actor called James Clark. Soon they were married, and her mother could not have been happier when she learned that they wanted to live in one of the converted flats at the top of the house. Sadly, their happiness was not to last long. One bitterly cold November, Grace's mother lost a battle against pneumonia and died soon after her daughter married. And if this hadn't been bad enough, her young husband was knocked off his bicycle soon after. He was in hospital for over two months with his injuries when he suddenly died from heart failure. They had barely been married a year when Grace was a widow.

To have lost both her parents and then the only young man that she had loved, had almost been too much for the young Grace to bear. But bear it she did, with the help of her numerous friends. These important links within her world of actors, writers and producers was what carried her through and helped her to rebuild her life. But over the years her friends had drifted away and she had grown lonely. At least she had been able to continue living in the house where she had been born. Now in her early sixties, Grace chose to live in the ground floor apartment – not only was it spacious, but it also saved her from struggling upstairs with her shopping. But the house still needed lively tenants to make it feel like a home. Gwen hoped that Molly moving in could be the start of happier times in the house again.

The next morning Molly lay in bed in her friend's spare bedroom with the smell of crispy bacon frying in the kitchen and the summer sun coming in through her window. She was more relaxed than she had been in a very long time – even with the thought of the unpacking ahead of her. She watched the dust as it danced in the ray of sunshine and wondered whether Patsy had enjoyed the dance. During her ride in the van with Rita they had chatted about Patsy and Danny, and Rita had said that when shopping at Hobbins she had more than once thought that he was a lovely chap as well as being handsome.

This had helped reassure Molly – but then Rita really was a brick. She had worked hard helping Molly to empty her cupboards and pack pots, pans and linen. And when Molly had given her a mug of coffee and some biscuits to nibble, she had continued to drive herself on in between sipping her hot drink. And not only had she worked hard but had also, in her own special way, made sure Molly had the confidence to carry out her plan. When she had slumped into her old armchair and asked Rita if she was doing the right thing by taking everything that she wanted and most of what she needed, Rita had reeled off good reasons to do so.

Once everything had been packed and loaded and was on its way to Wanstead, Rita had driven Molly to her new home using her husband Errol's van. During the journey the young woman had continued to tell Molly that she had to celebrate the fact that she had a lovely new life to look forward to. She also reminded her of all the years that she had suffered in silence before she had mentioned anything to anyone – Rita included. Molly had had to agree with her and, in doing so, the measure of guilt that she had felt in the pit of her stomach faded away.

By the time they pulled up in the pleasant street in Wanstead, Molly had shed a few tears – not only from relief but for joy. She had many times heard the saying freedom is sweet but hadn't in a million years thought that she would get to taste it for herself at this stage in her life. And because there had been so much unpacking still to do, Molly had taken up Gwen's offer to stay in her spare bedroom that night so that she could get a decent sleep.

Apart from this, if truth be told Molly was a little bit in shock at what she had done and appreciated not being alone that night. It also meant of course that she would be fresh the next day when she had to tackle arranging things in her new flat. Now that she was free from Joe, and with the move done and dusted, she knew that she had done the right thing. She hadn't felt so much at peace in a very long time.

Of course it had been a wrench to leave her house and Whitechapel, but once she stepped inside the flat that was to be her home, carrying boxes filled with her favourite ornaments, she knew she would be happy there and had felt a wonderful sense of a new beginning. Her back had been playing up after all the packing and lifting, but she had rubbed in her pain-relieving ointment last night and this morning she could feel it was beginning to work. Smiling to herself, she quietly murmured, *Never mind Molly. Everything aches for some of the time old girl, and something aches for most of it.*

This had been one of her mother's favourite sayings and it was comforting to bring to mind the memory of her mother's face. And as she lay in between the lily-white sheets, she felt not only the spirit of her late mother in that room with her, but also that of her first dearly beloved and long-since departed husband. She felt sure he was there, helping her to celebrate what she had achieved and willing her on to make the most of the years that she had left in this world.

Waking up this morning had been like waking from a long drawn-out nightmare – her life with Joe. Thinking about him now that she was free, Molly gently stroked one of her wrists and smiled. No more would the man be able to cause her pain. No more was she going to have to listen to him going on and on as to how *she* had driven him to drink. Never again would she be made to feel that it might be her fault that things had gone wrong within her marriage. It was over. He was out of her life.

And now, a safe distance away from him with time on her own to think, she realised just how stubborn and obstinate he was. Aside from his drinking, she also knew that he had been bad-mouthing her to all and sundry, especially to her neighbours who, quite rightly, had been reporting back to her. But she no longer cared. Still she could not forgive, forget, or excuse his wicked behaviour.

Molly could hear movement in the apartment so knew that Gwen was up and about. She got herself out of bed and, putting on her light blue dressing gown, caught sight of herself in a full-length mirror and noticed just how much weight she had lost with all the worry over the last few years. She hoped that eating whatever she liked whenever she liked would soon put some flesh on her old bones and also bring some colour back into her cheeks. As she stood there, she saw

Scamp in the mirror too. He was looking up at her patiently and waiting to be fed.

She patted her thigh the way she always had done and he was there in an instant. 'I expect you want your breakfast too,' she said. 'Well, don't you fret sweetheart, I've got five tins of food that I fetched with me from the cupboard.' She gave him his usual stroke, kissed the tip of her finger and tapped his nose. 'We'll be all right Scamp. You see if I'm wrong.'

Once in Gwen's kitchen, sitting at the old waxed oak table while Scamp ate from his place beneath it, Molly couldn't stop herself from smiling. 'I can't believe that I've done it, Gwen,' she said. 'At last I'm doing what I want. Not that I want much. Somebody else is welcome to all the tea in China. I just want a cup of good brew when I feel like it and a place of my own.'

'Music to my ears,' Gwen said. 'And your leaving him is not before time from all that you've told me and from what I've heard via the grapevine.'

'How right you are. Deep down I knew that it hadn't been me that had driven him to steal money from my purse when I wasn't looking. Nor had it been me that had driven him to drink, which he so often accused me of. He was already a heavy drinker when we met, you know, I just didn't realise until too late.'

'Oh Molly . . . you don't have to tell me that. I already knew. People are not stupid and I've now been filled in, don't you worry. You should never have blamed yourself for any of it.'

'No, I realise that now. I suppose I just wasn't thinking straight. But he did scare me at times Gwen.

And when I heard that his father, and *his* father, before him, all drank more than they should have and could be sour bastards at home, I felt better about myself. I knew that it wasn't me who was to blame, even though that's what he would say if I ever dared to mention his drinking.'

'Of course. I bet you he'll come looking for you though, with his tail between his legs. But don't you take him back just because he's realised where best his bread was buttered.'

'Oh trust me . . . I wouldn't even open the door to that man now that I'm free of him. Free to do just as I please and when I please.'

'Good for you, but don't let's forget that this might be a lull before the storm. He might turn up out of the blue. Just keep on telling yourself that you have every right to be happy and that you can jump all the hurdles. And don't fall into the old trap of rubbishing yourself again should he start with the accusations and insults. Because you can bet your bottom dollar he'll be slagging you off right now.'

'I know he will, and I know what you're saying. You're right. I can see things clearer now that I'm out of there. I loved my little house before he moved in. But I was lonely Gwen, and he seemed as if butter wouldn't melt. I was a fool and I've no-one to blame but myself. But there we are. It's never too late to make good a mistake. I remember my mother saying "Everything that goes amiss can be amended." '

Gwen spoke in a low, husky voice. 'Listen sweetheart . . . just you remember when you were a little girl.

Just look at old photos of yourself. Because that's the real you. That's the person you were before life and circumstance started to spit and kick. Look at Grace for example; she is a lovely woman and funny too. She makes me laugh without even trying and yet she's lost everything and everyone that she loved. In a funny way, that's what made me think that you would get on together. You've both been through the mill, and you're both unselfish and thoughtful people. She talks a bit posh but she can't help that. Once you're used to each other you'll get on like a house on fire. I feel sure of it.'

'So do I. And I know that my Patsy will take to her like a duck to water.' She smiled and then quietly chuckled. 'I wonder how she got on in South London . . .'

'You'll soon find out. From what you've told me about how close the pair of you are I reckon she'll be on the phone telling you once she's back home. You did tell Rita to let Patsy know that you've finally made your flit didn't you? Otherwise they'll all be worried sick when you don't answer the phone at your old place.'

'Yes. Not to worry – Rita will tell Patsy just as soon as she gets back from her night away, I'm sure – then I bet you Patsy will be round here soon enough. She's my little shining light in the dark is that girl.'

Across town, having woken up in Danny's family home, bright but not too early, Patsy was relieved to find she had the bed to herself now so that she could take things nice and easy with no rush. Aunt Vi was down below in the kitchen helping to prepare things for a hearty breakfast so Patsy was making the most of the peace and quiet to think about Danny. She knew that she would soon have to get her skates on and be ready for the first meal of the day which, from what she could make out, really was the most important of all meals in this household.

Once she had bathed, and dressed in a casual red blouse and black knee-length pedal pushers, she was unsure of whether she was meant to join the family below or wait until someone came to the bedroom to collect her. Looking around herself she saw a small pile of *Woman's Weekly* magazines. She picked one up to flick through and then sank down into one of the two pale-cream tub chairs. The walls of the house were thick and she could only just hear the movements from below, but the sounds of the birds singing in the tall trees of the garden were coming in through an open window and were just lovely.

As Patsy paged through the journal her thoughts were on Danny, how polite and caring he was compared to the lads that she was used to. Lads who she had had just as much fun with on the dance floor at the local dance halls had nearly always wanted to get their hand inside a bra of the girl that they were walking back home. But Danny had been the perfect gentleman.

Also, in her neck of the woods it was normal, once a dance was at an end and the hall was about to close, for there to be a last minute whip-round by the guys for beer and Babychams. A party in one of their homes was nearly always on the cards. This of course depended on someone mentioning that their parents were away on holiday and that their home was on offer, or something similar. Her thoughts drifting from one thing to another, Patsy didn't hear Danny coming up the stairs. He knocked and came in – dreased in jeans and a casual soft grey cashmere sweater, he looked more relaxed than he had done so far. More handsome and more soft and cuddly. He smiled at her and then kissed her on the cheek before saying, 'Did Aunt Vi snore and keep you awake?'

'No. I was out like a light and slept through the night. What about you?'

'Out for the count.' He then held his hand out saying, 'Come on. Let's go for a little walk before breakfast. There's no way out of this bizarre household without seeing the gaggle en route though.'

'Oh don't say that, they're lovely. Your parents are really kind. And look how they all welcomed me.'

'I know. I was only joking.' He escorted Patsy down the wide staircase and asked what time her dad planned to pick her up that morning. This made her smile because he had asked the same question twice the day before and in the evening during the party. Putting it down to nerves, she pretended that this was the first time and told him that he would be arriving around ten o'clock that morning. Glancing at the grandfather clock in the hall he shrugged. 'That gives us an hour, but by the sound of things, Sunday breakfast is about to be dished up so perhaps we could go for that walk afterwards if there's time.'

'That'll be lovely,' said Patsy, aware of the sun shining through a partly stained-glass window and onto her face. Going into the kitchen-cum-dayroom the smell of the bacon under the grill had her mouth watering within seconds. She hadn't eaten much at the dance the night before and she was hungry, which was just as well because it looked like it was going to be a hearty meal. There was even a wooden plaque fixed to the breast of the small inglenook fireplace that housed an old gas fire. The sign had been beautifully handpainted and read: *Eat Breakfast like a king, lunch as though a prince and dinner as if a pauper.* And from what she could see the advice was certainly going to be adhered to. On the table were matching blue and white patterned serving dishes from which the selection of scrambled eggs, fried mushrooms, crispy grilled bacon and grilled tomatoes was going to be served. There was plenty of everything to go round, and another serving plate piled with hot buttered toast. Two cut-glass jugs held freshly squeezed orange juice.

Aunt Vi was cooking over the hot stove, red faced and smiling. She waved Patsy and Danny out of the room and towards the back door that led out into the gardens softly saying, 'Out out out until the food is on the table. Into the garden with the pair of you. I'll call you when the table is full and we're ready to serve.'

'Are you sure I can't help?' said Patsy, not really knowing what else to say.

'Certainly not my dear. You are a house guest and must be treated as such.' She then glanced at Danny with a look to suggest he take his girlfriend away from the kitchen and the heat from the stove.

'Ten minutes?' Danny asked his aunt. 'Or fifteen?'

'Twelve to fifteen,' said Aunt Vi and turned back to the stove to fork sausages into a sizzling pan.

Outside in the fresh air Danny took hold of Patsy's hand and led her to one of his favourite parts of the garden, a timber corner bench framed by old-fashioned roses. Settling themselves down and knowing they were out of sight Danny pulled out his packet of cigarettes ready for a smoke. Once he had lit up he smiled at Patsy and said, 'I s'pose you've guessed that I'm the baby of the family around here?'

'I didn't have to guess. I saw it straight away. And you love it,' said Patsy. 'You're spoiled rotten – but in the nicest possible way.'

'And you're not?' He smiled.

'Fair enough,' she said. 'I'm a lucky only child, but I don't think I'm *that* spoilt. Do I behave as if I am then?'

'Course not. It's just that Mr Hobbins, who knows all the ins and outs, well when he heard I was gonna be going out with you, he mentioned that you'd been adopted. He said that you were loved to bits by your family. I can't imagine anything better than being chosen. I mean, I was born on the family bed and, ugly little rat or not, my mum and dad were stuck with me.'

Smiling at his own self-deprecating joke Danny looked at Patsy waiting for her to break into a smile. But the bewildered expression on her face changed as she narrowed her eyes and furrowed her brow. Swallowing against her suddenly dry throat, she slowly shook her head and only just managed to whisper, 'Say that again.'

'Say what again?' said Danny.

Drawing breath, Patsy looked into his face. 'I did hear right, didn't I? You did just say that your boss told you that I was adopted?'

Danny was now at a loss because, by the look on her face, he knew that he had perhaps just made the biggest mistake of his life. Realising what an idiot he had been by casually reeling off something that she might not have liked to talk about, he sighed loudly. 'Oh, Patsy. That was *really* stupid of me. I should have kept my mouth shut and waited until you told me.' He slowly shook his head. 'I'm so sorry.'

'Don't be, you've nothing to be sorry about. I'm not adopted. Your boss must be thinking of someone else. I'm an only child but I've got a mum and dad.' She paused, then went out. 'It's all right Danny, you've not done anything wrong. But you could tell your boss that he's talking out of the back of his head if he was referring to me.' She shook her head a touch bemused by it and then laughed. 'Adopted? You wait until I tell my gran. She'll split her sides laughing.'

Again Danny was lost for words. He was as certain that he had been told the truth, but perhaps Patsy had not been told about her birthright. It might be a very tightly kept secret. Not sure how to get out of this without telling a lie he shrugged and splayed his hands. 'I probably misheard what he said. Sorry.'

'Don't be. It's your boss who's in the wrong not you. You wait 'til I see him in the shop. I'll enjoy pulling his leg over it. He won't get off lightly don't you worry. I might even pretend that I believe that it's true and say

I'm gonna leave home and travel the world looking for my real parents.'

Danny gave a feeble smile but was only just able to look her in the face. He felt sure that Mr Hobbins had not made a mistake. He knew the Lamb family well because his folks had lived in the East End since time immemorial and so had Patsy's. The East End had always been a tight-knit community, and secrets had a way of spreading.

'It's all right,' Patsy chuckled. 'It's not the end of the world. Gossip can be like Chinese Whispers. He's got the wrong family that's all.'

Raising his eyes to meet hers Danny smiled. 'I'm sure you're right.'

'He probably got mixed up way back when children and babies had become orphans during the raids on our part of London.'

'Possibly.' He then offered her a cigarette which she accepted gratefully. She did smoke now and then but at this particular moment it was more to steady her nerves. Even though she had waved off Danny's gossiping it had actually pierced her to the core. Was it possible? Might her parents have adopted her? Could there be a family secret that she hadn't been told about even though she was at its centre?

Back in the kitchen where the table was already laid with a marvellous spread, the aunts showed Danny and Patsy where they were to sit – opposite each other. Taking his place, Danny looked across at Patsy and mouthed the words, 'Are you okay?'

Slowly nodding and with a little smile, Patsy once again felt as if she was in a kind of make-believe world and wondered what she was supposed to do next. She wasn't sure whether to help herself to food from the serving dishes or wait to be served. So she looked to her chaperone for help and Danny immediately saw from her expression that she wasn't used to sitting down to a feast first thing. 'Mum and Dad will be in directly and once we're all at the table everyone digs in. It's help yourself time.'

'Oh right,' said Patsy in a quiet voice. 'So where are they now? Your parents?'

'In the library reading the Sunday papers. It's a tradition. The aunts do Sunday breakfast and Mum does the lunch and Dad the supper.'

'And you?'

'I see to the washing up after breakfast and that's it.'

'And I'm allowed to help you with that am I?'

'I'm not sure. I've never brought a girl home for an overnight stay before. We'll play it by ear.' He smiled. 'I s'pose it must all seem a bit odd to you. I'm used to the routine though. It's part of my life so it seems normal.'

'It's not *that* different to most families. Why did you think that I would find it all a bit odd?'

'Because a mate of mine stopped over once and couldn't believe the way everything is so regimented, and mostly by the spinster aunts. It suits me down to the ground. My shirts are washed and ironed and hung up, my best suit's taken to the cleaners whenever there's a wedding or an important function and I'm spoiled rotten when it comes to being fed.

Breaking the little bit of awkwardness between the couple Danny's parents arrived, talking between themselves as to how wonderfully the dance had gone and what a success it had all been. Settling down at the table the mood was cheerful and noisy, with everyone seeming to want to talk at once. But Patsy, pondering on what Danny had said, felt queer at the thought of it. She only just managed to suppress the sick inner feeling that had crept into her and smile politely at each of her elders as they gave their little snippets of humorous gossip and goings-on about the evening before. But as the meal went on, the stories began to take her mind off what had been said. With silly thoughts of having been adopted pushed to the back of her mind, she gradually joined in the banter and found that the time simply flew by. Before she knew it her dad had arrived at the front door to collect her.

Once she had gathered her overnight bag and was ready to go home she thanked Danny's mother for having her and the aunts for the lovely breakfast while his father chatted to Andy.

'You're a bonny lass,' said Aunt Ada as she fondly squeezed Patsy's arm. 'And I hope that we'll be seeing more of you Patsy.'

Blushing, Patsy said that she hoped so too, but she avoided Danny's eyes because this was, after all, only their first date and she didn't know for sure whether he would ask her out again. To divert the attention from herself she turned to Aunt Vi and said, 'I hope I didn't fidget too much in bed.'

'Oh no, of course you didn't, Patsy my dear. But

then I wouldn't have known in any case because I was out like a light and probably snoring.' She then smiled. 'Was I? Snoring?'

'I don't know,' was her honest answer. 'I was out like a light as well.' Then, hearing her dad's voice talking to Mr McDonald, she excused herself and went to join him.

When Andy saw Patsy he smiled and said, 'Hello babe.' She could tell that Andy approved of this household and that the family that he had met so far were all right by him. Smiling at him, she then gave him a gentle hug to show how pleased she was to see him and grateful that he had taken the trouble to come and pick her up. While it had been an amazing night, she couldn't wait to be driving back home with her dad. There was something she needed to ask him . . .

Chapter Seven

On their way home in the family car – a five-year-old light-blue Anglia – Patsy's thoughts returned to Danny's casual comment. She couldn't get it out of her mind, remembering especially the way he had blushed and looked embarrassed about mentioning the word adopted.

Breaking into her thoughts, Andy asked, 'How did the dance go, babe? Was it an old-fashioned band?'

She looked at him and felt her heart melt. He was so sweet at times. 'No it wasn't Dad. It was good, really good. I had a lovely time. Thanks for letting me go and for trusting Danny to see I was all right.'

'The family seem all right,' he said, all casual. 'Friendly – even though they've got a few bob in the vaults.'

'They're really nice, Dad. I slept with one of the aunts, Violet, the one who doesn't break wind! I slept really well. I thought she might snore but she didn't.'

'Slept with an aunt who didn't break wind?' Andy laughed.

'That's right. The other aunt did apparently. All night long from what I could tell.'

Bemused, Andy slowly shook his head. 'I would 'ave

thought that with a big house like that they would have a spare room for guests.'

'They've got two but they're filled with stuff that belongs to all and sundry. You know the kind of thing . . . suitcases, trunks, tea chests and all of that.'

'So there's not a huge attic then?'

'Probably. Why do you ask?'

'Just wondering that's all. I should think they own that place. It doesn't look like a house that would be rented out. There's a bit of old family money there if you ask me. All that antique furniture . . . you've picked a good 'un babe.' He smiled cheekily and clicked his teeth.

'I don't know about that. And I don't really care one way or the other about the money. The house is a bit old-fashioned and not like ours, but I did feel at home funnily enough.'

Andy looked sideways at her. 'I can't see you sleeping with an old aunt, babe. I just can't visualise it.'

'I had no choice, but it was all right. It's not something I'd choose to do but there you go.' After a pause she added, 'Don't tell Mum whatever you do. You know she's a bit of a snob on the quiet. She'll think it's a disgrace them not putting me in a room of my own.'

'I won't say a word sweetheart. Oh, and Ritchie phoned last night by the way. He and a few friends are going to High Beech this afternoon and he wondered if you fancied going along.'

Patsy quietly chuckled. 'He won't give up, will he?'

'What d'you mean?'

'His mate, Johnny Blanks.'

'What about him?'

'Oh come on Dad! You know that he's interested. Didn't he ask you if he could take me out on a date when you were in the pub having a drink with him and his dad? At least that's what you told me. Stop trying to match-make. He's too old for me. There's four years' difference, and anyway he's a work mate of yours.'

'He's a lad and he's under me in the pecking order but he'll make something of himself. He's got a good brain.'

Patsy sighed with a smile. 'I know, and you're his boss and he'll learn a lot from you. It's a bit old-fashioned you know, parents trying to find a match and believing it's only they who can find the right man for their daughter. I can choose my own boyfriends you know. *And* I'm fussy. So, I suppose you don't like Danny then?'

'He's all right,' said Andy. 'Just different from us that's all. He's a South London boy.'

'So?'

'You know where you are with an East Ender. I'm not knocking the family but they're different from us. That's all. Forget I mentioned it.'

'I will, but you might not. I bet you say more or less the same thing to Mum when we get home. You won't let it drop, will you? I know you.'

'And I know you, babe. I'm not saying he's not a nice lad – he is – but he's just not one of us, and if you're gonna see him again and you don't want to share a bed with an old spinster . . . well, I don't want you schlepping home on a late-night bus after an evening out with him. And *we* don't have *guestrooms*. So we can't put him up.'

'Oh for God's sake, Dad will you stop it! I don't even know if he *will* ask me out again, but if he does I'm going to say yes.' She glanced slyly at Andy's profile and could see that he was chewing on his bottom lip, something he always did when he was agitated. 'I like him a lot. And what difference does it make whether he's from south, east, north or west London? Since when were we that fussy? And I'll tell you something else while we're at it. If he was black and I liked him I wouldn't give a toss about my being white. So I'll phone Ritchie and tell him thanks but I'm too tired to go to High Beech. It's fun there and a lot of people my age go, but I'm tired. And Mondays at work are always dead busy. So today I just want to laze about and do sweet sod all.'

'I shouldn't think you would give a toss that you're white,' said Andy, not really having listened properly to what she had just said, he was typically on his own track. 'But I'd care about him being black . . .'

Patsy scoffed. 'I might have known you'd pick up on that. You know what they call people like you nowadays?'

'Well you're gonna tell me whether I can guess or not.'

'Racist.'

'Don't be ridiculous. The lad's as white as we are.'

'I don't believe you at times,' said Patsy. 'I'm not talking about the boy you've got in mind for me or Danny for that matter. You just said *you'd care* if my boyfriend was black. Don't forget that my friend Rita, who you always said was a lovely girl, married a Jamaican boy who you thought was a good chap.'

'I never said that.'

'Yes you did.'

'Well then, if I did, then it shows that I'm not racist. You're getting your knickers in a twist over nothing.'

'If you say so,' she sighed.

'Enough said then, eh? Let's drop the subject.'

'Yes please . . . give it a rest,' she murmured.

'I'll give you a clip round the ear if you don't stop the cheek. Very nice example that lot in the south 'ave set you. It's not as if you were there for days. You only stayed overnight. I'm not so sure about that lad.'

'The *lad's* name is Danny. And he's a perfect gentleman. He doesn't swear or tell dirty jokes in front of me and he didn't try anything on. He kissed me goodnight and that was all. He might swear behind my back for all I know, but so long as he doesn't while I'm in his company why should you care?' She turned her head as if to look out of the window and smiled to herself as she waited for Andy's angry retort.

'Very nice I must say. You come out with swear words in front of your mother and I promise you that roof will come down.'

'That's all right. One of Danny's cousins is a roof repair man. He'll fix it on the cheap if the borough council won't cough up.'

Taking the corner a little too quickly Andy had to swerve to avoid a lad on his bicycle. 'Stupid little bastard!' he said, and pressed repeatedly on the hooter.

'Or stupid parents more like. Fancy letting a kid of his age out on the road.'

'He's not that young, Dad. I bet he's all of twelve. And you did have your foot down as you swung that corner.'

'That's enough of the backchat Patsy, I'm in no mood for it. And if stopping over in a big posh private house is gonna do this to you, you can forget going again.'

'It's not a posh house. They own it, true, but the furniture's hardly brand new and up to date like ours. It's all family stuff that's been passed down along the way.'

'Antiques, Patsy, antiques. Personally I can't bear them, but it's worth money – don't you fret.'

'I wasn't fretting. Why should I? I couldn't care less about the house or the furniture. I liked the family even if they are different from us.'

Miffed at the way his daughter was somehow controlling the conversation Andy went quiet. He wasn't sure he liked this new cocky attitude. She had always spoken her mind, just like he did, but she sounded different this morning. A bit too sure of herself. It was almost as if she was giving *him* advice all of a sudden instead of the other way round. He thought he would change the subject and bring her back to family matters.

'Ritchie also wanted to know if you were going to go bowling next Saturday. They need another player on their team. They're playing against the Blakes and you know how good they are. So it's every man and woman to the fore.'

'Well, that lets me out then. I'm not a woman, I'm a young lady,' Patsy teased. 'When is the match?'

'I just told you! It's next Saturday. And don't be sarcastic. You're a good bowler and that's what counts. Saturday is what I *think* he said, but check it in case I'm wrong. I don't want you having a go at me again.' Andy smiled wryly as he turned into the avenue where they lived opposite the church.

'Dad . . . I wasn't having a go. I was just telling you in my own way that I can be my own judge of people. That shouldn't get your back up, I'm only taking after you. Mum always said that one day we'd stand up against each other because we're so alike and maybe that day's come. I've got your family blood running through my veins after all. How many times have we heard that you and I are like two peas in a pod when it comes to being obstinate?'

'All right, point taken.' As he slowed down to find a parking place close to his house he had no idea that Patsy was about to drop a bombshell.

'Danny is so sweet. We got on really well. We got chatting about this that and the other and he told me that Mr Hobbins, you know how he's been running the corner store for years and was born and bred—'

'Get to the point babe, I've got a car up my bumper who's after that space.'

'Well, go in another one. It's not the end of the world. You don't have to wait for old habits to die – you *can* break them, you know.'

'No. That's my parking space, always has been, always will be. *He* can park somewhere else.'

'Oh whatever. Anyway, what I was saying about Mr Hobbins . . . as we know shopkeepers can be a bit like old women on the quiet but I wouldn't have said he was a gossip-monger, would you?'

'I've no idea Patsy, and to be honest I'm not all that fussed.' Andy was now looking at the driver behind him via his rear view mirror. 'Stubborn bastard,' he murmured.

'Well, Danny said that Mr Hobbins told him that I had been adopted. Can you believe that?' She laughed. 'Danny was so embarrassed when he saw the shocked look on my face. I put him straight though. Where on earth could he have got that from? You've known that man in the store since you were a lad. At least that's what you've always said.'

Feeling the blood drain from his face, Andy put a polite hand up to the chap behind and slowly drove forward to turn into another narrow back street where hardly anyone chose to park. 'Bloody people,' he murmured to cover his true feelings, as well as trying to change the subject. 'Coming into our neck of the woods and parking as if they live 'ere.' He was side-tracking and could only hope that his astute daughter would not pick up on his tone and change of mood. He felt sick inside and if truth could be given away by an expression then Patsy would know for certain that he was shocked to the core by what she had just said. The last thing that he had expected was to hear her use that word: *adopted*. He knew that a few old and trusted locals had picked up on the family confidence at the time of Patsy's birth, but he hadn't dreamt that any one of them would ever even think of mentioning a secret like that. Working-class Londoners didn't do that kind of a thing – not as a rule.

At a loss for the right words, Andy side-tracked by moaning about the shortage of parking places now that there were so many cars on the roads. But Patsy was having none of it. A seed had been sown. 'I laughed at Danny and said he had the wrong person and that I definitely was not adopted. I told him his boss must have been thinking about someone else. I might be an only child but I know who my mum and dad are. And I love them to bits.'

Andy could feel the heat rising from his neck to his face because he was not telling the truth, even though he was not telling a lie either. 'Daft sod,' he said. 'I'll put him straight later on in the week. I'll pop in on one of the days when I take an afternoon at home to do my paperwork.'

'Oh, Dad don't you dare do that! Danny could get the sack!'

'Well, maybe he deserves the sack for gossip-mongering. Another man not as soft as me might well sue him for libel for saying something like that.'

'Oh for God's sake! I wish I had never told you now.'

'So do I. But it's been said and we can't change that.'

'Oh thanks! Thanks a lot! What is this anyway? What does it matter? We know its all rubbish. Stop being silly. It's not as if we even care.' She slowly shook her head. 'His boss probably meant someone else and Danny got it wrong. Why are you getting your pants in a twist over it? I don't understand.'

'I'm not.'

'Yes you are.' Uncomfortable about how het-up her father was getting, Patsy decided to change the subject. 'Anyway forget all that . . . did you tell Cousin Ritchie that I would phone him back or is he coming round?'

'Neither. He said he'd phone again later on.'

'And did you tell him that I was staying out overnight with my new boyfriend?' she smiled.

'No I never. Which was just as well. We don't want another rumour up and running do we.'

'Oh for Christ's sake, Dad, stop it! And don't you dare go in and tell that lovely man off. Danny obviously got it wrong and I wish I had never mentioned it. Promise me you won't go in the shop. Just forget it, it doesn't matter. Promise me, Dad.'

Having parked the car to his satisfaction Andy pulled on the brakes and turned off the engine in silence. He didn't want to look into the face of his daughter. He now knew for certain that the day had come for her to be told the truth – and he'd just blown a chance to come clean. He couldn't help but inwardly curse and blame himself for not having told her before now, before it came out. Deep down he knew that he was at fault, that he had never wanted her to know that he wasn't her father. It had been him who, in his own sweet way, had always put off the day. All he could hope now was that it wasn't too late. Pray that when they did sit down and tell her the whole story, she wouldn't think that they were only telling her because she had found out for herself, from a lad from the south of London of all things!

Andy had never felt so worried and angry at the same time. Now the story was going to have to be told, and with an apology, when he and Alice explained to Patsy what was what. They had always said that they would plan it properly and do their best to try and make a celebration out of the fact that they *chose* to have Patsy as their daughter: that they had loved her from the moment she came into the world. All that he could do now was hope for the best and not try to do anything more than make a good job of a bad one. He was to blame. He would shoulder it.

Pushing the key into the lock of the front door, Andy drew a deep breath and prayed to God that Patsy wouldn't start going on to Alice about it straight away. He still couldn't believe that the family secret had, after eighteen years, give or take a few months, finally found a little crack from which to seep out. This would devastate Alice. He knew his wife better than she knew herself sometimes, and he was sure that she wouldn't be able to hide her anger once he told her what had happened. Never mind that the family secret had come from the mouth of a local man, a shopkeeper who she knew and liked. She would want to know who had said what to whom and when.

But he needn't have worried because Patsy, knowing her dad like the back of her hand, could tell that he was more concerned by her reaction than she was letting on or ever would let on. She wasn't going to throw more mud at the wall to see if it would stick. He was clearly worried and anxious. And the question was floating through Patsy's mind as to why he should be so agitated by a daft comment? As far as she was concerned that's all it was. But then, as she thought about it she reminded herself that she had asked as a child, and later on in life, why she didn't have any brothers or sisters and had felt as if she had touched a raw nerve.

Once in the house she followed Andy through to the living room and managed a smile for her mum, who looked up from reading her Sunday paper.

'I'm so glad you pair are home.' Alice leapt up to meet them. 'You'll never guess what. Rita's just phoned to say that Molly did a moonlight flit yesterday! She's upped sticks and moved to Wanstead, of all places. She's taken everything she owns and moved into a little place next door to Gwen, that mate of hers she met up with in hospital. I can't believe it! I mean, I knew her and that old misery Joe weren't getting on too well, but I didn't know it had come to this.

Andy stood there, amazed. First Patsy's bombshell and now this – it was turning out to be a heck of a day. He couldn't believe his mother had left her beloved house. A cold fear ran through him. 'Did Rita say anything more about Joe?'

'Only that he's had some kind of fall and is in hospital, which is what gave your mum her chance to make a move. Although she did hint that it's been worse than we feared behind closed doors,' said Alice.

Andy felt like he'd been punched. What had that evil old man been doing to his darling mother? He felt his anger rising.

Alice sensed Andy's mood and decided to change the topic. 'Anyway, it's not that far away, Wanstead. I told Rita we'd all be down there to check it out soon enough. So, come on, I want to hear about the dance – now the dirty little stop-out has returned to her roots.' Alice leaned back in her chair and smiled. 'How was it sweetheart? Did they look after you? A little birdie told me that Danny comes from a moneyed family.' She clicked her teeth and winked at her daughter.

'Oh leave it out Ali, for Christ's sake,' moaned Andy. 'We've barely walked in the bloody door.'

'Ooh-ah. Who's put salt your tea then?' She looked from Andy to their daughter and smiled. 'Didn't catch you having a good-morning kiss and a cuddle with that handsome devil of a boyfriend did he sweetheart?'

'No Mum, he didn't.' Patsy sighed and rolled her eyes. 'I'm going to make myself a cup of coffee. Any takers?' She glanced from one parent to the other as each of them slowly shook their heads.

'I've just had a cup of tea, sweetheart,' said Alice, glancing again at her husband, worried that Molly's news had really upset him . . .

'Go on then . . .' said Andy. 'I could do with a cup of tea as it happens, after driving all the way to South London and back again. It's thirsty work being a taxi service.' He waited only a few seconds for her to jump to his command and when she didn't he shrugged. 'Right, I'll make the fresh pot of tea then shall I? And then I'll wash up the cups and dry them. And if the roof leaks I'll fix that as well!'

'Coffee for me please Dad,' said Patsy, still worried

by his sulky mood. She knew it wasn't just her nan's move to Wanstead that was troubling him.

'Fine,' said Andy. 'But I'll go upstairs first if that's all right. Into the bathroom to freshen up after driving all morning. And then I'll wait on the pair of you 'and and foot.'

In truth Andy wanted to be by himself to sit down and think. There was a horrible sickly feeling in his stomach. And it was one that he recognised. It was fear and worry all rolled into one.

'What's got his goat up?' whispered Alice. 'I thought he'd be pleased his mother had left the old villain, even if it does mean she's a bus ride away.'

'He was in a funny mood before that Mum – I think it's just the traffic getting him all het up,' said Patsy, wishing to leave it there. 'And before you ask again, yes I had a lovely time. The dance was a great success, there was plenty of food and the band played a good mix of songs. Old ones from the old days that you would have loved and some from the hit parade that were my favourites.'

'Well, that was a bit of luck then, wasn't it? It could have been dull as ditchwater babe. And what about the house? Is it much bigger than ours?'

'Much. And the family owns it. And it's filled with family heirlooms and antiques and I shared a bedroom with one of the aunts.' She smiled.

'I'm sure that must have been fun,' said Alice, a touch sarcastic. 'You go all that way and end up tucked in bed with an old woman! But did you get on all right with Danny?'

'Like a house on fire.'

'Good. So next time there's a do maybe your dad and me will be invited. Kill two birds with one stone: meet the family and have a knees-up.'

'No Mum, not a knees up. They're not East Enders.'

'I was joking Patsy! What's the matter with you? I thought you'd be full of the joys of spring?'

'I'm a bit hung over, that's all,' she murmured, and flopped down onto a soft-backed chair.

'Fair enough.' Alice smiled then, as if it had suddenly struck her, she remembered what she had to tell Patsy.

'You had a phone call this morning. Maggie who married the Italian lad rang. She'd heard from Rita who married the West Indian boy about Gran doing a moonlight.'

Patsy couldn't help but laugh at her mother. 'You don't have to mention the nationality, Mum. Why can't you just say, Tony or Errol?'

'What difference does it make?'

'Well . . . it could be seen as you being a touch racist?'

'Oh shut up. Racist? How can anyone born in the East End be racist? There's not that many of us whose ancestors were born and bred. It's the first port of call when they get off of the boat. Anyway, Maggie said for you to give her a ring. So – Danny's family are mostly Scottish then are they?'

'Yes, but they don't have a strong accent. Just a very slight one. Is that all right? Acceptable?'

'Oh shut up,' said Alice. 'I'm not like that. The lad could be black or white or Jewish for all I care. We're all the same under the skin and behind the shape of our nose.'

Unable to keep a straight face Patsy said, 'Mum . . . that is a terrible thing to say. You should hear yourself. You can be so insulting at times.'

'Says you. Anyway, when you give your old school chum a call ask if old Aunt Naomi is still alive and kicking. It would do your gran the world of good if she were to meet up with her again. I might put on a little party, or maybe arrange an old timers' dance in the church hall. I would quite like to have gone to that one last night with you, but there you go. Your dad and me weren't invited.'

Ignoring the little bit of wind-up that was going on Patsy said, 'That would be a great idea Mum. Get everybody together again. Your old mates as well as mine. And Dad's of course. And all of our family, and your old neighbours from before you were married. You could bake hundreds of sausage rolls and butter loaves of bread for sandwiches—'

'Yeah all right, Patsy, point taken.'

'Good. And now I'm gonna have a lovely long soak in the bath. There was an old-fashioned shower for me to use but I didn't much fancy it.' Patsy hauled herself out of the chair. 'Thanks for letting me stop out over-night and for swaying Dad. You're a gem.'

'That's all right babe . . . but best not to make a habit of it, eh? You know what your dad's like. Too over-protective for his own good.'

'Of course I won't. I only stopped over because the party ended late.'

'I know.' Alice stood up and hugged her daughter and patted her back the way she had been doing since she was a baby in arms. 'Go on. Go and have a soak. I'm sure you're ready for it.'

'I am, but I'll say this much, Mum . . . it was an experience being in that house, but now I know what that old expression that you used to come out with means. You know the one: *There's no place like home.*'

Alice waved a hand through the air, saying, 'Oh go away . . . you'll have me in tears in a minute.'

'Well that's never hard to do is it? You're an old softie and you know it.' With that Patsy left Alice to herself.

'An old softie?' she whispered. 'Well she's not far wrong there when it comes to my girl.' She then looked around the room and smiled contentedly. 'No place like home . . . Long may you go on thinking it sweetheart. Long may you do it, because it suits me right down to the ground.'

Alice went into the kitchen and took a carton of orange juice – delivered by the milkman that morning – out of the fridge and poured herself a glass to take outside into the pretty walled garden. She thought of Molly and wondered how she was getting on in her new apartment and whether she would like it as much as she had loved her old house. But at least she was away from Joe, who no doubt would soon be on the lookout for another woman to prey on. Someone who might not only be desperate for a bit of male company but also have a home he could share and perhaps some cash from a life endowment policy.

Thanking God that Molly's friend Gwen had been in the hospital at the same time as her mother-in-law, she smiled at the woman's loyalty towards someone that she had not seen in years. Molly had been lucky to have found her and it had taken a lot of guts for someone of her age to clear out of her home to start afresh elsewhere. Of course, having freedom would help. Alice was close to Molly and she knew that she was going to miss her. Miss popping round to her house for a cup of tea or coffee and a gossip.

Her own mother had passed away a few years since and her dad had remarried a woman who had been born and bred in Essex and had wanted him to move into her house, a spacious detached chalet-style bungalow in High Beech. And ever since then her dad had got into the swing of playing tennis and lawn bowls and socialising with the members of each of the clubs. Occasionally he would come into the East End to say hello, but he had clearly moved on and seemed content to have left his roots. To Alice it was as if she had lost both parents. She supposed it was inevitable that she and her dad would drift apart because she didn't like her stepmother, and she knew that her stepmother wanted little to do with her dad's East End family.

In her ignorance, the woman believed that Stepney and Bethnal Green were filled with tramps, prostitutes and beggars. Of course there was a small number of each type surviving in and around Aldgate and Shoreditch, and the Old Jago in Bethnal Green, but her stepmother had not been interested enough to look or ask about the better side of this part of London. She never saw the parks and the museums, the greens dotted around here and there and surrounded by tall elegant houses that were once owned by the rich middle classes.

Pushing all of this, and the way she felt about her dad's stuck-up wife from her mind, Alice brought Molly back into her thoughts and decided there and then that she wouldn't mention that she had also heard from Rita that Joe had been discharged from hospital in Whitechapel after just one night. If she told Andy she felt sure that he wouldn't want to leave it there. He would want to go in search of the man now that he knew how wicked he had been to his mother, and he'd want to give him a good hiding. A hiding that he deserved but one that could land her Andy in trouble.

Imagining the ugly scene Alice felt herself go cold. She knew that as placid a man as Andy was, he could turn on the spin of a coin where bullies were concerned, and if he knew the full story he would go looking for Joe. Andy had never taken to the man and knew that his mother had only married him out of loneliness. When Alice had told him the news there had been tears in his eyes, and she felt sure he had gone upstairs to their bedroom to weep quietly in private. He blamed himself for not having been more attentive, for not picking up on what his mother might have been going through.

Chapter Eight

Leaving work the next day, dead on time after quickly having cleaned the surfaces and swept the little area in the hairdressing salon that was her own personal space, Patsy left the salon to go and meet Danny outside the corner store. She had had such a lovely weekend and now she couldn't wait to see him again, brief though their time together was going to be. Danny had to get home early that evening to help with getting things all tidied up in the church hall where the dance had been held.

As she walked along the pavement, oblivious of cars on the narrow roads or people walking to and fro, Patsy recalled the time spent with Danny on Saturday from the moment that they had held hands outside of the store and strolled to the stop to catch a bus to his home. She had loved being with him. They had spoken on the phone last evening and made arrangements to meet up after work today for a coffee in an Italian café that was close by to the stop where Danny would catch his bus. As she approached the store she could see him standing outside and enjoying a cigarette. In his casuals he looked even more handsome than when he had worn his best suit for the dance.

Smiling at him as she approached, she felt a warm

glow in her chest when he placed a gentle hand on her shoulder, and looked into her eyes. 'I'm glad you came, Patsy,' he said. 'I had a horrible feeling that you might stand me up.'

'Why? Why would I want to do that? I couldn't wait to see you again if you want the truth.'

'You look as lovely as ever,' he said, gazing into her eyes. Then, shaking himself out of this soppy love-struck mood, he took hold of her hand and led her across the main road to the little café that was tucked away in a side turning just off of the Cambridgeheath Road. Once inside and seated at a table for two that was covered by a red and white check cloth, Danny took her hand and lightly kissed her finger tips. 'I've been thinking about you all day long,' he whispered.

'And I've been thinking about you all day long,' Patsy confessed. 'I really did enjoy myself. At the dance and at your house.'

'Well . . . I think you're gonna have to pay another visit. The aunts think that you are "*so so lovely*".' He smiled. 'And my parents and grandparents were full of praise as well.'

'Well, I can't think why because I'm so ordinary – an ordinary girl from the East End. Weren't they in the least bit bothered about my cockney accent?'

'Of course not. I'm hardly posh Patsy. We're not so different to your family except that we live south of the river and you live east of it.'

'I know but . . . well, the house and everything . . . I just thought . . . they might have been disappointed that you chose to take a cockney instead of a well-spoken South London girl, that's all.'

'Hardly. Those kind of thoughts never cross their minds. Trust me. So long as you can scrape a good new potato you're okay.'

'But I didn't though, did I? I didn't do anything to help in the kitchen. I didn't know whether I was supposed or not. I could easily have helped prepare vegetables for your Sunday dinner. I help Mum in the kitchen and—'

'Patsy,' he interrupted, 'it's only a saying. You're bound to hear it when you're there next time as well. You know the kind of thing. "The girl's all right so long as she can scrape a new potato." Basically it means that so long as you're not the type who won't get their hands dirty you're okay. And anyway you did help – you gave Gran a hand with the drying up while I went off for my bath, didn't you?'

'True. I just hope it was enough.' Then, seeing the waiter on the way over, she leaned forward and whispered, 'Mine's a frothy coffee.'

'Anything to eat?'

'No thanks, I'm not hungry. And anyway Mum will have my tea ready soon after I'm in. But you go ahead. You have a slice of that chocolate cake that you've got your eye on.'

'Not me. I take a cigarette with my coffee.' He pulled a packet of Benson and Hedges out of his jacket pocket and offered her one.

Patsy took a cigarette and Danny lit it for her. 'Thanks,' she said, 'I've been so longing for a ciggy, but we're not allowed to smoke in the salon and I have to make do with having one in the back yard at lunchtime. And I can't smoke at home because Mum and Dad would hit the roof. They don't know that I have a cigarette on the quiet. Well, at least I don't think they know.'

Looking into her lovely face Danny leaned back in his chair. 'I wish I lived nearer to you,' he said, and then felt a touch embarrassed and foolish for saying it. 'Well, what I mean is . . .' he shrugged and then smiled. 'What *do* I mean? You tell me Patsy, because I'm not sure what day it is any more.' He leaned forward to look into her eyes. 'I know we've only just met but I think I might be falling in love with you.'

Patsy, blushing, replied quietly, 'And I feel the same. But – as you just said – you *think* you might be. Let's take it easy and see how we go and enjoy it as long as it lasts.'

Danny looked thoughtful, then nodded slowly. 'You're right, of course you are.' He smiled. 'We can meet up like this after work every day and see each other on Sundays. My parents said to let you know that you're welcome to stay over whenever you like and that they're clearing out the attic rooms in your honour so you won't have to sleep with an old aunt again. You've completely won them over, and that's saying some-thing. And I do mean all of them, the entire flock – including funny old Ada who's been miserable as sin ever since her friend left.'

'Oh, don't say that, she can't help the way she is . . .

and she was harmless enough and looked after me as if I was her daughter.'

'I was only joking Patsy. I love both my aunts to bits. Anyway, the offer's there.'

'Thank you and yes. But first I'll have to get Dad used to the idea that because we live on opposite sides of the river we will need to share the same roof now and then. Of course, it'll mean that you'll have to stay at our house. Dad will want to show that he can do as well as your dad can do.' She quietly laughed. 'He's a bit competitive on the quiet.'

'Good. I'll stay at your house whenever he invites me. Does your dad play snooker by any chance?'

'He used to play quite a bit, but Mum nagged him for hardly ever being at home on a Sunday morning so it's eased off.'

'Ah well, there you go then. If and when I do stay over I'll drag him to his favourite snooker hall.'

Patsy laughed. 'I wish my gran could hear you now. She reckons that Mum's got him under her thumb. That Dad has turned into a subservient boring old sod.'

'Well, there you go then, it'll be good for us to go out just men. Although from what I hear about this grandma of yours, she'd probably come along as well and beat the pants off us.'

'Nan? Playing snooker? I don't think so.' With that, Patsy cast her eyes down and gazed at nothing as she slipped back in that world of her own where dark thoughts had been put away. But now what Danny had told her about being adopted was surfacing again . . . She snapped herself out of it and said, 'I just hope that my nan has done the right thing by moving into that flat out there in Wanstead. It isn't exactly on our doorstep, is it?'

'She'll be all right,' said Danny. 'From what you've told me, she knows what she's about. You said she's a strong woman who knows her own mind. And if that means that she's anything like my grandmother she won't have gone without thinking it through.'

'You're right.' Then, biting her bottom lip, she said, 'Danny . . . I don't want to seem as if I'm going on about what you told me but I can't get it out of my head . . .'

'About you having been adopted?' he said. 'It was stupid of me—'

'No. It wasn't. I just keep on thinking about it. And do you know what – I think it might just be possible. Dad acted really strange when I mentioned it to him, so I don't feel that I can mention it again at home, and yet it won't go away.'

'Well . . . didn't you tell me that you're really close to your gran?'

'Yes, I am. We can talk to each other about anything.'

'Well, there you are then.'

Patsy looked at him and slowly nodded. 'So you think that she's the one I should ask?'

'It's only a suggestion.'

'I know. And you're right. It's not gonna go away so I have to do something. I think I might take a bus ride over to see her in Wanstead, but I'll leave it for a while.

I might change my mind and just see it as stupid, and that I've not been adopted and leave it at that.

'Why don't you go and talk to her about it in a month or so if you're still feeling like this. I wish I hadn't of mentioned it, it was daft, but I did.'

'No it wasn't. I'm glad you said something. I would hate to find out much later on in life. I mean, what if one of my real parents should pass away without me ever knowing. That would be horrible. I'll go and see gran but I won't rush it. She'll tell me the truth, and she won't think me stupid or nasty for asking such a thing. She knows that I am a bit of a worrier on the quiet. I'll go over there and talk to her about it when I think the time's right. Not that I won't pop in and see her before then, I will.'

Danny reached out and squeezed her hand. 'Good for you,' he said. 'And if you like – when you're asking her – you can lay the blame at my feet. I think a lot of you, Patsy. In fact I think about you most of the time. Don't break my heart will you?'

'No, Danny . . . I won't do that.'

One Sunday a couple of weeks later, after endlessly deliberating as to whether she should or shouldn't question her gran, Patsy decided that she should follow her instincts.

When she told her mother that she was going to see Molly, Alice told her to pass on a message from Rita. 'I bumped into your old school mate as I was coming out of gran's house—'

'What were you doing in there? She doesn't live

there any more! You can't just walk in and out as you please! You've got to give up that spare key, Mum. Honestly, I can't believe you at times.'

'I will give up the key, all in good time. I was making sure she hadn't left anything behind and it was just as well as it turned out. I found that little old-fashioned gold watch of hers at the back of a cupboard in the kitchen. It was in a cracked cup of all places. As if it was hidden.'

'It probably was. She hid things from that miserable old sod who would mostly likely have sold it down the pawn shop if he had got his hands on it.'

'And that's why I went back there. To have a little search in case he was still there. And, if I'm honest, for a touch of nostalgia as well. She and your real grandfather were happy in that little house, and I used to love popping in and out in the old days. And you loved going there with me when you were little, when your granddad was alive. It had a different atmosphere entirely.'

'I know it did, Mum,' said Patsy, touched by Alice's sentiment. 'And that's what we've got to remember. The good times and not the bad when that spiteful bastard was there and tormenting her.'

'Tut tut, Patsy. There's no need to swear. Don't bring yourself down to his level just because we're talking about him.' Alice became all thoughtful and shook her head. 'Just thinking about what your gran went through brings tears to my eyes. But it's over now.' Turning her face to the window, she gazed out as if in a world of her own, feeling a sickening sense of guilt. Why hadn't she picked up on what was going on, she asked herself. Why hadn't she noticed the extent of abuse. . .

'Thank God it is over. And do you know what, Mum? I don't think I've ever seen her so happy. She'll love that little apartment, as she likes to call it, and she'll love being in next door to Gwen. I take it there was no sign of the old man at the house?'

'No. He's gone. Let's hope it stays that way.'

'You can say that again!' With that, Patsy headed out to catch her bus.

On her walk to the stop and during her bus ride out of the East End, with the sun shining on her face through the bus window, Patsy told herself that she had every right to want to know who her birth parents were if she had in fact been adopted.

While Patsy was on the bus, Molly was in her apartment thinking how content she was. In her cosy new sitting room with all of her familiar furniture around her, she had nothing to worry about and nothing to fear. She'd settled in better than she could have ever imagined. As well as getting to know Grace Clark, she had shared more than one joke with the two young actors who rented the first-floor flat. Sadly though, they had been up at the crack of dawn to pack the last of their things into their suitcases so as to catch an early morning train to Surrey where their families lived. Both professional actors, they had been working at the Stratford East theatre in a play by a new young playwright that had been fairly successful, but had had to finish its run earlier than scheduled. The play had been given the thumbs down by the local press and tickets sales had immediately dropped. According to what the local papers had written, some of the scenes were too explicit when it came to romping around in the bedroom. It seemed that not everyone liked the changing attitudes this new decade was bringing.

Some of the reviews had been fantastic because this playhouse *had* bent the rules by treading on ground that playwrights had not trod since a century or so before, when Oscar Wilde had broken new ground. The actors were fun and their naughty off-the-cuff jokes had made Molly laugh, but at least, as Grace had told her, she knew that she would easily be able to re-let their apartment. The area had come to be seen as a desirable place in which to live because of its situation between the Essex countryside and the City.

Once she had had her second cup of tea on this sunny summer morning, Molly went to her front door to collect her favourite newspaper, the *News of the World*, which she had arranged to be delivered as soon as she had settled into her flat. As well as her favourite weekly paper she also saw on the coconut mat a folded piece of smart notepaper that was addressed to the owner of the house. The writing was beautiful and the paper impressive – it was edged in a lovely gold and red pattern. Seeing that this was addressed to the owner of the house and was meant for her landlady, she took it up to the main entrance door to the house and slipped it through the letter box, not wanting to disturb her new friend unnecessarily. Then, glancing along the turning, she saw Scamp and smiled. It seemed to her an age ago that he had been abandoned by his owner and that Joe, when tipsy and in a rare jolly mood, had invited the dog into the old house. Since that day Scamp had become their dog. When she had first given him scraps she hadn't known if he belonged to anybody or not. But he certainly did now. He belonged to her, he was more loved, and no longer had to fear the boot of Joe in a nasty mood.

Scamp now had a new collar with a tag that showed his address in Wanstead. He had a good home with people around that loved him. Whistling to him to come to her, Molly thanked God that she had brought the dog with her when she moved out here. Once back inside, with Scamp at her feet, Molly was ready to relax on her little sofa and read the Sunday paper in the peace and the quiet while her small piece of silverside was roasting in the oven.

In the sitting room directly above Molly's, also enjoying a cup of tea, Grace Clark had seen her new friend through the window and gone to fetch what she had pushed through the letter box. She had thought it was most likely something from the Boy Scouts or Girl Guides asking for bric-a-brac for one of their fetes, but saw that she was mistaken. She gave the note a quick once-over and realised that she would need her reading glasses because this was rather a wordy letter, beautifully composed but in small handwriting. Now, back in her chair in her spacious sitting room which was filled with inherited antiques, Grace began reading the note, and found the contents quite amusing. She had seen something similar to this that an elderly neighbour in a nearby road had shown to her.

The woman lived in a house very much like Grace's and had told her how she'd received a letter offering to buy her house. Grace's neighbour had been tempted to take up the offer – until she told her son who realised the price was scandalously low. Now it seemed that the same people were targeting Grace in a letter that was very similar to her neighbour's. It was filled with passion for the area, but concealed a darker purpose. It was clear that the sender had done their homework when it came to targeting prime properties – properties that looked a touch jaded from the outside, perhaps indicating that an elderly person might be the owner, living alone and struggling with the upkeep.

Grace had heard via the grapevine that there was quite a lot of this going on, that there were people on the lookout for houses owned by the older generation, who could be lured into selling at a price much lower than the market value. And Grace would seem like the perfect victim – elderly, widowed and childless. The writer clearly hoped there would be no one else to point out that the price mentioned was nothing short of a rip-off. Grace's letter hinted that she could continue to live in the property as a sitting tenant, rent free. In truth, the rogues were interested only in properties owned by those who could be nudged towards the grave soon afterwards by a little tormenting that might finish them off, so they would move in to the property with the old owner for a short while and do their work. The house would then be sold without a sitting tenant at a much higher price. To the old, lonely and frail who knew nothing about the scam, the offer sounded like a dream come true. To be able to continue living in their home, with an extremely healthy bank account and enough funds to enjoy the rest of their years in comfort. And with no responsibilities whatsoever for the maintenance of the property? Wonderful!

Keen to share the contents of the note, Grace made her way out to her back garden and through a little gate that led down into Molly's small but lovely part of the grounds. She tapped on the back door, hardly able to contain her excitement: the scam had given her an idea.

Molly opened the door to see her landlady was beaming. 'Don't tell me you've come up on the pools,' she joked. 'Either that or you've lost a penny and found a pound while looking for it?'

'Neither.' Grace waved the letter. 'You wait until you read this note that you slipped under the door for me. The one that was posted through your letter box by mistake.'

'Well, yes it was. I didn't like to disturb you on a Sunday so that's why I didn't knock.'

'Oh my dear I quite understand but I simply had to come down! I promise you will be amused.' She followed Molly into the sitting room.

'You're in luck. I've just put the kettle on the stove,' said Molly.

'Oh I'm far too excited for tea.' The woman could hardly contain her joy. 'And I mustn't stop, because I've promised the Women's Institute that I would bake and take a jam and buttercream sponge to the church hall for their Bring and Buy sale tomorrow.'

Molly invited Grace to sit down and asked what it was that had put the smile on her face. 'Is it a love letter from an admirer?'

'No, of course not, silly. Here you are. Read it for yourself. It's to do with what we were talking about just the other day. The fraudsters.'

Molly raised an eyebrow as she took the note. And, as Grace expected, a wry smiled crossed her face as she read it. 'Well I'll be . . .' she said. 'They don't give up do they?'

'What do you think, my dear? Shall we have a little fun with them?'

'In what way?'

'Well . . . let's have a little drop of that sherry you keep in the cupboard and then sit down and plot. I think that I might have an idea that would bring in more than a few shekels. And you know how we girls, and my friend Henry Jackson, are longing to go on a lovely long cruise one day? Well . . . this might just be the ticket we need.'

Molly read the note again, then looked at her new friend with a puzzled expression. 'I'm not with you on this one. You're not saying that you'd sell the property to them, are you?'

'Possibly.'

'But why? Are you in debt?'

'No of course not, silly. But I have an idea how to put one over on the rogues *and* have cash for a wonderful cruise for the four of us . . . it would be heavenly, would it not?'

'I should think so!'

'Well, then, let me explain my plan. I'll give you a clue and let's see if you can work it out . . . Now, as you know, I was an actress for quite some time.'

'Yes, and you miss the theatre. So?'

'Well, I think I'm ready to don one of my old wigs that will age me some thirty years or so . . .'

'I haven't a clue what you're thinking Grace, but I'm all ears,' Molly laughed. 'Calm your excitement and I'll pour that bottle of celebration sherry even though it's early for us.'

'It's never too early for a sherry my dear!'

'Good. Because I now fancy one myself. And as for that note and your plan, it had better be good because you've got me all worked up about a cruise now . . . and I know you'd hate to disappoint me.' Molly arched an eyebrow and then smiled wickedly.

'I wouldn't dream of disappointing you or myself. I believe I have a *foolproof* plan.'

'Have you now? Well off you go then. Let's hear what it is, Grace.'

'Well . . . if these rogues purchase a house with a landlady who is prepared to be a sitting tenant, and who looks as if she isn't long for this world, they would be prepared to pay more for the house – would they not?'

'Well, yes,' said Molly, 'I suppose so.'

'Good,' said Grace. 'And what if that said landlady should gradually, over a few weeks or months, start to look and behave like a much younger and more lively person that's been given a new lease of life?'

'Well I suppose that if they were only buying simply to sell on and make a profit they'd be gutted.'

'Precisely. And soon they'd be desperate to sell it on again – especially if we young-at-heart older generation drive them to distraction with our loud music and parties, and friends coming and going all the time. I have a feeling they'd be prepared to sell back to me – and I could name my price!'

'Heavens above,' said Molly. 'You are a clever girl. How on earth did you work this plan out?'

'Oh, I can't take all the credit. When the swindlers sent that letter to the old girl down the road, I talked about it with Henry Jackson and we came up with this plan. He made a few useful suggestions, such as getting down my old theatre costumes and wigs, etcetera, from the loft. I'll look as if I'm pushing ninety when viewers come, then only about sixty once they've purchased. They won't know what's hit them once they've moved into the flat above mine. My dear friend Henry also gave me some tips about the legal side – he's a retired solicitor you know – so we'll make sure they don't have access rights to the garden.'

'Well I never,' said Molly. 'That *is* clever. But only if you sell to the rogues we've heard about. You can't do something like that to an innocent young couple.'

'Molly my dear . . . the letter is all the proof we need that these are the same swindlers that have been so busy in this area.'

'That's true. Yes, I see where you're coming from.'

She started to laugh. 'You are one sharp lady, Grace! I take my hat off to you. You're so canny that I swear your ancestors must have come from the East End.' Then, thoughtfully, Molly added, 'But isn't it a bit of a gamble? Once they've purchased, what if we can't drive them out? You will have lost your home and they might kick us out.'

'My dear Molly, do you think I haven't thought this through? Never mind my lovely Henry and his quick brain. Trust me – they will want to go. And of course they won't be able to sell at the price they paid for it. Their crotchety old sitting tenant, yours truly, will have lost years within a week. I shall be lively and back to looking younger than my years again. And I'll drive them mad with my loud music if I have to. Now . . . who in their right mind would want to purchase a house with women as sprightly as us as sitting tenants with a water-tight lease?'

'Good grief, I'm seeing the light. That is clever. Very clever. So they will have to let a buyer have it at a cheaper price than they purchased it for.'

'Exactly. And we shall be around all of the time to put those buyers off. You see? I'm not as daft as I make out, am I?'

'No Grace, you certainly are not. It's not even a gamble really is it?'

'Hardly.'

'It's a brilliantly worked out plan.'

'Indeed it is. And we shall have fun when and while we execute that plan.'

'I can't wait for the fun to begin,' said Molly.

While Patsy's gran was behaving like a teenager, Patsy herself was sat on the bus on her way over to see her. She still hadn't been able to sort her head out one way or the other. As much as she wanted to find out the truth, the closer she got to finding out, the more scared she was of what she might learn. She could feel her resolve melting away. After all, she didn't know anything for sure. Feeling like a fool for even thinking of bringing it up and making a fuss she suddenly felt embarrassed by her own silly behaviour. Apart from anything else, she knew that if she made a fuss it could cause her parents heartache – whatever the truth might be. In a way she was in a no win situation, because if she *had* been adopted and everyone had wanted it to be kept under wraps, what right did she have to blow apart the family secret? She was loved and always had been, and she couldn't imagine having a better mum and dad. Feeling a touch guilty, she told herself that it was all a load of hogwash that she had spent too much time thinking about.

Yes, she decided, it would better just to forget it all. She didn't want to be a sneak and go behind her parents back and, if she *were* to ask her gran whether or not they were her real parents, it would be like sneaking around in the undergrowth to dig up some dirt. She would be all but accusing her parents of bringing her up under a cloak of lies.

On top of it all, she was worried about clouding her nan's new-found happiness. Molly had been through enough, and now that she had found a little sanctuary with new friends it hardly seemed right for Patsy to march in and cause upset.

With time on the bus to think things through, she could hardly believe that she had been stupid enough to think she had been adopted simply because it had been mentioned in passing by a man in a grocery store. So, having got as far as the skating rink in Forest Gate, she got off of the bus, crossed over the road and caught another bus back home. She was determined to push the whole thing right out of her mind.

A week later, having made an appointment for a viewing of the house with the young couple who had posted the note through her door, Grace, looked like an entirely different person in her new guise. Her professionally dyed chestnut hair, always cut and set in the latest style, was now hidden under an out-of-date, silvery grey, wavy wig and she was wearing an old-fashioned pale blue and pink floral frock that had once been part of a costume for a stage play that had been set in the 1940s. Over this she wore a paisley wrap-over apron and a baggy cardigan. Her legs were bandaged beneath thick lisle stockings and she wore a pair of check slippers with a pompom which she had bought especially in a local old-fashioned shoe shop. On the bridge of her nose sat a pair of national health glasses that she had found while rummaging through her box of theatrical ensembles brought down from the attic. These completed the look that she was after and seemed perfect for the performance she was about to give. She was sure she could now be taken for a woman in her early eighties once she went into character. All that she had to do was to act the part of a half-baked old girl who probably smelt of mothballs and who benignly smiled her way through life.

Checking her appearance in the 1930s mirror on the wall, Grace couldn't help but chuckle. Even the looking glass showing her reflection had been taken out of an old tea chest that had been in the shed for donkey's years. This had been spotted by Gwen when she was helping to search for Grace's props. As she admired her handiwork, Grace knew that she looked every bit the elderly woman at death's door. To top it all off, she was pleased with the way she had transformed the apartment. Over her lovely modern three-piece suite she had thrown a mismatch of outdated fringed covers that she had picked up during the week for next to nothing at a jumble sale. And on her beautiful antique mahogany corner table, now covered by a plastic patterned cloth, stood a ghastly cheap vase purchased in a second-hand shop, which she'd filled with grubby plastic flowers bought at the same place. On another table was a shabby fringed cloth and a tray of small iced cakes on a cracked plate, alongside a brown teapot and a selection of ancient china cups and saucers. A 1940s gramophone, also brought down from the attic was placed on a small table with a little pile of old records next to it.

Between them, Grace, Molly and Gwen had created the perfect setting for their purpose. Happy that the room was ideal for the little drama about to be played out, Grace went into the hall to double check that the wilting potted plants, collected from the garden shed, looked the part. She was more than satisfied that they looked as if the owner would have to be almost senile to have displayed such smelly, grimy foliage. Altogether, the house looked exactly as though it belonged to a docile elderly lady who could pop her clogs any time.

When the sound of the doorbell pierced the air, Grace took a long deep breath and then hunched her shoulders as she went into character. Slowly shuffling to the street door, she opened it very slowly and peered at the couple standing there as if she would be as blind as a bat without the spectacles that were perched on the bridge of her nose.

The young lady on the step was smart and looked to be in her early thirties. She leaned forward and smiled. Speaking in a loud voice as if she thought the old girl was hard of hearing, she said, 'Hello! Mrs Clark? I'm Lee-Anne Brown! I believe . . .'

Grace showed the flat of her hand to interrupt a touch impatiently and then said, 'Oh and so do I my dear! I read the Bible every day. I've always believed. Thank you for calling.' Smiling politely at the couple as she slowly began to close the door she saw the young man put his foot in the way.

'I don't think you quite understand, Mrs Clark! We're not here to convert you! We've come to view the house!'

Raising a phoney trembling hand to her mouth as she peered at them through the gap Grace spoke in a whisper. 'Oh how silly of me. I thought that you were the Jehovah's Witnesses.'

'And we are in a bit of a hurry,' said the woman

looking at the delicate gold wrist watch on her pale thin arm. 'May we come in? To view the property . . . ?'

'Oh, of course you must come in! I do apologise. It *was* silly of me not to remember that you were coming. I had quite forgotten . . . please . . . do come in.' Standing aside with the door now fully open, Grace caught a glimpse of the smug look on both faces of the couple as they slyly glanced at each other. She knew by their expression that she was on form and that she had not lost her acting ability. She had fooled them.

Once they were in the hall she feebly inched her way forward to close the door with a trembling hand, but the young man graciously turned around and obliged. He then smiled a touch patronisingly and with raised voice said, 'My name is Philip! Philip Drake!'

'Oh . . . now why did I write Mr and Mrs Brown in my diary. I do hope I've not got muddled again and gone and double-booked a viewing . . .'

'No, of course you haven't.' He smiled and, before he could say anything else, his partner intervened.

'When I telephoned . . . I said that *I* was Lee-Anne Brown! And that *we* would be calling around four!'

'Ah,' said Grace as if the penny had finally dropped. 'So you're not married, but are just good friends. Silly of me. Now which one of you will be buying my house?'

A touch excited at the prospect of picking up a bargain, the woman called Lee-Anne said, 'We are *both* interested in the house. And no, we are not married – but we do live quite happily together.'

'Oh . . . well yes, of course that's quite the fashion

nowadays isn't it. But there we are, times change and we must change with them. But I must say that you seem just right for each other.' She looked from the attractive but cold young woman to the young man. 'I thought that that was a Bible you were clutching.'

'Did you really? Oh . . . yes. I see what you mean!' He smiled. 'No! This is my notebook! I do hope we're not early. You *were* expecting us weren't you?'

'Oh yes! And I'm quite broad minded. Some people can't be bothered to get married these days, can they? Each to their own is what my mother used to say. Each to their own.'

'If this is inconvenient,' said the woman coldly. 'We could always come back another time. We do have *other* houses to look at.'

'Oh my dear, I wouldn't dream of turning you away!'

A touch impatient if not exasperated Lee-Anne looked distastefully at the plants in the entrance hall and then quite pointedly said, 'There's a very strange smell in here.'

Floating a hand across the dusty leaves going brown at the tips, Grace sighed. 'Yes . . . my babies are a touch neglected. I used to have such a good memory but now I do confess I forget to water them sometimes. Such a pity. Now when I was *your* age—'

'Oh I don't know . . . personally I *hate* rubber plants! Dusty fly collectors,' said the young woman, cutting in.

Grace laughed as she reached for a violently perfumed lavender air freshener. She sprayed the air, causing the couple to draw back. 'I didn't think that they would die . . . but there, at least I've managed to outlive them. I suppose I should throw them away. I suppose I had just got used to them being there and my eyesight is not what it used to be. I know I shouldn't use the air spray either because of my lung. One has collapsed you know. But the other works fairly well so I mustn't grumble.'

'The dustbin men will take plants away if you leave them outside the door,' said Lee-Anne, too impatient to be polite.

'Would they? Would they really take them? How kind. Now would you like some tea before you view the house or afterwards?'

'Oh, I'm afraid we shan't have time for tea. Very sweet of you to offer though,' said the young woman desperate to get on with it. The last thing she wanted was to have to sit in a room with an old woman who looked and smelled as if she had one foot in the grave.

The young man, however, looked daggers at his partner, saying, 'Oh I'm sure we could spare a *few* minutes *darling* . . . once we've viewed the property?'

'Most of the furniture throughout the house has been passed down from one generation to another you know,' said Grace, dreamily. 'I expect it will all seem rather old-fashioned to you, but I've just never found the time to get rid of it all.'

'Well . . .' said Philip Drake. 'We might be interested in buying some of it since it's part of the house. That way we won't disturb the ambience that you've been used to.'

'I'm so sorry,' said Grace cupping one ear. 'I didn't quite hear that.'

'I said that we might be interested in buying some of the furniture since it's part of the house! That way we won't disturb the ambience that you've been used to!'

'Oh that *would* be nice!' said Grace. 'I've got arthritis you know, so I shan't be able to help you with the furniture on moving-in day. I would love it if you or whoever buys the property were to take all of my family furniture with the house. I would pay someone to take it off my hands.'

Believing her to be fairly deaf, Philip raised his voice again. 'Would you really? Well, best get on then. After you Mrs Clark!'

'Oh, I shan't come up with you, my dear. I can't manage the stairs.' She then raised her skirt to show her heavily bandaged legs. 'And to think that I was once a dancer who danced every single day. I sometimes worked with the best you know. I remember . . .'

The young woman grimaced at the sight of the faded knee-length pink drawers that were just showing. Grace was delivering the best act ever and putting on an excellent show of approaching senility.

'Now,' said Grace. 'I've drawn a little map of the property so that none of my viewers will lose their way. Perhaps you would like to start at the top and work your way down? Or would you rather start at the bottom and work your way up?'

'We'll start from the top, then,' said the young man, impatient to see the rest of the house.

'Now that does sound sensible. And once you've viewed the inside you can look at the gardens. In the old days I used to be out there digging away for hours. But that's all over now. Now . . . would you like me to give you a guided tour around the ground floor? I could manage that I should think.'

'Oh goodness me no!' said the young woman. 'We'll find our own way thank you.' The couple started up the stairs, but just as they reached the landing Grace called after them. 'If you have any questions, I'm sure that I or Mr Jackson can answer them . . .'

Philip Drake stopped in his tracks and turned slowly around to smile before saying, 'Mr Jackson?'

'My solicitor. The law, sadly, insists that we do things properly,' said Grace. 'But he's not terribly strict about things.' She smiled demurely, trying her best to look angelic and not quite all the ticket.

'Ah . . . right . . . of course. The solicitor.'

'Well, when I say solicitor, he's more of an old chum really. He retired donkey's years ago. But he won't charge me any fees you see, he'll just sign the papers. He'll let me get on with it and choose who I want to sell my house to. He's elderly, you know, a bit like me really. Even though I'm probably closer to the grave than he is. But I've had a good innings.'

Of course Mr Jackson was as young at heart as she was. And when she had told him of her wicked plan he had roared with laughter. Leaving the young couple to it, Grace hobbled slowly into her sitting room and closed the door behind her, waiting for Molly to pop up as planned. She couldn't wait to tell her about the couple who had been taken in by her disguise.

*

In the flat at the top of the house Philip was checking the walls for damp while Lee-Anne was looking at the base of an ornament.

'Good Lord, Philip,' she said. 'This must be worth a fortune. It's a very early piece of Rockingham. This place is crammed with antiques.'

'I know it is Lee, but let's not start looting the place just yet, sweetheart. Be patient.'

The woman raised an eyebrow as she faced her lover. 'Can you imagine what it must smell like in her room? She's like a walking mothball and a urinal all rolled into one. A decrepit old woman on bandaged legs.'

'Yes, but if the old bat doesn't take to you she could very easily not sell us the house, so do try and be nice to her.'

'That's true. But my God – old people! I would rather take tea in the monkey house, than sit in a room with ageing bodies.' She shuddered and then murmured, 'If she was a cat or dog they would have put her down by now. But still, I'll find how to help her on her way. I haven't failed yet.'

The man turned to face his woman, saying, 'You are so deliciously evil, you gorgeous woman.'

'Yes, aren't I?' Lee-Anne smiled seductively, and went on, 'I've got a good feeling about this one. She's even more decrepit than she sounded on the phone. Not with just one foot in the grave but both dangling and ready to go. We'll have to act quickly or our little find will slip right through our fingers, my sweet.'

'I couldn't agree more.'

'Yes, I wouldn't be surprised if that old woman is six

feet under this time next year. Once she's popped her clogs we can get the decorators in and have them go through the entire house with brilliant white and then have light carpet fitted from top to bottom. We should make a handsome profit.'

Reaching out for her, her handsome co-conspirator pulled her close to him and smothered her with kisses, then whispered in her ear, 'You're a wicked, wicked woman.'

'Not wicked, Philip, just thinking ahead. And I shall go on like this . . . it works well, buying property dirt cheap from an ancient owner and then selling it for much more when they drop off their perch. And from the look of the old bag downstairs, I don't think we should have to wait very long for this one.'

While the viewing couple were investigating every nook and cranny above, Grace was relaxing with Molly.

'I think that that young couple will be perfect,' said Grace, pulling some folded pages taken from a cruise brochure from her apron pocket. She turned a page to look at a picture and sighed. 'Just think of all that money I'll have in my bank account once I sell to them. The cost of a cruise will be peanuts by comparison. And it will do all four of us the world of good. You'll like Henry Jackson. Gwen thinks him a perfect gentleman. As well as being a retired solicitor, Henry is also a talented amateur actor – though not as good as me of course.'

'I shouldn't think that anyone is,' smiled Molly. 'But although I see how well this part of the plan is working,

I still don't see how you're going to get your lovely house back once you have sold it . . . and what if whoever buys it loves living here and never wants to leave?'

'Oh, I shouldn't think that will be the case. All will become clear in Act Two. And as you so kindly just said, if nothing else, I *am* a good actress. Possibly the best, for my age. That couple think me old and silly and frail, and not long for the grave. Well – if they become the new owners – they're in for quite a surprise. And I daresay you will be rather taken with my performances too.'

'You don't have to tell me. I'm already impressed.'

'Good. I think I was quite persuasive and convincing, even if I do say so myself.'

Molly smiled. 'And apart from that you're a very funny lady, Grace. You look every bit the part you're playing. I would never have thought you had it in you. I can't wait to tell my granddaughter about this.' Molly started to laugh. 'That wig is just wonderful!'

'Well let's hope that I've managed to persuade those two that I'm on my last legs.'

'I'm sure you have. I'd be taken in by it. I think that you're a genius for thinking it up. I take my hat off to yer.'

'Well, I have been working on it for a good few days my dear. It's almost as if I have been writing my own play just so that I can be the leading lady, with a very nice income at the end of it.' Then as both women giggled at the way Grace had pulled the wool over the couple's eyes there was a ring on the doorbell.

'Well I never!' said Grace going into the hall. 'Who-ever can this be?'

Molly smiled. 'What happens in this household as far as I'm concerned, Grace, is anyone's guess. Go and open the door. Although if it's someone who knows you they'll have a heart attack seeing you the way you look now. Or they won't recognise you at all and think that they've knocked on the wrong door.'

Grace laughed. 'This will be the real test as to my acting ability. I shall now go into character.' She shuffled her way out of the room and into the hall to open the door, leaving her friend quietly giggling at her antics.

'My God,' Molly muttered to herself. 'And I thought that it was only East End people that were canny. Grace Clark might be posh and 'ave come from a wealthy family, but I reckon there's some cockney blood running through those veins.'

Coming back into the room, Grace smiled broadly and said, 'I take that as a *marvellous* compliment whether I was meant to hear it or not.' She then she stood aside the door and said, 'I have a surprise for you my dear. Look who's come to see us.'

'All right Nan?' smiled Patsy as she came into the room. 'I was gonna say boo but thought better of it. I don't want either of you two old girls dropping down dead with fright.' She looked from Grace to Molly and slowly shook her head as if trying to wake herself from a dream. 'So what's all this about then? What are you pair up to?' She turned to look at Grace again and smiled. 'I know we've not met yet but my nan told me that you looked really young for your age. How old are you? A hundred?'

'There! You see Molly? I told you it worked!' said Grace. 'We've even fooled your grandchild.'

'She's an actress, Patsy, in costume. Now what are you doing here? And why didn't you phone first? What if I had been out? I would have hit the roof if that had of happened.'

Patsy could hardly take this in. Here was Molly, her Nan, who no more than a couple of months ago, if that, had been ready to give up on life. And she looked not only happy but full of life.

'Never mind me. What's going on Nan? What are you up to? I can tell by your face that you're in mischief mood.'

'Oh . . . we'll explain later on my dear,' said Grace answering for her friend. 'First things first. I've been so looking forward to meeting you. Your grandmother told me how close you both are, and how you saved her from that bullying husband of hers.'

'Is that right? Well, I'm here now, so you can both calm down and fill me in on what you're up to.'

'Oh, I do so much prefer you working class people! You always seem to speak straight from the shoulder.' Then with a faraway expression on her face she said, 'Of course I got to know quite a few cockneys when I was in theatre. Backstage was far more interesting than front – and much funnier when it came to the antics of those who changed sets and so on. I remember one lad who was a runner—'

'A runner?' Molly cut in. 'Shouldn't he 'ave been on a sports field rather that in a theatre?'

'Not that kind of a runner, my dear. No, a dogsbody. The one who makes the tea, runs the errands, mends the props and so on.'

'Oh right . . . well, anyway, you'd best keep your eye on those two in case they pinch your silver.'

'Pinch her silver,' said Patsy. 'What *is* going on?'

'Yes, I must . . . but why don't you come with me . . . both of you? You've got to see this couple. They simply ooze money-grubbing meanness.'

'Oh do they now? Well we'll wait until they come down the stairs Grace,' said Molly.

Waiting for Lee-Anne and Philip to appear, Grace and Molly filled Patsy in. She could hardly believe what was going on. She hadn't seen this side of Molly before. Here she was, her gran, in Grace's sitting room with the pair of them behaving like teenagers. She loved it!

'I'll just have a listen at the bottom of the stairs,' said Grace. 'I shan't be a sec.'

'So what do you reckon to my landlady then?' Molly smiled.

'I don't think that I know what I think any more. I feel like I'm the parent here and you two are the kids.'

'She'll see that as a compliment,' said Molly. 'Well help yourself to a drink then. She won't mind. And have a rummage in the kitchen and you'll find a fruit cake on a stand. Cut yourself a slab.'

'Right . . . with another fruit cake on a stand that makes three,' murmured Patsy to herself as Molly also went to listen to what was going on in the hallway. 'I must be still in bed and dreaming all of this', she thought. 'And the press write that we teenagers are the troublemakers . . .' She slowly shook her head and then went into Grace's kitchen to get herself a drink.

Outside in the spacious hall Molly and Grace could only just hear the couple looking around in the upstairs apartment, and even though neither could quite make out what they were saying, Molly could tell by the spontaneous little bursts of laughter that they probably believed themselves to be one step ahead of the woman who owned the house.

They went back inside Grace's flat, quietly closing the door behind them just in case the couple suddenly came down. Lowering herself into her favourite armchair, Grace drew another holiday brochure from a magazine rack beside her and sat back to flick through it. 'Oh, this should do very nicely,' she said. 'Look at the lovely pictures of ships, sea and sunshine, Molly.' She held up the brochure to show her friend the double-page spread.

Molly gazed at the page. 'Perfect. Absolutely perfect . . . a long and lazy cruise,' she said. 'I just know that those two won't be able to resist buying this house. You look all of eighty and on your last legs. You must seem the perfect vendor for that pair. Look at you. Yesterday you didn't even look anywhere near your sixty-one years and now you could easily be taken for an eighty-year-old who's about to keel over any day.'

'I know, but then I *was* in the theatre for years let's not be forgetting! And even now should a part come up I would jump at it. Once an actress always an actress!'

Finding it almost impossible to get a word in, Patsy held up a hand as if she were in a classroom at school and said, 'May I please use the lavatory?'

'Oh my dear of course! It's just through there, dear.'

Molly smiled at her new friend. 'You certainly are the best, and in more sense than one, Grace, and you're just as wily as me and Gwen. My life has turned around since you pulled me into your world. I've you to thank for my new found freedom. You *and* Gwen. I know you've let me have the garden flat at a rent I could afford. You're a diamond.'

'Well, they say that diamonds are forever – so let's hope so. I'm ready to have some fun Molly, my dear. I've had my fair share of tragedy and now the tables have turned, thanks to our lovely Gwen. It was she who brought me out of the doom and gloom. And *she* who brought *you* into my life. I think that between us we could teach the young a thing or two.'

Molly laughed. 'I think so, Grace. And as for your life having been turned around, what about mine? I'm away from Joe and I've got a lovely apartment and my own little garden down there. And I've got my old friend back and gained a new one in you in the process. Thank you from the bottom of my heart for every-thing.'

'You're more than welcome, Molly. And if I have to, I shall say this a million times over until you believe me . . . you have given me a new lease of life. Both you and Gwen have. All that we can wish for now is that the couple up there buy this place. I want money, and with my plan I'll get money *and* keep the house in the end.'

'How wonderful that would be, Grace,' said Molly. 'Right now I feel much younger that I did three or four weeks ago, or however long it is that I've been here. The time seems to fly by now.'

'I know what you mean. And I'm sure your granddaughter must have played a part in your coming out of the gloom. What a lovely girl she is. I've only just met your Patsy but I felt an instant rapport. She'll be good for all three of us. I don't think that any one of us should ever be prepared to lie down and get old without having a bit of excitement. And excitement and fun we shall have. I feel it in my bones.'

Coming back into the room Patsy slowly shook her head. 'I don't think any one of us stand a chance in high heaven of making you two lie down. I don't know what the pair of you are on but I wouldn't mind some myself.'

'Oh it's post menopause my dear!' said Grace in a laughing voice. 'And it cannot be bottled and sold. Now we must call in Gwen and then all four of us—'

'No!' said Patsy, showing the flat of her hand. 'All *three* of you! Not me! I'm going down into Nan's flat for a bit of peace and quiet. Have fun.' With that Patsy slipped via the back route to the basement flat.

'I had better go, Grace,' said Molly. 'My Patsy must have come for a reason, perhaps for a little advice from her wise old grandma. She's in love you know. I hope she's not come to tell me that she's got herself in the family way.'

Back in her own flat and enjoying a cup of milky coffee made for her by Patsy, they chatted first about the dance and then about the woman who owned this house until Patsy said she was ready to leave. Yet again she had had the wind taken out of her sails and hadn't spoken one word about whether or not she had been adopted. It was why she had come, but it didn't seem right to dampen her nan's spirits. So now she had it in mind to forget it again and just go back to the East End and pay a visit to her Auntie Eileen and Uncle Tom. Telling Molly that she had only come into Wanstead for a ride out and to make sure that she really was happy, Patsy finished her drink. 'I hope you don't mind if I pop in and out like this, Nan. It's really nice to hop on a bus and visit.'

'Of course I don't mind, but you could stay a bit longer . . .'

'No ta. Just seeing you having a bit of fun with your new friend has done me the world of good.' She kissed her nan, hugged her goodbye and then slipped out of the house, only too happy to let the older generation enjoy themselves without her.

Once back in her own neck of the woods and knowing that her Auntie Eileen was bound to be at home and by herself, Patsy made her way there. She knew that on Sundays her uncle and cousins spent time together bowling. While on the bus she had thought again about the possibility that she was adopted. In her heart she was beginning to believe that this might be the case, but she wanted to know for definite – if she could only get up the courage to ask. She didn't feel that she could broach her parents on the subject, just in case she was wrong. It would be soul-destroying for them to know she was even thinking such a thing, although the seed had been sown by someone else and not her.

So, her Aunt Eileen, who she had always been able to talk freely to ever since she was a little girl, seemed like the next best choice. She felt she could trust Eileen to keep it all close to her chest.

Once her ride was over, she strolled through the backstreets until she arrived at the wide steps of the terraced house with its bottle green door and highly polished brass knocker and letter box. Drawing breath as she pressed her finger on the doorbell, she hoped that Uncle Tom and her cousins weren't going to be in. Luckily, when the door opened it was her aunt who smiled broadly at her. With her shoulder-length curly ginger hair and bright smile, Eileen always looked pleased to see her.

'What do *you* want?' said her aunt in her usual sparkly saucy manner. 'Your belly grumbling is it?' She then stood aside and opened the door wide. 'Well, move yourself then. It might be a sunny Sunday but that wind's a bit chilly.'

'Is Ritchie about?' Patsy asked innocently as she made her way through to the kitchen.

'No. He and his brothers have gone to play snooker with your Uncle Tom at the Golden Eagle pub. So it's just you and me sweetheart. Sorry.'

'*I'm* not!' Patsy called back over her shoulder.

'Ah . . . that's nice. It's me you've come to see then.' Happy as ever to have Patsy's company Eileen couldn't help but smile. She still loved her as if she was her daughter. Her little girl. The child she had had to give away.

Closing the door behind Patsy, Eileen followed her through the passage to the small kitchen with the door that led out into the back yard. 'I was just gonna pour myself a fresh cup of tea out as it just so happens. So you're in luck unless you want coffee. If you do, you can make it yourself because I never get it quite right, do I?'

'You're like a bloody record at times Auntie Eileen. And a cup of tea will just hit the spot. And a biscuit would be nice.'

'As if I didn't know,' Eileen said, opening her larder door. 'Ritchie finished off the chocolate digestives before he went out so you'll 'ave to make do with a couple of custard creams, like it or lump it.'

'That'll do me,' said Patsy, as she slumped down into a comfortable chair with wooden arms that was usually reserved for her uncle. 'I've got something to ask you and I'll come straight to the point. Because I know that's what you do.'

'I should think so. I've been telling you that for long enough. Go on then,' said Eileen as she poured a little milk into two cups. 'At least you take notice sometimes so my breath's not entirely wasted.'

'Well, you know I went to the dance with Danny . . .'

'Oh I might 'ave known. You've come to tell me all about it. Was it good?'

'It was brilliant. I'll fill you in on the details later, after I've asked the question that I came here to ask.'

'Go on then. And if it's anyfing to do with that lad such as him taking liberties I'll give it to you straight. Keep—'

'Yes, yes I know. Keep both legs in one stocking. You and Nan are as bad as each other.'

'Well did he try anyfing on?'

'No. He never. But he did tell me something that his boss told him, and that's what I want to ask you about. And I'm not gonna beat about the bush. Right?'

'Yeah, all right . . . get on with it.'

Patsy took a deep breath. It would be best just to come out with it. 'Was I adopted?'

Feeling as if someone had touched her with a live wire the woman stopped what she was doing and almost stopped breathing. She turned slowly to face Patsy. 'Say that again.'

'You heard what I said, Auntie Eileen. Stop acting. Was I or was I not adopted?'

'Who did you say told you that?'

'Ah . . . So I was then?'

'I said, who said it.'

'Danny said something but it was probably only a bit of gossip gone wrong. He heard it while in the shop. And I'm not gonna let it lie there, I'm not having people gossiping about me.'

'No, you wouldn't would you.' Eileen then lowered herself into a kitchen chair by the small table. 'Why ask me? Why not ask your mum or your dad?'

'Because you tell it straight, Auntie Eileen, you always have done and you know that. Well? Come on.'

The woman, clearly not ready for this, pinched her

lips together as she looked up at the ceiling to avoid her daughter's eyes. Hesitating, Eileen couldn't think what to say. She knew if she let Patsy carry on asking about her real mum that she wouldn't be able to stop herself telling the whole story. But maybe it was already too late. Patsy wouldn't stop asking now, and after all these years perhaps it was time for her to let go of the secret she'd guarded so closely.

'I can't answer you Patsy. You must ask your mum or your dad. Or both of them when they're sitting down together. That might be best.'

Patsy could hardly believe her ears. In her own way Eileen was giving her an answer. Her voice much quieter she said, 'So they did adopt me. Why? Why did they have to do that? Couldn't they have children? And why didn't my own mother want me?'

This was going far too fast for Eileen but Patsy had always been direct. And today it would seem that she hadn't time for niceties. She didn't know how to answer the girl and yet she knew that to fob her off would be wrong. Then, knowing that Patsy was not going to leave it alone she said, 'And what if your mum and dad don't want you to know . . . if you *had* been adopted that is?'

'That'll be a shame because I intend to find out. I haven't slept very well since Danny told me because it just keeps on coming back to me. And then I started to add silly little things up. Things that I had heard or seen or whatever. I can't really explain it. I went to see Nan to ask her but couldn't bring myself to ask.'

'All right,' said Eileen, looking into Patsy's face. 'I suppose it's as much my responsibility as it is your mum and dad's'. With tears in the back of her eyes she pushed away the memories of the time when she had held her baby daughter in her arms before passing her over to Alice. She clasped her hands together, let out a long sigh and then reluctantly said, 'I hope to God that neither one of us will regret this conversation, sweetheart, but I can't see that I've any choice but to tell you. To tell you that, yes . . . you were adopted. I don't suppose for one minute that if I were to ask you not to tell your mum and dad that I told you, you would agree?'

'Of course I would agree. So I was then? Adopted?'

Sighing as she leaned back in her chair and closed her eyes the woman nodded and then said, 'And for good reasons Patsy, not bad ones. Remember that. I suppose you want the full story?'

'No. I just want to know who my real mum and dad are. And why they didn't want me. That's all.'

'They *did* want you. But they already had three children whereas your mum and dad had none. Your dad had mumps as a child and was left infertile. And they so wanted to have a child. And at the time the mother—'

'The mother?' said Patsy in a slightly broken voice. 'Don't you mean my mother?'

Correcting herself, Eileen said, 'Your mother . . . already had three children and could only just afford to put bread on the plate to feed them never mind butter or jam. Your father was a hard-working man but at the time there was not enough work for labourers to go round. He ducked and dived and worked every God-given hour . . .' Her voice now breaking and her eyes filling with tears, she only just managed to carry on. She cleared her throat and stared in front of her at nothing. 'But they loved you so much. You were their first daughter after three sons and they so wanted to keep you. You were a beautiful tiny baby girl and it was so hard . . .'

Unable to say anything else and with her throat seeming to close up Eileen covered her face with her hands. She then said, 'Forgive me sweetheart. Forgive me and your dad but we couldn't see any other way forward than to give the best gift we could ever give to Alice and Andy. At least we knew that we would be able to see you and cuddle you and watch you grow up.'

As Eileen faltered, Patsy could hardly believe what she was hearing. She had come to her aunt for answers, half-prepared to hear her confirm she was adopted. But finding out who her mother was? And for that mother to be so close to home? It was all too much to take in. It didn't bear thinking about. Stunned by this totally unexpected confession Patsy stared at Eileen, speechless. She watched the woman, who she thought of as her aunt, rocking to and fro as tears trickled from her eyes and her face creased with grief.

'I didn't want to give up my baby girl. But at least I knew she would be looked after and loved.' Eileen then quietly wept as she said, over and over, 'My baby . . . my baby girl . . . my baby Patsy . . . I'm sorry. I'm so sorry. I never stopped loving you. And Andy and Alice love you. And we all stayed in the same area. And—'

'It's all right,' said Patsy in a whisper as she stared

down at the floor. 'It's all right. What you and Uncle Tom did was kind. And right at the time. Please don't cry. Please Auntie Eileen, don't cry or you'll have me wishing that I'd never been born.'

Her body suddenly jerking upright Eileen said, 'No! No Patsy. Don't say that. Please don't ever say that! Please Patsy . . . don't ever say that or think it or anything. It happened, and it all seemed to work out all right and none of us wanted to spoil it. We're family! And I still got to hug you and so did your dad. It's not that we didn't love you, we did. We really loved you and we still do.'

'I know that.' Patsy, with the flat of her hands, wiped away the tears that were trickling down her face. 'I should have guessed really. You've both been like a second mum and dad. What about my cousins . . . my brothers. Do they know?'

'No. One minute I was fat and the next I wasn't but I had been in hospital for a week or so and your dad, who was looking after them with the help of your gran said that I was in hospital with influenza and that the food was so horrible that I had lost weight. I didn't put that much weight on when I was carrying you in any case. But then there wasn't that much food to go round at the time. And I've never been a big eater. I was always skinny. It hardly ever showed – my bump – as I called it. My bump that was you, all tiny and perfect inside me.'

Patsy hadn't known how she was going to feel, but standing here with Eileen in front of her, she knew that everything that had been done had been done for the best. More moved and choked by the second as she listened to her aunt, who seemed wracked with heartache, Patsy reached out and placed a hand on Eileen's and looked into her face and smiled through more tears. 'I'm glad I came round and I'm glad you've told me. So what do I do now? Call you Mum or Aunty Eileen? And Uncle Tom? Do I call him Dad?'

'Oh Patsy please – don't say that. Don't call me Mum. I can't bear it. I've missed out on that for all these years. Think of me as your aunt who loves you more than anything in the world. Please Patsy. Do this for all of us. We told the boys that Auntie Alice had had a baby girl and they were young enough not to want to know where it came from. Babies were being born all over the place at that time – during and after the war.'

'Stop worrying and stop crying,' said Patsy, clearing her throat. 'I won't say anything to the boys. They're my cousins and that's enough. More than enough. Brothers, cousins, what difference does it make? We're family.'

Slowly shaking her head Eileen looked into her beautiful daughter's face. 'Don't think too badly of your mum and dad for not telling you. Alice will always be your mum – although we've both loved you, and always will, she's the one who's brought you up. I know that they always meant to tell you but just couldn't do it. And I for one was happy to go along with that. We're all right. We all live close by to each other, don't we?'

'I know. And I think you're wonderful. And I love you as much as ever. And I love Mum and Dad as much as ever. I can't imagine what they must have been going through at the time when they knew they couldn't have children.'

'None of it was easy for any of us at the time,' said Eileen, gazing out at nothing. 'Not at first that is. But once we did what we did it . . . well, it seemed the most natural thing in the world.' She looked at Patsy and shrugged. 'So you're all right about it then?' she whispered as she dabbed her handkerchief at the tears that were filling her eyes. 'You won't run away from home or do anything silly like that?'

'Of course I won't. Silly thing. As if I would leave you? I mean . . . you and Uncle Tom could have left me, couldn't you? In a children's home? But you didn't. You did the next best thing to bringing me up yourself. You gave me to your brother, my dad, and my mum.'

Then slowly nodding and smiling, her birth mother just managed to say, 'That's right darling. That's what we did. And it's not all bad is it? We all love one another like one big family, don't we?'

'Of course we do.' Patsy smiled affectionately at the poor woman who looked destroyed. 'And long may it last.' She then took both Eileen's hands in hers and quietly said, 'Would you mind very much if we don't tell the others about this? If we go on as we were? For a while in any case. I don't think I could cope with it. Let me keep my cousins as my cousins. Until the day comes when you and me both feel ready to tell the tale with a smile and not sad tears.'

'Oh sweetheart,' murmured Eileen. 'You are such a lovely girl.'

'Well, that's not that surprising is it? Look who my

mum is.' She then wrapped her arms around Eileen and neither of them said a word. There really was no more to say. They now shared a very special secret. Just the two of them. Mother and child. Deep down Patsy knew that she wasn't going to be able to just leave it there and knew that Eileen would be thinking the same thing once she had gone. But it would do for now. And it really didn't feel all that bad. In fact, now that she knew, it all fitted into place. Apart from a strange nervous sensation in her stomach she was quite calm. Too calm perhaps?

She told herself that she would go to see her gran and let her know that she knew. But not just yet, not for a while . . . not until she'd had time to let it all sink in. Until then she would throw herself into her work at the hairdresser's. At least she had that. And she had Danny. And she knew that she would be able to talk to him about it whenever she wanted. The way she saw it was that she now had two sets of parents and not many people could boast that. And, of course, she now had three brothers that she had always seen as cousins. Suddenly, something that had been kept a secret was making her feel warm inside. She loved Eileen and always had. And she loved her uncle Tom and her cousins. It was enough.

Chapter Nine

A few weeks later, having had more flying visits from Patsy than she could have expected, Molly was in her flat, sipping a cup of refreshing tea after having done her ironing and was wondering if her granddaughter was all right. Of course she loved to see her but something didn't quite sit right and she couldn't put her finger on what it was. Her one and only hope was that she hadn't let the lad, who she was clearly in love with, have his way with her. Not that she would blame him or Patsy if this was the case. She had been a bit of a wild one herself when young and beautiful and the men were all over her like honey bees. But she knew that she had to wait for Patsy to spill the beans if this was what was on her mind and worrying her. The girl had to live her own life in the same way that Molly had had to live hers. It seemed that there were changes going on all around her, and not just in her own sphere. This new decade seemed to have brought about a fresh outlook on life. Have fun and laughter whenever and wherever you could get it was the motto.

Molly herself wasn't short of fun and laughter. Grace's plan was proceeding well. The sale of her house had gone through and Grace was feeling very pleased with the way she had executed her plan. She had pulled off the old and feeble act, but of course this was soon to change. Now she could dress flamboyantly and youthfully again. And the best of it was that the young couple, believing Grace's act, had not much cared about the clause in the contract that confirmed she was to live in the property until she popped her cork. The carefully worded tenancy agreement drawn up before the house went onto the market meant that *both* sitting tenants could continue to live there until death. She and Molly.

The next stage was to drive the couple to want to sell at any price to get away from the madhouse Grace was planning. Meanwhile, Grace could continue to live in her apartment, enjoying a little of the money made from the sale of the house, with more than enough left to buy it back once the plan had been executed. And while she set about her plan, of course Molly would have the freedom of her apartment and garden.

Outside, Lee-Anne and Philip were pulling up in their dark blue estate car and could clearly be seen through the ground floor window of Grace's apartment. They had gone out shopping on this Saturday and, of course, Grace was intrigued to see more of the kind of para-phernalia they were going to furnish their rooms with. She could see that Lee-Anne was carrying some rather classy looking carrier bags from John Lewis in Oxford Street. Grace recognised the bags straight away because the store just happened to be one of her own favourites for a shopping spree. Philip, lagging behind her, looked a touch pathetic, puffing and blowing as if the bulging bags were filled with concrete rather than lovely new clothes or bits and bobs for the flat.

Tempted to go into the hall and annoy them a touch by being over friendly, Grace decided against it and told herself to behave. There would be plenty of time for amusement and she didn't want them to catch on too quickly. Then, creeping to the door, she heard them struggling with the parcels and the young woman bitching at her young man as they went upstairs and into their apartment on the first floor. Ready for a little nap, Grace went to lie on her comfortable feather-cushioned sofa with a satisfied smile on her face. Here she was, happy in her apartment, as if nothing in her world had changed except for the fact that she now had thousands and thousands of pounds in her bank account. And, of course, once the young couple found out that they had made a mistake in buying a property with a sitting tenant who got younger by the day, she would buy it back at a lower price – how much would depend on how desperate they were to go. It had been such a special house to her, the home where she and her late husband had spent the first years of a very happy marriage before he died, before they even had a chance to have children. She wondered if she would feel differently about the house now it had changed hands, but she felt confident it would be hers again soon enough, as well as having provided her and her chums with a nice little nest egg.

She had been through too much heartache for one person to have to suffer and she knew that. But all of this was now in the past and she felt that she was being given a second innings, that at last things were on the up. She had been given a new lease of life thanks to her new friends. With no more thoughts of what had been and what was to come Grace closed her eyes and drifted off into a doze.

A little later that afternoon after the shopping had been unpacked and put away, Lee-Anne was slumped in one of a matching pair of armchairs purchased at Heal's. As far as she was concerned it was a case of, 'so far so good' where the old lady below was concerned. She seemed to be a wretched old soul who wouldn't be troubling them for long. She was probably barely able to look after herself. The young woman shuddered at the very thought of ever having to rely on a visiting carer to attend to such basic things.

Relaxed now, a smile crept onto her face and a warm glow spread through her chest. This was it. This was a little paradise of a house that she and her lover had picked up at a good price, all things considered. The sitting tenant below was old and senile and not long for the coffin. She praised herself for being astute and getting in before any other viewers came along. Glancing at Philip, her bed and business partner, she smiled. He was in a chair, looking around the room at the fitted cupboards that looked to be the same period as the house although they had had far too many coats of paint over the years. As did the lovely period shutters on the windows, through which the late afternoon sun was now flooding and casting patterned shadows on the walls of their sitting room. Gazing across the room at her lover, Lee-Anne smiled triumphantly and raised an eyebrow as she said, 'So far so good, sweetheart . . . the barmy old bat is as quiet as a mouse down there. That must either be because the floors are deep and solid or that she thinks it's night-time during the day and has nodded off.'

Turning his head to look at her, Philip said, 'Or she might simply be having an afternoon nap, or knitting, or even looking at a magazine. Try to act as if she's a normal person who you like, Lee-Anne. For at least a few weeks or so.' He smiled and got up from the chair. 'Right . . . rest break over,' he said. 'Just a few more bits and bags of shopping to fetch up and we're done. I think we deserve a Chinese takeaway this evening don't you? I read in the local paper that one has opened just down the road. What do you think?'

'I think that would be just the ticket. Wonderful. But I *would* like that new coffee table brought up now . . . if you're up to it?'

'Not a problem my sweet.' Once at the door he turned around to look at her. 'And yes . . . before you ask me again, I love the house. Well found dearest, well found.' He then went down the stairs and once in the entrance hall saw Grace as he glanced through the open doorway into her sitting room. Taken aback by her appearance he could hardly believe his eyes! Could this be the same woman from whom they had purchased the house? She had cast off the grey wig that she had been wearing when he had viewed the property and was back in her normal clothes, wearing a fresh and pretty blue dress. And her little cat nap had done her the world of good. She did now actually look a touch younger than her years.

In one hand she had a sack into which she was putting her props – and the horrid dying plants that had been purposely placed in the entrance hall when the couple had first come to view. In their place now was a beautiful arrangement of coloured silk flowers. There was also a new, large, and healthy rubber plant hidden beneath a delicate table cloth. Watching from the staircase as she energetically dropped another dying plant into the sack, Philip was overcome with suspicion and bewilderment. He covered his uncertainty with a wry smile, telling himself that he had to be patient, that she was bound to have her good days. So, trying to be no more than a little concerned at how youthful she looked, he passed her by and went outside to collect the things from the car. On his return, however, while he was struggling with the awkward and quite heavy new coffee table, he was stopped by Grace, who smiled radiantly at him.

'Oh, Philip my dear!' she exclaimed. 'I *am* glad to have caught you on your way back up. I've a little something for you and Lee-Anne. Now then close your eyes and don't move. It's a surprise.'

'Well, actually Mrs Clark . . . this table is rather heavy,' he just managed to say. 'Do you think I could just carry on up the stairs with it and then come back down to receive the gift?' He was clearly having difficulty and his knees were beginning to buckle under him as he tried to keep his balance.

'Oh, it won't take a second. Just close your eyes like a

good boy.' Once he had reluctantly done as asked she removed the delicate cloth that was covering a huge rubber plant and in a sing-song voice said, '*Open*!'

Obeying the irritating command, the young man was faced with what he considered to be a ghastly house plant. He was speechless but Grace wasn't. 'It's always difficult to know what to get for you young people,' she said, 'but I think I've chosen wisely. At first I thought I might buy you some nice linen. Then I set my heart on a rag mat. And then I changed my mind again and—'.

'Mrs Clark . . . I really must keep on going and this table is quite awkward in any case. So if you will excuse me . . .'

Behaving as if she hadn't heard she continued tormenting him. 'But then I thought that rag mat would be cheerful but a touch out of date! So I thought, what about a nice mirror for the bathroom. I'm sure Lee is always looking at herself to make sure that she's top notch for going out to work. Well, she would have to wouldn't she? It wouldn't do for her to go out looking like a monkey's bottom.' She chuckled.

'Absolutely. But I really am going to have to put this table down Mrs Clark. So if you could just move aside . . .'

'No, there's no need to put it down. I'll just pop the plant on top.' This done she smiled serenely at him. 'There! A gift to welcome you into your new home!' Horrified at the thought of Lee-Anne's face when she saw the large rubber monster of a plant, he couldn't think of anything to say. 'Ah, yes. Words fail me. It should fit perfectly into the corner of this lovely hall. Where we shall all enjoy it.'

'Oh no! I wouldn't dream of it! No . . . this is meant as a gift for you and Lee-Anne. A house warming gift. I ordered it specially.' She looked from the plant to his face and, feigning disappointment, said, 'Perhaps you would have preferred one that blooms? I suppose I could take it back and change it for—'

'No,' exclaimed the now exasperated young man. Then lowering the table to the floor he just about managed a polite smile that was more of a grimace and said, 'I wouldn't dream of it. We . . . we love rubber plants. Really.'

'Do you? Oh I *am* pleased! I do so want us to be friends. Friends as well as neighbours. It will be lovely having young blood around. Do me the world of good.'

'Yes. Right. Well . . . best get on, Mrs Clark. Lots to do.'

Picking up the table again and longing to escape, even with the plant balanced on the table, he gingerly made his way upstairs, only narrowly avoiding being caught in a black bin bag that Grace had left there. Philip eventually climbed the stairs with Grace watching him as he went and telling him to be careful. With a wry smile, she then eavesdropped from the stairs to hear Lee-Anne's reaction.

Once inside the flat Philip very carefully lowered the table to the floor and – to Lee-Anne's horror – the toppling plant. 'What the hell have you got there and why have you brought it up here?' shouted Lee-Anne.

'Take it downstairs and throw the bloody thing out into the back yard! You know I can't bear the hideous things!'

Having heard enough to satisfy herself, Grace left them to it and went inside her apartment to put her feet up for another five minutes telling herself that all boded well. The couple were already at each other's throats. She congratulated herself on the fact that life was sweet and that things were going well. But she had not long sat down when she heard the sound of her doorbell. Back on her feet she was in the hall and opening the door to a young lad holding a beautiful bunch of flowers. 'Oh good. Bang on time.'

'Whose birthday is it then, Mrs Clark, eh?' said the lad, all friendly and cheerful and hoping for a tip.

Grace laughed fondly at him. 'Thank you so much. They are beautiful, aren't they?' She took a sixpenny coin off the windowsill where she kept small change for times like this and tipped the lad.

'So you were expecting them then? They're not a surprise present?'

'Yes and no.' She then leaned forward and whispered in his ear. 'I sent them to myself. A little treat.'

'Ah . . . doesn't anybody ever send you flowers then?'

'Oh yes from time to time. But I just felt like treating myself. And I wanted to brighten up the hall for the new people who are now living in the upstairs apartment.'

'Oh that's nice. But why didn't you come in for your flowers Mrs Clark? You usually do. Why didn't you do that this time? We were a bit worried at the shop. Thought you might be ill or somefing.'

'Oh no. I'm as fit as a fiddle. But I'm rather busy and I did so want to brighten up the hall with a special arrangement. Thank you so much for bringing them.' With that she gently closed the door and laid the bouquet on the hall table, then gave the place a couple of squirts of unscented fresh air spray, which she much preferred to the ghastly lavender-scented one she had used when first showing the young couple around the house.

Back in her apartment once more, Grace continued with the work in hand, then stood back and admired her room, which was almost back to its former glory as was the grand entrance hall. The horrid dying plants were now out on the compost heap, and she couldn't wait to get rid of the drab old-fashioned throws that had also been part of her props. Slowly, one by one, she placed everything into her sack and then opened a small cupboard fitted into the wall next to the elegant fireplace and reached in for more of her beautiful silk flowers that she had hidden there.

Next to come out of hiding were her favourite cut glass vases, very much in vogue and kept especially for her silk flowers. She placed one on each of her matching side tables and admired her room once more. 'Much better,' she whispered aloud. 'Everything back to normal again. Everything just right and my lovely things placed where they belong.'

Happy and smiling she turned to her gramophone and placed the needle onto her favourite record, 'I'm in the dancing mood,' she thought. And so she was – and dance she did. And while she danced, she decided that she would invite people in for cocktails this coming Sunday. She knew that she could phone a local number and contact a lovely woman who had started her own little catering business. She had heard very good reports on the quality of the dishes that she supplied as well as what was now being referred to as finger food. Apparently it was the best cold buffet to be found.

So, once her record was at an end, Grace went to her collection of cards kept in a little ebony and ivory box, and took out a printed business card that read, *Christine – dishes to tantalise the taste buds*. She made her phone call and to her delight the girl had a space in her diary and said that all she would need would be a couple of days to shop, bake the selection of quiches mentioned, make an assortment of sandwiches and prepare a variety of tossed salads.

Grace was beside herself with joy at the thought of holding her party and was now ready to phone her friends and invite them. She wanted to have a mix of old chums and new and was so excited at the prospect that she poured herself a large sherry. She felt that she was at last getting the spirit of joy back into house, the way that it had been so many years ago when she was a small child and her mother had entertained so very frequently. She wanted the place to be filled with music, laughter and conversation, and of course young people as well as those of her own age. She had been lonely, but now that Gwen and then Molly had arrived, she woke in the mornings with a sense of peace in her heart and a smile on her face.

But there was no time for day-dreaming. She knew that she was going to have to get moving with phone calls because now, instead of having a little too much time on her hands, there was lots to be getting on with. She was going to bring the house alive again. Her first port of call would be Gwen who she would tell to invite whoever she wanted. Then she would tell Molly that she could also invite her family. Grace wanted a marvellous get-together that would fill the entire place with laughter. She picked up the phone and dialled Gwen's number. Of course she could have popped next door to tell her about the party but she didn't feel like it. She felt far too comfortable where she was.

'Is it a special occasion?' said Gwen, once she had heard Grace excitedly explain her plan for a party. 'And if so, what is it? An anniversary of some sort that you want to celebrate?'

'The beginning of my new life my dear!' Grace laughed. 'And I shall tell Molly the same. I shall ask her to invite all of her family too. And talking of Molly, you and I are going to take her shopping into the West End quite soon. All three of us are going to John Lewis and into the ladies clothing department. And you, my dear, are going to spend some of your post office savings on yourself. Money that you've been keeping for a rainy day. Well, it may be the summertime and not raining but we all three are going on a spending spree. Molly can afford to buy a new outfit and so can you. But I want to treat both of you to an appointment at the hairdresser. To show my appreciation. The pair of you have made my world a very happy place to be in again. I can't tell you what it means to have good and trusted friends such as you two. And I won't accept any resistance!'

'Well, you won't get any from me, girl. I'm up for it,' said Gwen. 'You can rig me out with lovely clothes as well if you like, and don't you worry about Molly. I'll drag her there screaming blue murder if I have to. Oh yes, I'll join the pair of you at the hairdresser's for a cut and style.'

'So you really will come with us, even thought you always prefer to perm your own hair?'

'Well yes, in the past. But I'll have a cut and style as well. Sod it. Let's all push the boat out.'

Highly amused at the way her friend swore in such a humorous way, Grace said, 'You cheer me up no end Gwen. What would we do without friends, eh?'

'Be as miserable as sin!' Gwen laughed. 'They say that life begins at forty. Well, let's prove them wrong and show that it can begin whenever we want it to. Pensioners or not!

'But about the party, Grace . . . what did you mean when you said family too? You don't expect me to get in touch with my lot do you? Because I can tell you right now that they won't come in from North London – the remaining few that are living, that is. We hardly speak to each other on the phone let alone pay visits. But I should think that a couple of my close cousins might come. They don't live that far away. One's in Walthamstow and the other in Leytonstone. I haven't seen them for months so we'll be killing two birds with one stone.'

'Oh well, then never mind about those in North London, just invite whoever you fancy. And I'll tell Molly to invite as many of hers as she wants. I'm going to fill the apartment with a mix of posh and poor and old and young, and a mix of music to please each. Let's bring everyone together.'

'Sounds like it's going to be a lot of fun,' said Gwen. 'I'm actually just about to go to Molly's for a cuppa so I'll fill her in on everything while I'm at it, shall I? As long as you don't ask me to prepare any of the food for you because I'm past all that.'

'And so am I my dear!' Grace chuckled. 'I've called in a caterer, and the caterer's husband is going to fetch the drink. I shall order twelve bottles of champagne.'

'Champagne? Twelve bottles? Good grief woman. That'll cost a small fortune.'

'I know, and I don't give a monkey's toss. We are a long time dead my dear – a long time dead.'

That evening Grace spent time talking to a few of her old chums on the phone and inviting them to the party. She had told Molly to phone her family straight away and left Gwen to get in touch with her relatives who were fairly local. By the time she had talked to everyone that she needed to she was ready for a gin and tonic. And this is what she poured herself before lounging in her armchair, imagining what it was all going to be like with such a wonderful mix of people. It was all coming together just as she'd hoped and she was delighted that she had managed to nail down one of the best home caterers in the area. But, telling herself to calm down, she picked up her address book from a side table and called the hairdresser to book the three women in for next Saturday morning, before the party. It was a time for change for all three of them. She couldn't wait for her short-notice party to kick off. Champagne and delicious substantial eats. Marvellous. And music of course.

Molly had had to do a little more explaining than she would have liked when she phoned Andy to invite him and the family because he wanted to know all the ins and outs and whys and wherefores. But she had expected this. Then, when she spoke to Eileen she was a little surprised at the way her daughter-in-law seemed to be a touch guarded, because this wasn't like her. But then, Molly had no idea about Eileen's confession to Patsy.

Twenty guests were now expected and although they would not necessarily be arriving at the same time, this was exactly what Grace had hoped for. She wanted it to be friendly and informal.

Not everyone was quite so excited at the thought of the party, however. Patsy, at home after a busy day at the hairdressers was in her bedroom lying on the bed thinking about how her life had been turned upside down . . . Even though she liked the sound of this drinks party that her gran had invited the family to she was wondering whether she and Eileen were going to be able to stand in the same room as the rest of the family and not let on that *they* now shared their own precious secret. Her thoughts flew back to when she had stood on the doorstep outside of their house having no clue whatsoever that it was actually her mother that she was visiting and not her aunt. She had been pressing her finger on that doorbell since she had first been able to reach it on tip-toes, and all the while having no idea about the secret behind the door.

She wondered why she hadn't questioned herself as to why she and Eileen had always been so very close. They had always got on and had seen the funny side of things, and Eileen had always looked so happy whenever she turned up out of the blue onto her doorstep. The woman had always said the same thing: *What do you want? Your belly grumbling is it? Or are you after a threepenny bit for a toffee apple.*' And it hadn't been just her who had greeted Patsy as if she were part of that family but Uncle Tom too. She recalled times when she had spent hours with him in the small walled back garden where he grew prize-winning roses that had a lovely perfume.

She had always felt close to both her uncle and aunt and had always been able to get straight to the point if ever she wanted a favour or a question answered. And now she could see why she had always been able to talk to Eileen about things that she wouldn't have broached with her mum. Silly little things that didn't seem to matter that much now but had done at the time, like being told off by a teacher for something that she hadn't done and how unfair it was.

Of course, she realised that her aunt had been behaving quite naturally, as if she was her mother –

221

which she actually was. And apart from this they had always shared the same sense of humour and saucy jokes. Her aunt had been the first to tell her always to keep both legs in one stocking once she was a grown-up and going out with a lad. And Patsy had known even from the age of thirteen what she had meant by it because she had made Eileen explain. They had always had a special bond, the unknowing daughter and the mother who had to give up her newborn baby girl, her only daughter.

But that was then and this was now and Patsy and she were as close as they had always been. The only difference now was that *they* held a secret that the family weren't in on. And in a way, it felt good that as mother and daughter they now shared this between them – at least until they were ready to tell others. They'd agreed that neither of them yet wanted it to be discussed openly within the family. Now Patsy hoped she could hold her nerve at the party.

The days simply flew by and the day of the party seemed to arrive in the blink of an eye. Grace looked lovely in her pretty new red and white sun frock with its matching bolero and red Cuban-heeled soft leather shoes. Her hair had been cut into the latest style with a few highlights to lift her now greying soft auburn. She looked and felt wonderful.

Looking around her sitting room she glanced at the table where she had sat as a child with her parents in this very room so very many years ago. The leaves had been pulled out to their fullest and could now, as it had done in those early days, easily sit fourteen people. And covering it was a beautifully ironed white linen table-cloth that was brought out on special occasions such as today. When her parents had had dinner parties this cloth was one of four that was used regularly, and a time when the silver, the best china and the cut-glass frequently came out of the cupboards.

Today though, it was being used quite differently. Cold buffet parties hadn't been something that her mother had gone in for as they had not been as fashionable at that time as they were now. Checking her appearance in the mirror above the grand period fireplace, Grace heard the sound of her doorbell.

In the hall within seconds Grace opened the door and broke into a smile. Not only was the young caterer on her step but her husband too. This was Martin, who sometimes helped his wife Christine with deliveries. Today he was also fetching the champagne.

'Well . . . don't *you* look beautiful,' said Christine.

'Oh, thank you so much my dear. What would I do without you? And as for you Martin, I can't thank you enough for running the most important errand. My handsome champagne carrier.' She leaned forward and kissed him lightly on the cheek. 'Now do come in the both of you and if you've just a few minutes extra to spare I would love it if you were to open the first bottle and drink a toast with me.'

Christine, with a smile on her face led the way in. 'I think that would be lovely,' she said. 'And while I'm having a drink you can tell me what you're on to give you such energy.'

'What I'm on?' said Grace, once all three of them were in the room with the door closed behind them. 'Surely you don't mean marijuana?'

Placing the cardboard boxes she was carrying onto the table the local caterer quietly laughed. 'Marijuana. Listen to it. How do you know about things like that? I thought you were a sweet and innocent old lady.' She turned around and gave her the once over. 'I know you like to entertain now and then but what's brought all this on? You've not found yourself a boyfriend have you?'

'A boyfriend? No my dear, there's only my lovely old friend Henry Jackson – he is still around, wearing his old-fashioned suits and flirting with me to cheer me up.'

'So what's put the roses in your cheeks then? I mean to say – just look at you. You never did look your age, but there's more than just a spring in your step now. What's going on?'

'Friendship as a matter of fact,' said Grace. 'I have a lovely lady renting the flat below who is a marvellous companion and who has brought me even closer to Gwen, the woman who lives next door. They're both from the East End you know, and have known each other for years. It was Gwen who told Molly about the flat below when it became vacant. But apart from that I've sold this property to a couple who live in the flat above! And now I've got thousands and thousands of pounds in my bank account!'

Bursting with laughter, Christine looked from Grace to Martin, who was quietly chuckling. 'Well, if that's the case, all I can say is – yes – let's open one of those bottles. Let's celebrate the new you.'

'I wish my mother would do something like this,' said Martin. 'Her house is far too large for her now that Dad's gone. And obviously you've done a deal whereby you're allowed to stay in this flat. Very clever. Well done.'

'Well yes, I rather thought so too,' said Grace, deciding to leave it there. As excited as she was she didn't want anyone else to know what a cunning hand she was playing in case they thought badly of her. 'Yes . . . we simply must have a toast! The three of us.'

'I'll drink to that,' said Christine as she flopped down into an armchair. 'I'm worn out if you want the truth. Next time give me more warning when you have a party. I've been working round the clock. And all because you were a good friend to my mother once upon a time. You brought her out of the gloom when she lost Dad. And that's something special that can't be bottled or bought.'

'Absolutely,' said Martin as he expertly pressed two thumbs under the cork of a champagne bottle and sent it flying to the high ceiling.

Once the drinks were poured the three of them stood by the window where the sun was flooding in and made a toast to each of their futures and, especially, to Grace's second flush of youth.

Having met Danny on her way home from the hairdresser's, Patsy was enjoying a slow stroll with him as well as looking forward to getting dressed up ready for the drinks party, as Grace was calling her little soirée. Danny had brought his lightweight summer suit and a clean shirt, and the night before Patsy had laid out her favourite navy blue miniskirt and a lovely pale blue long sleeved blouse to make an outfit when put together with her powder-blue pointed-toe shoes and matching handbag. The plan was for Andy to drive all four of them to Molly's apartment in Wanstead and Tom and Eileen and their three sons to make their way in their own car. Apart from liking the idea of this little party that they had been invited to, some of the family had not yet been to visit Molly in her new home, so the excitement was doubled.

Alice, all at sixes and sevens, wasn't sure what to wear and had been trying things on in her bedroom. Normally she wouldn't have been quite as fussy as to whether an outfit was or was not right for this kind of casual Sunday night do. But she had heard via Molly that the woman who owned the big house in which she was living was from a wealthy upper-middle-class family. Andy, meanwhile, was in the bathroom shaving and was whistling the tune to a song that had been in the charts. Alice could hear him, and was a touch surprised when he stopped whistling and sang along to the words, changing some of them: '*Quivers down my backbone, Yeah the shakes in my knee bone, I got the tremors in my thigh bone, Shakin' all over. Well you make me shake, la-de-da baby . . .*'

Marching into the bathroom in a bit of a snit, Alice glared at him and then said, 'It's all right for some! Singing as if you've not got a care in the world! I haven't a clue what to wear! You and Patsy can go, I'm stopping right here. Fancy reminding me that it'll be all la-de-da!'

'Oh for Christ's sake Ali . . . leave it be. How many more times do I have to tell you that my mother said the woman was posh but ordinary and not the least bit a snob.' He then relaxed with a sigh because he had seen by the look on his wife's face that she was ready to burst into tears.

'Darling, you know that I think you look lovely whatever you wear, but all right, if I think about it and to be honest I have been while I was shaving . . . I think that you look the best ever when you wear that black and white dog-tooth two-piece costume with your plain black top.'

'That's not party wear! That's something I put on when there's a staff meeting at work!'

'Well, all right then. Wear my second favourite – that lovely red and green striped dress with the full skirt. Then, when we have a jive you'll be able to show off them lovely long legs of yours.'

'I don't think that an old woman will be putting records from the hit parade on, but, as it happens, I did pull that frock out of the wardrobe and it'll go with my shoes.'

'Well, there you go then.' He winked at her and went back to seeing to himself while singing, '*Quivers down my backbone, Yeah the shakes in my knee bone, I got the tremors in my thigh bone, Shakin' all over. Well you make me shake, and I like it, baby . . .*'

Smiling now that she had settled the question of

what to wear, Alice went over to give her husband a peck on the cheek. 'I'm glad that we're going really. I've not seen you this bubbly in a while. Is it because your mum's a lot happier now that her life's turned around?'

'Probably. But there is something else. I've got a little surprise for you and once you've made up your mind for sure of what you're wearing and got kitted out, I'll show you something that'll put a smile on your face. A big smile.'

'Oh, will you now? Cheeky sod. I don't think there'll be time babe.'

'I wasn't thinking of that. Go and get dressed and be quick about it.'

'Fair enough,' said Alice. And then cocking an ear added, 'That's Patsy coming in with Danny. I hope she doesn't expect me to have a bit of tea ready. Your mum said that there was gonna be plenty of food so I—'

'Alice! For Christ's sake go and get ready!'

'All right, all right. Keep your shirt on.' With that she left him to it and went back into their bedroom, slamming the door behind her. Patsy could take care of herself and so could her boyfriend. She was going to have to get a move on with getting ready, especially if she was going to find out what Andy's surprise was. 'Something that'll put a smile on my face?' she murmured. 'Now I wonder what that's gonna be? A new sparkling ring perhaps? Maybe even a diamond eternity ring?'

Almost an hour later, with the four of them all smartened up and on their way, Andy was no longer singing as he seemed to have been doing all afternoon, having been out of the house for most of the morning. But he still had that certain look on his face that Alice couldn't fathom. It wasn't like him to be this happy just because they were going to see his mother. It was out of character. But she had enough of thinking about it and walked with Patsy and Danny while Andy took the lead, walking more quickly than he usually did.

'Something's different about your dad today Patsy, and if I'm honest he's not been himself all week. Singing every morning while getting ready for work? I mean . . . he's never done that before.'

'Maybe he's found a gorgeous woman to keep on the side, Mum,' she teased.

'On the side? She can take the plate. I won't be second fiddle to no-one darling. Look at him! Two more strides and he'll be round that corner and out of sight. And look at us. We're walking faster than we usually do to keep up!' She then deliberately slowed her pace. 'Well sod him, he can stand and wait like a lemon by the car for us.'

'I don't know what you're going on about,' said Patsy. 'He's happy and very obliging at the moment that's all. And he was the same yesterday when he gave me five shillings to get these flowers for Nan's land-lady.'

'Exactly my point! Why is he being all nice and cheerful and not moaning about having to pay for things? I got a big box of Black Magic yesterday. Now what was that all about?'

'Oh well, buying you chocolates is a sure sign of

guilt. I read that in a woman's magazine. That's what men who are spoiling themselves with a lover do. I wonder what she's like?'

Laughing at Patsy winding her mother up, Danny was longing to tell them why Andy was so happy but it was more than his life was worth. He had been surprised when his girlfriend's dad had taken him aside and into his confidence . . . even if it might have only been to brag a bit. But as far as he was concerned the bloke was beside himself with joy and he wasn't going to spoil it or ruin the surprise that Alice and Patsy had in store. Turning the corner he glanced at his girlfriend and then her mother to see if they had spotted the car that was in Andy's usual parking space. And Alice had. 'Oh God . . .' she moaned. 'Someone's car's in your dad's space and I bet you he's gonna leave a note on it or do something stupid. That's what all the smiles have been about I bet you. He's like a bloody kid at times when it comes to what he insists is his personal parking space. Just because we've lived here for years and—'

'Oh Mum . . . give it a rest.'

'It's all right for you. You can switch off when he goes on and on about that bloody space as if he owns it.'

'Let's hope he doesn't run a nail along the side of it,' said Danny doing his best not to chuckle.

'He wouldn't do a thing like that,' said Patsy. 'It's brand new by the looks of it. That's probably what the matter is. He's jealous.'

Arriving at his side, Alice said, 'One day sweetheart. One day. And whoever that beauty belongs to . . . he couldn't have known that was your space. So don't go on about a neighbour rubbing it in that they've got a new motor.'

'A neighbour rubbing it in?' said Andy. 'Why would I want to do that?' He then walked around the car to the passenger side and used his key to open the door. Doing his utmost to be casual and keep a straight face he looked at Alice and said, 'In you get then. We don't wanna be the last ones there.'

Looking from her parents to Danny, Patsy was wide-eyed. 'Jesus . . . what's going on?'

'He's about to take his family for a drive in his new car.' Danny winked at her. 'He was keeping it a surprise but I was let in on it.'

Patsy smiled and slowly shook her head as she murmured, 'I should have known shouldn't I. I should have bloody well known.'

Danny squeezed her arm. 'Don't bring him down Patsy . . .'

'Bring him down?' she whispered back. 'Not likely. If he wants to keep up with the Jones's that fine by me. And you know who I'm talking about.'

'Of course I do. My dad's Jaguar made him think that it was time he treated himself to a nice car.' He spoke in a quiet voice meant only for her ears.

Turning from her boyfriend to look across at her father, she said, 'It's fantastic, Dad! You crafty sod!'

Laughing, Andy got into the driver's seat and reached across to unlock the back door of the beautiful, sleek, dark-green Humber Hawk saloon. 'In you get then!' he said, his voice raised. 'Let's be on our way.

We've got a party to go to!' He then slyly glanced at Alice who was sitting there as if she was already at home in the smart new motor car.

'Oh . . .' said Alice, 'are you talking to me, driver? Because if so I would rather be driven in silence. And please do not brake sharply, I am used to a smooth drive, thank you.'

Andy glanced at her and smiled, glad that Alice had accepted it enough to joke around. He had always wanted a car like this but hadn't been able to afford it. Now he could, thanks to part exchange and part hire-purchase. But, truth be known, the furthest thought from Alice's mind was the cost or the repayments. If Danny's family could drive around in a Jaguar then she could ride in a Humber Hawk saloon. There really was no more to be said and they couldn't wait to see Molly's face when they turned up in this brand spanking new car fit for a film star. Alice was in her element.

'I was thinking the other day,' said Andy, all casual as he drove his beautiful car away from the backstreets and headed for the Mile End Road, 'I was wondering if it was time that we thought about living a bit closer to trees and fields instead of roads, shops and office blocks. Somewhere like Wanstead would be ideal. I might look into it.'

'It would be closer to where my father now lives with his new wife in Essex,' said Alice. 'But not too close. Would we be able to get an exchange, that's the thing?'

'Of course you would, Mum,' said Patsy. 'A couple of girls who work at the hairdresser and come in from

Loughton and Redbridge used to live in our neck of the woods. Their parents moved out a couple of years ago. They live in council maisonettes that were built for the East End overspill not long after the war.

'But that would mean that you and Danny would be even further apart. South London would be a bit of a drag from there,' said Alice, nicely relaxed and enjoying her ride. In fact she was secretly hoping that someone she knew might just be strolling along so she could open the window and wave.

'Oh, I won't be stopping in the house for that much longer,' said Danny. 'Once that land's been cleared I'll be overseeing the building work of the supermarket.' Danny had decided that now was the time to let Patsy's parents in on his family's plans. Patsy had reassured him they would be just as happy as she was about the new development plans.

'What supermarket?' said Alice.

'The one that we'll be having built where Hobbins and the other old shops are – once the land's been flattened. It won't be for a year or so that we're at that point but what's a year in a lifetime?'

'Oh, so whoever's buying the land to build on has asked you to oversee have they?' There was just a touch of disbelief in Andy's voice.

'My family owns it. The contract's been signed and it's all done and dusted. We only owned the ground that the store I work in at the moment is on but we've clinched a deal for that whole strip.'

Andy could hardly believe what he was hearing.

'Good for your family,' he said. 'So they're getting into the building trade?'

'Well not exactly . . . they've been in it for years. Not building properties though, just owning some . . . and land beneath them. My great-great-grandfather kicked it all off years ago. Buying bits and pieces here and there when it was dirt cheap. When there was plenty of wasteland up for grabs. That's how it all started from what I can gather.'

'Good for him. It takes a clever man to do that. Someone with plenty of foresight and self-belief, never mind guts. I take my hat off to him. I've always said those old shops have had their day. It's time for a bit of modern convenience round here – and I'm chuffed that it's your family that's behind it.'

Taken aback by this and finding it difficult not to smile or laugh, Alice could hardly believe what she was hearing. The boy, who was clearly head over heels in love with her daughter, came from a very wealthy family by the sound of it. 'So you might rent a little flat then when you're managing the project,' she said.

'Possibly. But then as Dad said, some of the privately owned backstreet terraces that were built back in the early eighteen hundreds and not brilliantly will likely be on the list for demolition within, say, the next ten years or so. Especially those around the Brick Lane area. So I could pick one of those up easily enough.'

'Oh, but you wouldn't want to live there, surely?' said Alice.

'Why not? It would only be for a few years so it would be a bargain. And don't forget that my family have been in the trade for years. It wouldn't cost us much to sort out the place. The men that work for my dad and uncle are good blokes. Totally reliable.'

The conversation went from one thing to another without a hint of awkwardness between Danny and Patsy's parents and there was no sense of having to fill a silence when one fell. There were even a few off-the-cuff jokes sprinkled here and there about paupers becoming princes. Danny's family, a few generations back, had owned little else other than the clothes they wore and the shoes they walked in from what he was now telling Andy. Patsy could hardly believe the way that her boyfriend was getting on with her parents. And she was relieved that Danny had never again mentioned what he had let slip to Patsy about her having been adopted. Patsy felt Danny's eyes on her face. Tilting her head a little she glanced at him and smiled happily.

Slowly pulling up outside the house where Molly now lived, Andy was a happy man because in this wide and quiet tree-lined turning he knew that his beautiful brand new saloon was as safe as houses.

'Makes a nice change not to have to worry about pinching someone's space. Or one of the kids running a nail along it,' he said.

Alice got out of the car and left him admiring the motor. She couldn't wait to see Molly and tell her what Andy had gone and done. She could almost see her reaction, the slow nodding of the head, then the shaking of it from side to side as she murmured, 'Who does he think he is?' And this is almost exactly what she did say – except that she threw in an expletive in her usual way.

An hour later – once everyone had arrived and with one of the records playing that had been borrowed from Christine the caterer, Grace was in her element. She hadn't ever imagined hearing the sound of Frank Sinatra singing 'Nice 'n' Easy' in the background, here in her apartment and in this very room where, long ago as a child, she had loved the excitement of people talking and laughing at her parents' parties. She adored having a mix of people from all walks of life in her house. They were all chatting to one another with no sign of anyone feeling out of place or awkward. Glancing at the two women from Molly's family who were talking together in a corner, Grace went over and topped up their glasses with champagne, saying, 'I can't tell you how pleased I am that you've taken the trouble to come all this way. I do hope that the traffic wasn't too thick.'

'It was fine,' said Eileen, who was standing with Alice. 'And I love your house. This room is beautiful.'

'Thank you my dear, and I will say that I quite agree. And it's all down to my mother. She had a flair for making sure that everything blended beautifully and I've tried to keep that up.'

'Well you've made a good job of it. But my mother-in-law, Molly, was telling me that there's a young couple who live in the flat above who are like sharks.'

'Oh they're not as bright as all that. In fact, they're a bit dim beneath the surface.' She then smiled as she looked into Eileen's face. 'Oh my dear, you do so look like your daughter. Or rather – Patsy looks like you.'

Feeling the blood rise to her cheeks, Eileen cleared her throat and then said, 'But I'm not Patsy's mum. Alice is.'

'Really?' said Grace, 'you do surprise me. Well there we are . . . that shows my age when it comes to my eyes doesn't it? She then turned to Alice and said, 'You have a wonderful daughter. You must be very proud of her.'

'I am,' said Alice.

'And I think that that young man of hers is not only very handsome but terribly polite. They seem made for each other.'

'Let's hope so,' said Alice.

Then, seeing that someone else's glass needed topping up, Grace excused herself and went over to Patsy's cousins who were chatting away to Molly. She was immediately drawn into the conversation that they were having and, just as Grace had hoped, from what she could tell they were just as comfortable in her company as she was in theirs.

Watching her, Alice then turned her attention back to Eileen. 'That was a close shave. If Patsy had been standing here I think I would have gone redder than a poppy.'

'Me too,' said Eileen, a touch down in the mouth that she was sworn to secrecy despite the fact that Patsy now knew the truth. Even so, she wasn't going to leave it there, because she felt that this was an opportunity not to be missed. Drawing breath she said, 'You know what Alice . . . I've been thinking more and more lately that it might be time that we told her what we did.'

'Well, you know my opinion on that, Eileen. I've always said that we should have told her when she was a kid but old enough to understand why we did what we did. But Andy wouldn't hear of it.'

'I know. I suppose we're just gonna have to see how it all pans out. But the four of us do need to sit down and talk about it. I mean . . . my boys don't even know do they. So it's going to be tears all round I should think. Tears and questions.'

'That's why we've put it off for this long.' Alice shrugged and then smiled. 'But then, you and me are the best of friends and I reckon that that alone will pull us all through. I mean to say – we're hardly gonna be at each other's throats, are we?'

'Hardly.' Eileen smiled and then clinked the tip of her champagne glass with Alice's. 'I think of you as a sister.'

'And I love you like the sister I never had, and the same goes for Tom, that lovely husband of yours, who's been like the brother I always wanted. What more could an only child have asked for?'

'I'm glad you feel like that. And even though my boys think that Patsy's their cousin, they love her like a sister.'

There really was no more to be said so the girls winked at each other and each had the same thought in mind. That they should socialise with the others. And so they did, and in no time the room was filled with the laughter and talk that Grace could have only wished for just a few months ago. Everything was going the way she had hoped it would and Christine had come up trumps with the food. It was delicious. All that Grace wanted now was that the little secret hope shared by herself and Molly that they touched on now and then would come to fruition. Molly had said that she thought Patsy might want a bit of independence from her protective parents and might like the idea of moving into the one-bedroom apartment above . . . once they'd driven out Philip and Lee-Anne and got the house back. As she turned to Patsy and watched the way she chatted to her cousins, Grace heard three loud thumps on her door that led into the entrance hall. She knew exactly who it was going to be and bang on time as far as she was concerned, because the party was now in full swing with everyone happy and chatting.

Opening the door with a false expression of expectation as if another invited guest arrived, Grace wore a demure smile. On seeing Lee-Anne looking all cross she pretended not to notice.

'Oh my dear . . . it's you. I *am* pleased that you've decided to pop in for a glass of champagne.'

'I have not decided to pop in – I am here to tell you to turn the music down! You are not the only one living in this house!'

'Oh, you mustn't worry about Molly . . . your other tenant. She's not going to mind one bit because it's her family that this little drinks get-together is all about. They're all here my dear. Why not come and meet them? They're all cockneys you know. Marvellous people. Salt of the earth!'

'No thank you. But will you please switch off that record player! I will not have this kind of thing going on in my house!'

'Oh . . .' said Grace. 'You must have missed the clause in the lease that gives a tenant the legal right to have family parties?'

'No, I didn't miss it, but it clearly said "Family". *Only* family. And from what I understood from you before we purchased you have no living relatives so therefore this cannot be a family gathering. So you are indeed breaking the rules!'

'But I *don't* have any living relatives – well none that I'm interested in seeing. Do you know none of them got in touch with us all of those years ago when daddy went abroad never to be seen again. I said at the time—'

'Mrs Clark . . .' said Lee-Anne, speaking between gritted teeth. 'I don't give a damn about your relatives. That music is too loud, and that is not a family gathering. It's a beer party for East Enders!'

'Oh my dear, you must be very careful. You don't want to sound prejudiced. That's against the law these days you know. And it *is* a family party. It's a party thrown for Molly who lives in the flat below. Thrown by myself so that she can have all of her family under one roof. Isn't that a marvellous thing to want to do? I said she could use my apartment because hers is a touch on the small side. We're having a lovely time and later on we'll be having a knees-up. Apparently there's a song called 'Knees up Mother Brown.' And that's what we'll be singing!' Grace laughed joyfully but more because she was getting one up on this woman than anything else.

'Well, if it gets too rowdy, I shall call the police.'

'Oh that won't be necessary, my dear. One of the in-laws is a policeman apparently. A high-ranking officer by all accounts. And he should be here with his wife and one or two of his brothers quite shortly. You can take it up with him when he gets here. I'll send him up, shall I?' Of course she was fibbing a bit but she didn't care.

Red in the face and looking ready to burst a blood vessel, Lee-Anne said, 'Please do *not* send *anyone* up to my apartment!' With that she stomped off up the stairs, leaving Grace quite proud of the way she had so convincingly told a little white lie about a couple of her guests being in the police force.

Feeling very pleased with herself, Grace quietly closed the door that led into the main hall and went back to her little soirée, which was clearly a wonderful success. At last her family home was truly alive again.

Chapter Ten

A few weeks later, having had more than enough of living above Grace, who seemed to have a string of people coming and going, the house's new owners were beginning to think that they might possibly have made a very big mistake in buying this property – not only with two sitting tenants but with one who had suddenly rediscovered her youth. And who wasn't, as it turned out, anywhere near as old and decrepit as they had first believed.

Now, trying to avoid yet another row with Lee-Anne about it all, Philip was all togged up in his suit and tie, eager to get out of the house and off to a client meeting. Checking that he had not forgotten anything, he examined himself in the mirrored wardrobe door to make certain that he looked pukka. Seeing Lee-Anne's reflection as she lay on top of the bed, wearing only her long pink satin nightdress, he felt a touch of anger rise from within. She had been nagging at him from the moment he'd opened his eyes that morning. And now she was sipping from a cup of coffee as she leisurely flicked through the *Financial Times*.

Trying to smooth troubled waters so that he wouldn't return to a moody woman later, he spoke softly as usual as he adjusted the knot of his tie, still observing her in the mirror. 'All that I was saying earlier on, Lee, is that it was a nice gesture her giving us that plant as a house-warming present – not to mention the fact that she did order lovely fresh flowers for the hall.'

Continuing to flick through the newspaper, the young woman replied in a quiet, but bored and irritated tone. 'If you say so Philip, you know best. I'm just being a silly female again. That's what it will be. Or the time of the month – which it does just so happen to be. I'm so sorry I couldn't oblige in bed last night, but women will be women and have that bloody period every month. I do understand that it's put you in a grumpy mood though. So don't fret. Don't worry about me and the pain I'm in. I'll work through it all.'

'I am not in a grumpy mood and neither did I imply that you were behaving badly because you are having a period! I'm just suggesting that since she seems to be trying her best to be nice we should go easy on her. That's all.'

'Whatever. Let's leave it there shall we? I'm trying to concentrate. It *is* part of my work project let's not forget. I might look as if I'm lounging but I am working. Stocks, shares and failing companies. And let's not forget our original plan.'

Pausing for a moment, Philip sighed. 'Yes. Of course you're right. I'm sorry.' He glanced out of the window at the garden below. 'But we do need to keep on the right side of the old bat for a little longer if for nothing else but to be able to spend time in her garden.'

'It's ridiculous that we can't have use of our own grounds,' said Lee-Ann, 'but the lease that the old bag had drawn up is water-tight. Whoever advised her – probably that ageing solicitor – knew exactly what they were doing. Sole use of her part of the garden? And the same going for the tenant in the basement whose rent is so low as to be peanuts, but can't be raised for five years? I don't know how we let that slip past us. But then it wasn't me who checked the lease, it was you.'

'You were in a rush to get the deal in the bag and the sale completed, Lee. Remember? It's not entirely my fault that we didn't study the small print more thoroughly when we purchased. I did warn you not to rush things.'

'Yes . . . and if you remember I was up to my eyeballs in paperwork. I do have work commitments too, let's not forget.'

Philip then went over to the bed and gave his beloved a conciliatory peck on the cheek. 'How will you spend your day off? Not working around the clock on figures for the boss, I hope.'

'It's not an *official* day off. I told you that already. *Remember?* I am working from home because it's quiet and I have to concentrate. Try not to go too soft when it comes to the old bag below, let's not forget why we're here.' She looked up at him and smiled, then rubbed her thumb against her fingers to indicate money making.

'Yes. Silly me. How could I forget?' Philip smiled weakly then left the room and made his way downstairs. But leaving was not going to be that easy. Grace was in the hallway below wearing one of her pretty housecoats. Smiling at him as he arrived at the bottom of the stairs, she could see that he was a touch surprised to see her in her doorway and looking so radiant.

'Ah Philip,' she smiled. 'I am glad to have caught you.'

Deliberately looking at his wristwatch to try and give her the message, he said, 'I am in rather a hurry to get to work Mrs Clark . . .'

'I know. But it's just that Lee-Anne seems to have got the wrong impression about the housewarming gift. The silly thing has brought it down here into the hall.'

Again he glanced at his watch trying hard not to show his impatience. 'Mrs Clark, I really am in the most frightful hurry—'

Continuing to smile at him as if she hadn't heard, she said, 'You see I wanted to give you a gift to symbolise the beginning of a new friendship. A friendship that I hope will grow with the years. I wanted it to be part of your new home. Of course the hallway is part of the house but I really meant for the plant to be yours and only yours. You may be my landlords now, but I see no reason why we can't live together as if we were close friends or family. I never did have children you see . . . and if I had done, I expect they would be your age by now. So, having you in my house – I mean *your* house – is really rather nice. I feel as if my life has just begun all over again!' She smiled demurely at him, then lifted the plant and offered it to him, all warm and friendly. 'I know it's not much . . . and I don't mind taking it up to your apartment if you're in a hurry?'

'No, I don't think that's a good idea. Lee is working

at the moment. Complicated paperwork. Figures and so on.'

'Oh well, then I shan't disturb her. I should think that her line of work must be quite wearing. And yet she always looks so attractive. Beautifully set hair and lovely make-up. You don't think she could do anything with my face, do you? Of course it's quite an old "front view", but—'

'Actually, Mrs Clark . . . it's funny that you should say that. I was only just this minute thinking how you've changed since the first time I saw you. You seem so, well, so much younger somehow. More youthful. And far more attractive and lively.'

'Do I? Oh, well, that can only be due to you and your lovely wife. It's doing me a mountain of good having young people around. I think I can honestly say that you've taken twenty years off me. And do you know, I've taken to the idea of painting in the garden again. I haven't done that in years! Your presence has given me a wonderful new lease of life, and I am so looking forward to you and Lee-Anne joining me for afternoon tea together one Sunday. Now I know that you're in a hurry, so I'll take the plant back upstairs and leave it outside of your little home sweet home. Then, when Lee-Anne comes out to use the bathroom, she'll see how lovely it looks.'

'Yes. Quite. Well, whatever Mrs Clark. Whatever.' With that he smiled, nodded and left the house.

A fortnight later, Philip and Lee-Anne, coming in from another shopping spree, with each of them carrying a few more classy carrier bags as well a couple of boxes, were quickly up the stairs before Grace had a chance to come out into the hall to annoy them by talking about nothing of any interest or consequence. But this suited Grace because she was quite crafty about when she would irritate them and liked to leave a few days in-between doing so, just to keep them off-guard. And today she hadn't a mind to be mischievous because she was studying her holiday brochures and trying to decide on the kind of cruise that she would choose for herself, Henry Jackson, Molly and Gwen.

Relieved that they had escaped a barrage of super-fluous questions about work and life in general, Lee-Anne and Philip went into their flat and closed the door behind them with a thankful sigh. 'So far so good. Neither sight nor sound of the barmy old bat. Maybe she thinks it's night time and is still in her bed.'

'Don't count your chickens before they hatch my darling . . . she may well knock on that door yet. And if she does, at least try to act as if you like her.' He winked and smiled and then left to go back downstairs to collect more shopping from his car. And whether by co-incidence or not, Grace was pottering about outside her doorway in an attractive up-to-the-minute frock that gave her a kind of arty look. Grace had always been a bit of a bohemian, having worked in the theatre amidst creative actors, writers and producers for so long, and she was delighted that the look was back in fashion.

'Ah Philip,' she said, as a smile spread across her face. 'I've got another little gift for your new home. At first I thought I would buy a pretty table lamp for the bedroom but then I thought you've probably got lots of good lighting since Lee-Anne always turns out looking immaculate. So, this being a period house, I've bought you a tablecloth that was made by an old woman at the Women's Institute.'

'Um . . . well I think that's a very nice idea. I'll collect it later and put it on display straight away. Thank you very much.'

'Oh I am pleased. It's been washed but I think that it still smells a little of mothballs.'

'No problem Mrs Clark. Now I really must soldier on.'

'Of course. I mustn't stop you.' And then, just as if she had suddenly remembered, she said, 'Oh! The plant!' She then pulled the rubber plant from inside the door of her flat and smiled at Philip. 'Do please take this present back upstairs to Lee-Anne. The silly girl doesn't seem to realise that it is meant for *her*. For the flat. The silly thing has gone and brought it back down yet again!' She giggled, hoping to annoy him.

Sighing with exasperation, Philip took the plant and made his way back up the stairs, inwardly telling himself to stay cool. To not lose his temper. That soon the old bag would be dead because, if he had to, he would lure her up and then push her down the stairs.

Satisfied that she'd antagonised Philip enough for now, Grace went back into her apartment and placed the needle onto the record that was on the turntable and ready to go. She smiled and stroked her old radiogram as, 'I'm in the Dancing Mood', began to play.

Coming back down the stairs again, feeling sure that his path was clear, Philip arrived into the hall and, as he reached for the door-catch to let himself out of the house, he stopped in his tracks. Listening at Grace's door he had his suspicions confirmed. The woman was singing! She sounded nothing like the old girl who once had bandaged legs and who dressed as if she was eighty years old. She had a beautiful singing voice that was perfectly in tune and had obviously at one time or another been a professional. Confused, he pulled open the street door, but before he had a chance of escape he heard Lee-Anne calling out to him. Going back up into the flat he smiled at her and as she glanced at him he saw the rubber plant on their landing. She went back to the fashion journal that she was now looking at and spoke between almost clenched teeth, saying, 'I could hear you downstairs creeping about, and I've just seen that bloody rubber plant is back again. Take it down-stairs, Philip, please. And tell that woman to turn down her music, would you?'

'There is no point in taking the plant back down. If I hadn't brought it up when I did she would have done so herself!'

'Well, if you leave it in this room I shall throw it out of the window.'

'And *she* will fetch it back again. It will be like throwing a ball for a dog. Look, there's one very simple answer, Lee. Just don't water the plant! It'll soon die off.'

'I wish that she would die off.'

'Yes well, I'm afraid the chances of that get less by the day. We've given her a new lease of life.'

'Oh, have we now?' She swung her legs over the side of the bed. 'Well then, I shall have to go into action sooner than I thought. Manoeuvres will be brought forward.' Striding to their wardrobe she pulled open the door and searched through her footwear until she found her tap shoes. She then sat down on the edge of the bed and tapped the heels together while sporting a wicked smile. 'I'm going to enjoy this.' She kicked off her slippers and pulled on her dancing shoes.

Philip ignored the pot plant and headed for the door. His face taut and his eyes showing contempt, he spoke with a tone of exasperation saying, 'I have a feeling our frail old lady is tougher than you think.'

'Don't you believe it my love. I shall tap right through this day if I have to. She'll be a quivering old wreck by the time you get back. I'm an old hand at this, don't forget.'

Staring at the woman he once thought that he loved, he wondered if he really knew her at all any more. And now they were stuck in this wretched house together. 'Yes – well – good luck. As for me . . . I'm going for a walk around the block and to the park before I do anything else.' He then turned away and left, knowing that it was time for him to cool off. He was a more troubled and angry man than he had been in a long while.

As soon as Lee-Anne heard the front door slam shut after her partner she, with revenge on her mind, determinedly pulled back a rug that lay on the old polished pine floorboards, chose her spot, and began to tap dance. She was hardly the best dancer in the world but she did have a newfound surge of anger-fuelled energy. So while Grace was casually thumbing through another holiday brochure that specialised in cruises, the young woman above tapped as she had never tapped before.

At first Grace thought little of it because she had other things on her mind apart from cruising the ocean. She was all dressed and ready to go with Molly and Gwen on a bus tour around the East End of London later that day. This was something that she had not ever thought of until Molly had mentioned it, and she certainly wouldn't have got round to considering such an outing. The tap-dancing going on above her head really hadn't bothered her but now, after fifteen minutes non-stop, it was beginning to get on her nerves. For one thing it was hardly a professional performance and it sounded to her as if Lee-Anne was simply tapping the same shuffle over and over again as if she were a would-be child star.

After another ten minutes or so she knew that she could no longer ignore what was happening above her. Covering her ears she murmured, 'Oh dear . . . that simply will *not* do. Dreadful. Quite quite dreadful. No. We can't have this. It will drive me quite mad.' So, after yet another five minutes of the repetitive noise, she decided to take things into her own hands and let battle commence.

Lee-Anne, quite out of breath, irritable and dripping with sweat in her pink slinky summer frock, no longer felt or looked as sophisticated as she had done when she first started her little tap routine. The sweat was running down her face and neck as well as oozing from her armpits. But still with firm conviction that she was doing the right thing, she continued to stamp those feet on those floorboards.

A few minutes later Grace, looking bright and cheerful, was applying a little lipstick. She now felt certain of what the girl was up to. Lee-Anne must have decided to play her at her own game and try to make her life a misery in the hope that it would all became too much, that she would leave and move into rented accommodation elsewhere. How wrong she was. Grace was about to turn the tables on this young woman. She had a bit of time to spare and was ready for a battle with a bit of fun thrown in.

With her small portable gramophone in her hand she left her apartment and made her way to the first floor to knock on the door of the young couple's apartment. Listening at the door she knew that she had been heard because the awful tap-dancing had stopped.

Inside the room, Lee-Anne was regaining her composure and was ready for battle. Smiling she whispered *Bingo! Let the battle commence.* Opening the door wide, she made every effort to look cool and calm but, before she had a chance to say anything at all, Grace raised a hand and strode into the flat, saying, 'I'm so sorry to interrupt you, my dear, but if you are going to take this thing seriously, you really ought to know from the very start that there is a right and a wrong way to go about it. You're looking at an old pro my dear!'

Stunned by the nerve of the woman, Lee-Anne was

not only exhausted and out of breath but also quite speechless. She stared at the woman who was her rent-free lodger and could hardly believe the change in her. She seemed to have gone from a frail old woman to a bright, sparkling pest. Lee-Anne felt like pinching herself to see if this would wake her from the nightmare that she hoped she was having. She had to ask herself again, was she really looking at the same woman she had met on the day that she had come to view the house? The elderly woman who hadn't seemed as if she would be that long in this world and who now appeared to be more of a live-wire than she herself was. She watched dumbfounded as Grace rested her small portable player on a side table, put a record on and then said, 'Now . . . watch me, and learn how it should be done. Tap dancing is an art and to do it well takes proper training my dear.'

She then gave a lovely light tap-dancing display – a routine that she had often gone through on stage in theatres around the country in her youth. She was quite carried away with herself and having a lovely time as she danced to the music, and even managed to smile demurely at Lee-Anne while doing so. The young lady, who seemed quite pale and sweaty from all of her tip to toe tapping was looking at Grace in bewilderment. Grace was clearly in a world of her own and enjoying every minute. Speaking in a kind of singsong voice above the lyrics and music, she said, 'You know Lee-Anne . . . I could give you a few lessons on *how to step the right way.*'

So carried away was Grace, it appeared that she

couldn't even hear Lee-Anne call her. Raising her voice as she folded her arms defiantly, the young lady all but shouted at the top of her voice, 'Mrs. Clark? Mrs. Clark! I think that will do!'

Stopping in her tracks, Grace smiled demurely 'Oh, I am so sorry my dear. I was away with the fairies.' She giggled. 'I get quite carried away with it all. How the theatre does come flooding back.' She then smiled and sighed. 'I used to be so very much applauded when on stage . . .'

'I'm sure you were, Mrs Clark, I'm sure you were.'

'Oh,' said Grace, showing a theatrical hand. 'Please . . . do feel free to call me by my Christian name. It's Grace my dear! As it is to all the young people that I know and sometimes mix with.'

Ignoring the irritating niceties, Lee-Anne folded her arms defiantly. Grace was rattling her cage and she had a feeling that the woman knew exactly what she was doing. This woman she was stuck with and who was living rent free in her house was not only an ageing Shirley Temple but, more damagingly, a freeloader who would be a serious hindrance should she and Philip want to sell the house. And the way she was feeling right then, selling up was exactly what she wanted. But this ghastly woman would have to be considered part of the fixtures and fittings for anyone who bought the place. Unable to keep her vile mood in order she all but screamed the words: 'Mrs Clark! If my memory serves me right, the first time we met your legs were completely bandaged and you couldn't manage the stairs!'

Grace, showing a look of mild astonishment, said,

'How funny! And you assumed it was because of some awful disease!' Not wishing to shout back at the woman a moment longer Lee-Anne marched over to the portable player and switched it off. 'Well then, why were they bandaged?'

'Oh . . . you young people. If I couldn't manage the stairs that day it meant I had overdone it a bit. And besides, I always bandage my legs after a good tap. Now, why don't I give you a lesson or two?'

Furious for more reason than one, Lee-Anne could barely speak, managing only a curt 'No thank you.'

Grace then looked from her to the rubber plant and said, 'Oh dear, the plant needs watering. It's far too dry. Well, never mind, we can't win them all. That's what I was told when at drama school. Of course, then I was taking my exams in both music and drama. I passed with flying colours, my dear. I can't think why!' she laughed. 'I really am quite slow on the uptake . . . as a rule.'

'Really? You do surprise me. I would never have thought it!'

'Wouldn't you?' The expression on Grace's face was all innocence. 'Not even on the day that we met when I was feeling quite low and poorly?' Smiling, she then looked again at the plant. 'At least Philip talked you into keeping my present. That plant's a tough old specimen, dry or not, I shouldn't think you could kill it off if you tried. But there – I've taken up far too much of your time already. I'll see myself out. After all, I was brought up in this house so I should know the way.'

Once she had gone Lee-Anne stared at the plant and

then dropped down onto her sofa, exhausted and angry. She tried to kick off her tap shoes but couldn't manage it. She finally pulled them off and hurled them one by one across the room. Sweaty, dishevelled and furious she cursed Philip, blaming him for not picking up on what the old woman, their now non-paying sitting tenant, was really like. And not only did she have *her* to contend with, but her bloody friends who seemed to be in and out of the house all of the time.

Back in her own apartment, Grace switched on her record player and turned up the sound nice and loud. She picked up one of her cushions and danced around the room as if the was holding a lover. She danced and sang along to, 'Let's Face The Music and Dance.' And while she danced, she imagined herself throwing lots of little parties to which she would invite some of her old theatre friends and of course her new ones too. This idea made her want to sing even louder. She felt as if she was beginning to live like a young woman again and it was a quite marvellous sensation. When the record was at an end and she was exhausted from all of the excitement, as well as from her tap dancing upstairs, she was only too ready to flop down onto her sofa. Once she had her breath back to normal she chattered to herself as she eased off her shoes. 'Yes, Grace . . . I think a summer garden party is the order of the day. Yes . . . a wonderful garden party!' She then drew her legs up onto the sofa and reclined while she ran through a list of possible guests that she might want to have around on a Sunday afternoon.

Preparing for her garden party meant time raced by, and soon enough the day arrived. On what had turned out to be a warm sunny day, Grace was to be found happily entertaining some of her old acquaintances as well as her new chums, Molly and Gwen, Patsy and Danny. Having a wonderful time in the garden, drinking white wine and sampling some of her tasty triangular sandwiches and vol-au-vents from the local delicatessen, Grace looked lovely in her delicate and flowing pink and green summer afternoon frock. Looking even younger than her years today, she was clearly enjoying the limelight, the music and the laughter.

The window of the young couple's sitting room overlooked the garden of course and Philip, who could see what was happening as he drank from a can of beer, was none too pleased. The old woman's music was too loud and her friends were rowdy. Lee-Anne, in a temper, was trying to take pleasure from dumping the house plant into a black bin liner. She was trying to stay calm but her temper was rising.

'The place is crawling with decrepit old people as well as that woman's relatives. That Polly woman who rents the basement flat for peanuts is out there as well. I can almost smell them from up here!'

Keeping his cool, Philip said, 'The woman's name is Molly not Polly and the relative is a granddaughter who is down there with her boyfriend. Of course if we were to go out, you wouldn't have to listen or look at any of them. We'll stay out until midnight if you like.'

'I don't think so! I will not be driven out of my own

home thank you. If it has to come to that, I would rather sell up and go.' She then dropped down onto the sofa and stared up at the ceiling, her anger spilling over. 'You should have said no when she told you she was going to have a bloody garden party!'

'That was not an option. This may be our house, but we have no legal right to stop her having a few friends round. Read the lease properly and you'll see it in black and white.'

'A few friends?' she said, glaring at him. 'There are at least a dozen old crocks out there. One with a Zimmer frame, one in a wheelchair. It's like a cemetery come alive. Garden parties at her age. Who does she think she is?' She pinched her lips together and drew breath through her nostrils, anger oozing from her pores. 'It's all going wrong! We're meant to have driven her to the grave by now – or the loony bin! Not the other way round.'

Turning to look at her, Philip saw another side to the person he knew. This woman, who he once thought to be full of fun and dangerously ambitious was nothing more than a spoiled brat. Staring back at him, tight lipped, Lee-Anne said, 'If you were to get off your backside and decorate the hall it might help. We could spill paint on her carpet, leave doors and windows open, forget to put stepladders away . . .'

'Oh for Christ's sake, will you give it a rest!? And I see no point in decorating, while you keep threatening to sell. Our original plan was to—'

'I know what our original plan was, thank you!' she screamed. 'And I don't actually *want* to leave this house!

I *like* it here! And it'll be worth twice as much if she were to oblige and kick the bucket! But I don't know how much more I can take of her and her crippled friends. If it's not a Bridge party or a Bring and Buy for charity it's something else. It would be just our luck to sell and then hear she'd dropped dead.'

'Exactly. So let's just stay cool and ignore it. Be patient, and we'll get our reward.'

Paying no attention to what her partner was saying she narrowed her eyes and wracked her brain as to how best to come out on top when it came to this house and the woman below. 'We just need to find her weak spot and aggravate her in a thousand small ways,' she murmured. 'Maybe she's got a weak heart? Who knows? That would certainly help.'

With both hands cupping his head as he perched on the edge of the sofa, Philip said, 'Lee . . . I think that you're getting carried away.' Then sighing, as if to say he had had enough of the whole thing he continued. 'If we do have to sell, and lose a couple of thousand doing so, it's not the end of the world. We've done all right so far with buying and selling property. We can't expect to—' The sound of Grace outside in the passage calling stopped him in mid-sentence. 'What the heck does she want now?'

'Hello-o. Hello-o – is anybody there?' came the irritating sing-song voice that Grace liked to use when trying to get under their skin.

'Oh for God's sake!' Lee-Anne covered her ears with her hands, trying to blank everything out. It was all getting too much for even a strong-willed woman like herself. 'I'm not listening.'

Staring down at her, Philip sighed with frustration – and with contempt. 'I'll see what she wants then, shall I? Don't you go and exert yourself Lee-Anne. Don't tire yourself out.' He then turned to face the door, his hands on his hips as if ready for battle. He pulled the door open and stared at Grace, waiting to hear what she had to say. Because as sure as it rained in the winter he knew that there would be something on her mind. Something to annoy him.

'Oh, Philip my dear, I am so sorry to trouble you like this but we appear to have another little problem.' Grace then walked straight into the room as if she owned the place. She glanced at Lee reclining on the sofa.

'Oh, I wish you wouldn't shut yourself up in here like this my dears. There's plenty of food left. Won't you join us? Just this once?'

Ignoring the invitation Lee spoke tightly, saying, 'What little problem are you referring to this time, Mrs Clark?'

'Well . . . it's my friend Agnes. She needed the lavatory rather badly, and as there's a bit of a queue for mine—'

'No. Absolutely not.'

'It's just that I didn't want her to have an accident, especially as the hall carpet is quite new. And of course your new lavatory is so nice . . . Are you sure you won't have some sandwiches?'

Lee-Anne could hardly believe what she was hearing. 'Are you being serious Mrs Clark?'

'Of course my dear. Why wouldn't I? There's egg mayonnaise, cheese and pickle, a few anchovy—'

'No. I mean, is there an old woman sitting on my toilet?'

'Lavatory dear, not toilet.'

'Oh for Christ's sake,' murmured Philip. 'Get her out of there, now!'

'Oooh, dear . . . I don't think that would be wise. I really do think we ought to wait until she's finished in there.'

Lost for words, Lee-Anne could do little other than stare. And then, to cap it all, Molly began calling Grace from downstairs. Smiling at Lee, Grace said, 'Oh dear . . . that sounds rather urgent doesn't it?' Then, assuming an expression of apology, she said innocently, 'Please do excuse me. It might be important – or it might simply be that my friend can't find the tomato ketchup. You know what we old people are like.' She left the couple to themselves, but she hadn't got far when Lee, who could hardly take this in, called after her.

'Mrs. Clark! You're not really going to leave the old woman in there are you?'

'Oh, you mustn't worry about Agnes, dear, she'll be perfectly all right in there.' With that Grace drifted away, leaving Lee-Anne speechless and Philip to stare out of the window that overlooked the back garden. He was flabbergasted at the nerve of the woman who no longer owned this house but continued to behave as if she did.

Furious, but not quite knowing what to do next, Lee-Anne strode across the room and picked up the plastic sack that contained the rubber plant to storm out with it. Once on the landing she threw the lot down the stairwell in a frenzy and, as luck would have it, just missed Grace by inches. With an angelic expression Grace, quite unruffled, looked up at her as if she was waiting for an explanation for the sudden outburst . . . as if Lee might be unwell and perhaps having a mental breakdown. 'I hate rubber plants Mrs Clark! I loathe them!'

'Do you dear? I'm so sorry, I had no idea. Dislike, or the fear of plants could be seen as a phobia. I should let your doctor in on it if I were you.'

Storming back into her apartment Lee was beside herself with fury. She glared at her partner and said, 'I really can't take much more of this Philip.'

Doing his utmost to remain calm the man shrugged. 'Yes . . . I know what you mean. But there we are. We can't expect to win them all, I suppose. Third time unlucky. We'll have to vet the tenants more closely next time. Although selling up doesn't mean we necessarily lose out. We could possibly come out even or with a couple of thou' on top. Property prices never stand still. Who knows?' What he actually meant was, who cares? He had had enough and seen enough to know that he wanted out.

'A couple of thousand on top? Think on, lover – think on. We bought this place with what we believed to be a dying tenant. And we are now going to have to sell it with a healthy woman who's got something of the devil about her. And apparently it's all thanks to our youthful presence in the house. Brilliant!'

Deliberately using a droll voice to give her a bit of her own medicine, he said, 'Of course that's supposing that we *can* sell it. She's got sole use of the ground floor and garden and her lease is water-tight.'

'Well, it's a pity you didn't think of that before!'

'Oh, I think I did mention it . . . but you were so sure she was at death's door and needed only a little bit of nudging that—'

'Of course, it had to be my fault!'

A sudden shouting stopped them in their tracks *'Hello! Are you there? Is anyone about?'* It was Agnes, calling from the lavatory.

'Oh, for Christ's sake,' murmured Lee. She then raised her voice with a change of tone as she called back, 'Bugger off!'

'Lee . . . let's not lose our sense of dignity.'

Again the old woman called out. 'Could someone come and give me a hand with my knickers . . . ? *Coo . . . ee. Is anyone there?*'

Throwing herself down onto the sofa, Lee was determined not to shed angry and frustrated tears. 'This isn't happening. I refuse to believe that this is happening!'

'I think that you'll find that it is. And I think that you'll find that this is only the beginning,' said Philip, a strange faint smile almost of satisfaction on his face.

Since living within these four walls, he had seen a very different side to his girlfriend. And he didn't like it.

And as for poor Agnes in the lavatory, Grace was up there in no time at all and giving the old actress her cue to come out of character. Both retired actresses then went below doing their best to muffle their bursts of laughter.

Chapter Eleven

Now very much settled into her new home and still with no sight or sound of Joe, Molly felt as if she had been given the greatest gift from God that could be asked for: freedom. Waking up each day in her old but comfortable bed and knowing that she hadn't anything to feel depressed about was just wonderful. And of course there was no nagging worry going on as to what *he* might be up to. Even if the sun didn't shine into her room first thing, the way that it had done in her little two-up, two-down, it wouldn't have mattered, but by the grace of God it did. Ever since she was a little girl, sharing a bedroom with her sister, she had loved to feel the early morning sun on her face.

On this Sunday morning as she sat drinking her first cup of tea of the day, she was feeling nostalgic. She had woken up with her sister Marjorie on her mind and didn't know why, other than now she had found peace and quiet she liked nothing better than to reminisce. And to her surprise she found that she could now recall so many happy times from her childhood; times that she thought, with age, had faded from her memory. Had her sister still been around, Joe would never have got past *her* with his nice-guy act. She and Marjorie had been very close and had hardly left each other's side before fate had seemed fit to separate them when Marjorie was twenty and Molly no more than eighteen.

It had been too awful to talk about it all those years ago – or ever since for that matter. Without even realising it, Molly had been bottling up her grief for all these years. After the funeral, Molly, who had been the shyer of the two sisters, had withdrawn into her own private, silent world of make-believe: making believe that her sister was still by her side, still talking to her and exchanging jokes and confidences. And now, for some reason that she couldn't account for, Molly could actually think about Marjorie without feeling grief. She could see her sister's smiling face in her mind's eye and all but hear her quiet, contented laughter.

Molly's parents, and her aunts, uncles and cousins, had done all they could to make it easier for her way back then, but nothing and no one had been able to shift the deep sense of loss when Marjorie lost her battle with leukemia and died in hospital. The grief at her loss had been buried deep inside and now she could see that this was probably how she had preferred it to be – locked away like a special trinket that she hadn't wanted anyone else to see or touch. After the tragedy, still living in a small and cosy house with her parents, down by the river Thames in Wapping, Molly would sit and watch children mucking around and having fun the way she and her sister had when they were kids. She hadn't a best friend at the time because her sister had always filled that role and she hadn't wanted to replace her. But now she had found her old mate Gwen again and, thanks to her, had a good friend in Grace Clark.

Gwen hadn't known about the tragedy of Marjorie's death at the time because they had only met a year or so afterwards and Molly by then had all but pushed it from her mind into a secret place deep inside her, along with the memory of the black funeral and the masses of flowers. Why all of this was surfacing now she wasn't sure, but she didn't mind. Perhaps it was because Patsy had told her how Danny had also lost a sister. And now, just as Danny had moved on and found happiness with Patsy, she too had found not only peace but happiness too. With a warm feeling inside, she smiled and thought that she would like one day to tell Grace and Gwen all about Marjorie. She felt strong enough now to share her story.

Grace, meanwhile, was in the room above. In a contented mood she too was feeling that her life was turning a corner. The little triangle of friends was, to her mind, like three ships sailing on calm waters after coming through tidal waves and storms. Philip and Lee-Anne had now announced their decision to put the house back on the market and Grace was optimistic about buying her home back – although she hadn't given the game away to them. But now the couple was leaving, Grace had been thinking more about whether Patsy might be tempted to move in. Gwen had asked her if she'd like Henry Jackson to move in, but even though she had a wonderful relationship him, he – like her – was of the opinion that it was better for them both if he remained independent in his own little terraced house in Bromley by Bow.

Things couldn't be going better as far as Grace was

concerned. Since the present owners went out to work five days a week as a general rule, she had been the one who had 'kindly' shown five sets of viewers around once the property had been advertised. To her delight, she had managed to make each of them back off pretty sharply. Her acting skills to the fore once more, in the most delicate way she had scuppered every possible sale. She had chatted away as friendly as you like and invited each of them to one of her many charity garden parties that she supposedly held for the poor and destitute of London. And she explained in detail the water-tight lease that gave tenants every right going. On one occasion, while a couple were viewing the flat above her, Grace just so happened to be on the staircase dusting her immaculately clean banisters, when she overheard one of the viewers discussing her. They had said that she was a lot younger and more vibrant than they imagined, and not at all on her last legs as had been suggested by the sellers. This, it seemed had put them off wishing to purchase.

Although most of the viewings were down to Grace, sometimes the young couple saw to it, but even then Grace made sure she was around just so any buyers could see that their potential tenant was fit as a fiddle. So all in all, it was going rather nicely . . .

The shrill sound of the telephone ringing broke through Grace's thoughts. Picking up the receiver in a light-hearted mood, she heard Henry speaking in his usual charming voice, saying 'Hello, my darling Grace. How are the viewings going? Any new ones on the horizon?'

'Oh yes, dear Henry,' replied Grace. 'I have a landscape gardener coming round at three. The house looks so much duller by afternoon when the sun shines on the rooftops and not through the windows. And of course I shall set a tray and insist that he sits in the garden for tea beneath the gnarled old apple tree. It's such a delightful spot – so close to the compost heap where I leave old fish skin and bones for the cats.'

'Cats?' said Henry with a giggle. 'Since when did you have cats?'

'Oh not real cats my dear – fabricated felines, strays, that come and go and are always clawing away at the roots of plants.' She laughed.

Enjoying the joke with Grace, Mr Jackson said, 'And you're sure it's not getting too much for you to cope with?'

'Oh no! Not at all. I am much more young at heart for it. And I love to bore the viewers with my many tales of when I was in the theatre! I'm thoroughly enjoying myself.' She chuckled wickedly before saying goodbye and blowing him a kiss down the line.

Gazing out of the front window and inwardly thanking heaven for sending the lovely lady in the flat below to her, she saw Patsy unlatching the small gate that led down to Molly's apartment and waved at her. Thinking how nice it would be to have a girls' get-together, she picked up the telephone and dialled Gwen's number to ask if she was free to come round. After just a few short rings she heard her neighbour's voice. 'Hello my darling girl. I wondered if you would like to come in for a cup of tea, and whether you think it a nice idea for me to invite Molly and her granddaughter . . . who has just arrived.'

'Oh, I think that would be lovely, Grace,' Gwen said. 'Give me five minutes and I'll be there.'

'Marvellous,' said Grace, feeling on top of the world. She slipped out of her back door and down the steps into Molly's garden to tap her knuckles on the sitting room window. Coming to the door with a lovely big smile on her face Molly said, 'You'll never guess who's here.'

'I don't have to guess my darling. I have just seen a lovely young lady – your granddaughter – going into your flat, and I would simply love it if you and she were to come up and join me and Gwen for a cup of tea or coffee.'

'Well, now that is nice of you and yes, we will. Give us five minutes and we'll pop up.'

Back in her apartment, Grace set to with the business of taking her best china from a mahogany cabinet before she filled the kettle and put it on the stove. She then reached for the biscuit tin that she had had since the Queen's coronation when there had been street parties everywhere and gifts given out, such as her biscuit container. And no sooner had she set a side table than Gwen arrived, soon followed by Molly and Patsy.

'Come in, come in,' said Grace. She looked at Patsy and smiled warmly at her. 'I do hope you don't mind coming into an old lady's apartment but I promise not to keep you long. Now then would you like a cup of coffee, my dear?'

'Yes please,' said Patsy looking around the room. 'I really enjoyed your party. And I love my gran's flat but this is even better. It reminds me of the day that we were taken to Hampton Court on a school trip. There was a room just like this in the maid's chamber.'

'Well then, we simply *must* have scones with fresh cream and jam the next time you come. Afternoon tea fit for royalty and fit for us.'

'So,' said Gwen, 'here we are then. Four ladies in the chamber. And I must say it's good to see you again, Patsy my girl. You do look well. Not in love are yer?'

Rolling her eyes Patsy looked from Gwen to Molly. 'So you told 'er all about Danny then?'

'Me?' said Molly all innocent. 'Course not. She's a spy, that's the truth of it. Once I told her about your young man she probably went back to Stepney and hung around outside that shop to have a good look at him.'

'I'm sure.' Patsy laughed and then sat herself down on the sofa. 'I love this house,' she said, looking around herself. 'I could live here.'

Grace looked across at Molly and raised an eyebrow, a silent message between them about the possibility of the girl moving in above once everything had been settled and she owned the house again. 'Well . . . you never know my dear. One day you might.'

Smiling at the woman, Patsy raised an eyebrow and said, 'No, I'd never move in with Gran. I love her to bits but I couldn't put up with her twenty-four hours a day. Although I think that her flat is really great. Nice and cosy.'

'Well, you never know,' said Grace. 'There is a delightful apartment above where we are sitting that you might like to rent. I'm sure that Molly would be able to help you out financially – if not Danny . . .'

Patsy laughed. 'You're all the same, you lot – never mind where you were born and bred, rich or poor – you're all crafty. And no, I'm not thinking of marrying the boy I've not long met . . . who my nan here has no doubt gone on about.'

'I never said a word!' exclaimed Molly, although in truth she hardly stopped talking about her lovely Patsy and how she had got herself a very nice handsome boyfriend.

'I don't think so,' said Patsy, and turned to Grace. 'But it's a very nice idea,' she said, 'and it didn't take long to get here by bus, so I might just take you up on that one day. I could to and fro easily enough to get to work.'

'Oh, I almost forgot – this afternoon I've got another viewing to scupper, girls,' Grace said as she sliced the fruit cake. 'A landscape gardener. I've got all sorts of schemes to put him off!'

Patsy glanced at Grace who was in her early sixties, which she had always thought to be very old, and yet she was blooming and seemed more like someone in her early fifties. She wondered what she had walked into and couldn't help smiling. It was no wonder her gran was happy living in this house, she thought. The old girls always seemed to be behaving like teenagers. She thought it was great. Brilliant in fact.

'Well, if this is how you lot spend your time, I'll be

back for more. And I'll fetch Mum with me. She'll love all of this!'

'I hope so. And may I say that I think it is just lovely the way you jump on a bus and visit your grandmother every now and then,' said Grace. 'I love it when I see you arrive through that little gate.'

Patsy smiled warmly back and said, 'It's really nice to have somewhere away from the East End to visit. So . . . long may it last, eh?'

Two weeks later on a pleasant Sunday afternoon and after several more failed viewings of the house, Lee-Anne was sitting on their bed painting her fingernails while Philip reclined on the bed, listening to one of his favourite LPs and drinking beer. He was clearly agitated but trying desperately to take his mind off things by humming along to his record. But, unable to settle, he got up and began to pace the floor, talking as he went. 'Not *one* offer. *Nothing*. Except for *that* woman's man friend. I dread to think how many interested parties have been traipsing through this house while we've been at work to be put off by that ageing Shirley Temple down there. I would have thought that the landscape gardener would have shown interest. He seemed quite keen on the phone when he made the appointment.'

Blowing onto her wet fingernails Lee-Anne spoke in a quiet and slightly reproachful manner. 'Don't say I didn't warn you sweetheart. I think I did say that we shouldn't have left the viewings to the old bag to see to.'

'You did, but you didn't offer to take many of the days off from work, did you? And you know how busy *I've* been. I've not even taken a lunch break for a while, it's so hectic in the office.'

'You should learn to delegate, lover. You should have got an estate agent in. I told you that placing ads in the *Evening Standard* would get you nowhere. Especially when the ad is so small. You must learn to trust others to do things as well as you can, if not better.' Glancing up at Philip she saw that he was glaring at her and so smiled sweetly. 'As you said before, we'll just have to drop the price, lose out on a few thousand pounds and put it down to experience. We've done well in the past, but I doubt that anyone in their right mind will want to pay top whack for this place with a sitting tenant who refuses to keep quiet or still for more than five seconds. Never mind that woman Molly. A broader cockney you could not find even if you trawled the backstreets of Aldgate.'

'Yes, well, you wouldn't be so calm if it had been *my* idea to buy this place, would you?'

Continuing to blow her nail varnish dry, Lee shrugged. 'Probably not. It really is time you stopped whinging though, Philip, and faced up to it. We must cut our losses. I'm sure we won't be the first to have to do that. Playing the property market has always been seen as risky, and the old bat did say that she had a gentleman friend who would buy it. She even offered to buy it back herself.'

'Yes – but for several thousand pounds less than we paid her for it.'

'Sometimes lessons have to be learned, lover. Let her or her gentleman friend have the fucking place. I don't want to live here any more in any case.'

Squashing the empty beer can with his hand, Philip hurled it across the room in anger, only for it to crash against one of the four brilliant white walls. 'You can be so bloody annoying at times!'

Remaining composed and cool, Lee-Anne shrugged. 'You're entitled to your opinions but, as far as I'm concerned, it'll be worth taking a loss just to get away from that irritating cow, never mind her bloody friends.' She spread the fingers of her delicate white hand to admire her fingernails, only to see that she had smudged one of them rather badly. 'Oh damn! Now see what you've made me do!' She slammed down the bottle of nail varnish, cursing him and Grace Clark.

Downstairs, glancing at the woman who was helping her to get her life back on track, Molly couldn't help but smile. Grace was the same age as herself, give or take a couple of years, and she was full of life with energy to spare. She was holding the telephone receiver, having just dialled Mr Jackson's number, while Molly was on the sofa looking at a magazine. Grace smiled when she heard the familiar voice answer.

'Oh, hello my darling Henry! It's your ageing sweetheart here!'

'And hello to you, wicked woman,' replied her friend and part-time solicitor. 'How is it all going?'

'Oh, wonderfully well. I've so enjoyed seeing every interested party and putting them off.'

'You are a very clever girl. How do you do it, one wonders?'

'Oh, it was nothing other than my youthful looks and spirit that frightened them away,' chuckled Grace, while winking at Molly who was now sharing in the amusement. 'And as for the couple above, I can honestly say that I've driven them up the wall and across the ceiling. They can't wait to get out so I think that it is definitely time for you to make an offer. They're ready to sell and, I should imagine, at any price.'

'And you're sure that they haven't cottoned onto your little scheme?'

Flattered, she said, 'They know I plague them, but they haven't guessed that I planned it from the moment I first got their note. They're much too slow. And what does it matter in any case? Even if they have caught on, there's nothing wrong with one buying back one's former home . . . and if one gets it at a considerably lower price than one sold it for it's hardly breaking the law, is it.'

She smiled with pleasure as Henry sang her praises on the other end of the line then, replying, said, 'I've enjoyed every minute of it Henry. We'll all be able to go on that lovely long luxurious holiday with the money I make. And I've loved this little bit of acting too! Goodness knows what the neighbours must have thought. I was wondering if we might do it again sometime . . .' She chuckled. 'But first I thought that we could start by taking a lovely cruise along the Nile . . . then we could come home for a breather and then maybe jump aboard the QE2.' After a few more minutes of banter, the call ended. Grace replaced the receiver and glanced at her friend who was shaking her head in amused disbelief.

'You make me die,' said Molly, chuckling. 'Your little bit of play acting is going to pay dividends in more ways than one.'

Clearly, Lee-Anne and Philip couldn't wait to go because less than a fortnight later, Mr Jackson's offer had been accepted. He never mentioned that the mysterious party he was working for was in fact Grace – although they had their suspicions. Still, bang on the day that the contract had been signed, Grace saw a removal van pull up outside. She had told the couple that they could stay a day or two longer if it had all been too much of a rush for them, but of course they had declined her charming offer – they couldn't wait to go. They had in fact found themselves what they believed to be an even better deal, a spacious two-bedroom flat in a refurbished late Victorian six-storey block down by the river Thames in Wapping.

Standing in her doorway and smiling demurely as Lee-Anne came down the stairs to let the removal men in, Grace asked if there was anything she could do to help.

'No thank you. Except go back into your apartment and stay there. We would like to make this as swift as possible if you don't mind.'

'Oh, of course I don't mind. But the removal men might want tea. I could put the kettle on and have a pot made within minutes. You are obliged to give them a tea break I believe?'

'I said no and I meant no,' said the young woman as she opened the door to the men and then led them upstairs, cursing Grace and her bloody sing-song voice under her breath.

Going back into her apartment, Grace closed her door and sat down. At last they were going, and the house was hers again. And she did have something to thank them for – her coffers were the better for their association. She leaned back in her chair and closed her eyes to enjoy a ten-minute nap, but then she heard a tapping on her back door. Molly had come up to see how it was all going.

Pleased to see her, Grace poured them both a small glass of sherry and, while they relaxed, Molly told her about her suspicion that all wasn't well with Patsy. She explained about Patsy having been adopted, and that the man Patsy believed to be her father was in fact her uncle and her mother her aunt. 'The thing is, Grace,' she murmured, 'I feel sure that everything is going to erupt like a small volcano if Patsy finds out from someone else who her actual birth parents are. And this is why I feel that my granddaughter will need some space should it all come out. A place of her own not far away from me.'

'Well, you know how I feel about that, Molly. I told you when you first touched on your worry over this, earlier on in our friendship.'

'Yes I know you did, but I thought that you might have had a change of heart.' Molly had steered the conversation this way now that a little bit of time had passed since she had first mentioned it. She had wanted Grace to have time to think it through.

'Not at all – I'd love to have Patsy here. And I don't know why you seem so worried. Surely you can see that I would rather not let that apartment to strangers too quickly after that horrid pair.'

'Well, you've put my mind at rest. It might not come to that but I just feel that there's something in the air. Don't ask me why.'

Smiling at Molly as she cocked an ear, Grace whispered, 'Hark at Lee-Anne giving those poor removal men their orders. Why can't she just let them get on with it?'

'Who knows with someone like that. Anyway, forget them, they'll be out of your life soon. And let's face it – you don't need to rush in and get tenants do you? You can afford a little space to enjoy having no-one up there.'

'Absolutely. I shan't be rushing in like a fool where angels fear to tread. No, I've made a nice profit and I do have some savings tucked away. Still, I would love to have Patsy up there. That's what will keep us young at heart, you know. Young people around us.'

'You're right as usual, Grace,' said Molly. She finished her drink and hauled herself out of the armchair, leaving Grace on her own to enjoy the welcome sounds of the couple above moving out.

After her chat with Grace, Molly had been delighted that Gwen had popped in to see her on this lovely sunny afternoon. They were enjoying a chat about the antics of Grace and how she had managed to handle the couple upstairs, who they were all glad to see the back of. In no time at all the van outside had been filled with their belongings, and they had departed without so much as a by-your-leave.

Coming into her sitting room with a tray of fresh tea, Molly smiled and then caught a glimpse of the laundry in her oval basket that was waiting to be ironed. She had promised herself she would do it that very morning. But she shrugged off any sense of guilt because, in the bigger picture, it didn't matter any more what she did or when she chose to do it. There was no-one to nag her and no-one to demand that a particular shirt be ironed there and then. And of course there was no-one to call her a lazy cow or make her feel as if she was useless.

As she poured the tea, she said quietly to Gwen, 'Do you know what? This morning I found myself thinking about the old days . . . the early nineteen thirties, when I lived in the same street in Hoxton as Violet Kray.'

'My God . . .' said Gwen, 'so much has changed since then I can hardly believe it. She loved those twin boys to bits, didn't she? Reggie and Ronnie. She treated them as if they were royal princes, and all the while her old man was no more than a dealer in old clothes and scrap metal. But he was a lovely chap, and he liked to do a bit of prizefighting when he was younger. And he was good in the ring from what I heard.'

Easing herself into a more comfortable position with her feet up on a footstool, Molly smiled as she remembered. 'That's right, he was in scrap and he ducked and dived a bit, but then who didn't in those days? He was a lovely man and Vi was a very good mother. It's mothers like her that I feel sorry for. If that woman had known how things were going to turn out I should think she would have wished to have been sterilised at birth. What mother wants to see her sons imprisoned for life – which is what will happen to those young men, you mark my words.'

'What a terrible waste,' murmured Gwen. 'But the twins were mischievous little sods, even when they were cute kids. And sharp with it. They might 'ave behaved like little princes in the presence of their elders but not out in the streets with other kids of their age. Personally I always thought they were very intelligent. People said that they had a dark side to them even then, but I don't go along with that. I think that they were just spoilt little brats that took things too far.'

'You could be right there,' said Molly, all thoughtful. 'Lads don't start out evil – it's when they get to puberty that they change one way or another.' She sighed. 'But we lived in the East End, sweetheart, and it's got a history of villains as long as a ball of string.'

'Mind you . . . thinking about it, the other kids did use to say that they were a bit weird the way they could almost read each other's thoughts. And from the mouths of babes comes the truth,' said Gwen.

'Well, I can't dispute that. But you know what, I can't say that I ever saw them courting a girl the way the other lads did when young teenagers. And all they ever seemed to want to do was form a little gang. And yet . . . you couldn't help loving 'em when they were little.'

'I know. I feel sorry for their aunt though, Molly. She loved them boys and yet she once if not twice was heard to say that she thought the twins had been born to hang.'

'She wouldn't have meant it. That's just something that people say when they've had one drink too many. Or when overly worried.'

'I'm not so sure.' Gwen shook her head. 'I felt for all of the mothers whose sons went down the wrong road during that period of time – before and during the war, and then when it was over. I suppose we were all a bit mixed up. A bit all over the place. I mean to say . . . can you imagine what it must have been like when that sixteen-year-old-lad from Hackney was found beaten up. Kicked and beaten with bicycle chains? What must the lads' mother and father have felt like? It doesn't bear thinking about. I'm not saying that the twins did that by any means, but someone did. I heard one woman once say that since they had lived by the railway viaduct at one time it was a pity that the twins didn't play on the tracks when they were young teenagers. Now that *was* a wicked thing to say.'

'Yes. It was.' Molly glanced at her mate. 'They couldn't have meant it.'

'Maybe not. But what I don't understand are men in general. Most of them work hard for a living and see their children have food on their plates and yet they let all of that gangster business go on under their noses and do sod-all about it. How could they have stood by and done nothing when gangs slashed each other with knives? How could any of us?'

'The place was full of thieves,' Molly said, 'but beyond the villains I should think that it'll always be the friendly old East End with a mix of religion and race. No-one can change that . . . can they?'

'We'll see,' said Gwen. 'We'll see. Don't forget what Mosley said. That if we're not careful all of London will be filled with people from overseas and there will hardly be English born and bred to be seen.'

'Poppycock,' said Molly. 'Britain will always be Britain, regardless of the colour of skin of whoever lives here. And soon enough we'll all be the same after black and white 'ave jumped in bed together.' She smiled wickedly and then said, 'You know what they say about those West Indian men, don't you?'

'No. But you're going to tell me, I feel it in my bones.'

'They're hotter than the curries they eat!'

Chapter Twelve

At the same time as the women were having a bit of fun, Patsy, who had been meeting up with Danny each day after work and, if truth be told, falling in love with him, was on her way to see Molly. One evening during the week, while she and Danny had been enjoying a coffee in their now favourite Italian coffee bar, he had talked through Patsy's secret with her. He had been all for her bringing it out into the open and having done with it. And now while Danny was involved in a friendly bowling match in South London, Patsy was thinking about his advice. Maybe it would be better to get everything settled once and for all, but she didn't know where to start.

She hadn't mentioned the adopted bit to her dad again but neither had he, not even in a joking way so as to take the rise out of her for being silly. But the one person who she knew would give her good advice was her gran. So this, she decided, is where she was going: to see the head of the family tree. It was time to confront Molly, and this time there would be no backing out. She would tell her that she knew everything. And she wanted to be reassured by her gran that she would be doing the right thing if she were to tell her parents that she knew what had happened to her at birth.

Molly and Gwen were quietly listening to the Archers on the wireless when they heard the doorbell. 'I bet you any money you like that's our Patsy with that young man of hers. If it is, don't probe.'

'As if,' said Gwen, all innocent. 'And anyway what makes you think it might be?'

'Instinct.'

'It might be your old man come to fetch you back.'

'It had better not be!' Molly exclaimed as she went to open the door. And, as predicted, there on the doorstep stood Patsy, but without Danny and wearing a smile that her astute gran saw at once was false. Molly knew her granddaughter was not as emotionally strong as she would have herself and others believe.

Patsy's eyes were a touch red-rimmed because, on her way over, she had not been able to stop a few tears from coming. Although she'd told Eileen that she was fine, in truth she was more upset than ever. The thought of the adoption was waking her up in the night and it was there again first thing in the morning, before she had even opened her eyes. Now she wanted her gran to make her feel all right, the way she always could.

'You all right, Mog?' said Molly, reverting back to what she used to call this granddaughter of hers when she had played on bomb sites and was a scruffy little urchin.

'I don't know if I am all right or not. Is anyone in your flat?'

'Only Gwen. What's the matter?'

'Can you ask her to go? I need to talk to you.'

'I won't need to do that. She'll pick up on the fact that you're upset, don't you worry. You go through to the bathroom and I'll give her the nod.'

'Thanks, Nan.'

While Patsy went to the back, Molly and Gwen exchanged a look. 'I'll see you later Molly, sweetheart,' said Gwen, who was just astute as her friend, and left to go back next door.

Gwen knew just about everything when it came to Molly's family and especially to that particular girl. She knew that Molly loved her to bits, and she was now thinking that maybe Patsy had got herself in the family way, or that she had somehow found out about the family secret which, to her mind, had always sounded like a ticking bomb waiting to explode. Molly was going to need her support if this was the case. The woman had been through enough as it was. She had got rid of one horrible problem, Joe, and now she just might have another crisis much closer to the heart to contend with.

Molly had an uncanny feeling that Patsy had found out who her real parents were, and her instincts were telling her that this was why Patsy had come and why she was in a two-and-eight. Her heart sinking, she waited for Patsy to come out of the bathroom, steeling herself for what was coming because, as sure as salt was white, her granddaughter was in a turmoil over something. She wasn't the sort to get upset easily. Of course, it could be that she and that handsome boyfriend had fallen out, but knowing her the way she did, she knew that she would be cursing and swearing and giving her side of the argument, had that been the case.

When Patsy finally came back into the room, Molly felt herself go cold, because her beloved granddaughter was as white as a sheet. 'Come and sit down, sweetheart,' she murmured. 'You're shivering.'

'No I'm not,' said Patsy. 'Its summertime and it's not cold. I'm just shaking a bit after walking from the bus stop. I walked too quickly I suppose.' She sat in her favourite armchair and looked down at the floor. 'I've found something out and at first I was all right about it. It wasn't a dreadful thing really. Not really . . . But ever since I found out I keep waking up in the night with tears in my eyes and a horrible strange feeling in the stomach. Why didn't anyone say anything, Nan? I've tried to keep this to myself since I found out but I feel like I'm gonna explode into a million pieces.'

'Stop being melodramatic Patsy and tell me what's wrong.'

'I mean to say Nan . . . I would 'ave understood. It's not as if it's something terrible. That's what I keep telling myself anyway. I didn't know whether to pretend I don't know and go on as usual or talk to Mum and Dad about it. I told Auntie Eileen that I would keep the secret. Her and my secret that is. I think you know what I'm talking about.' The tears were trickling from her eyes now and she was still shivering.

Molly wasn't quite ready for this. Here was her granddaughter, who she had always seen as her baby, in a state of shock from what she could tell. 'You tell me first what it is you've found out so I've got something to go on at least.'

'I will in a minute.' She glanced at her gran's face and then shrugged before she wrapped her arms around herself. 'Auntie Eileen? Uncle Tom? Me?'

'Right . . .' murmured Molly and pinched her lips together. She had always known this day would come eventually. 'So how long have you been keeping it to yourself and bottling it up?' she said.

'Not long. I heard an old rumour from Danny that once went about. So I went to see Auntie Eileen. She told me everything and we decided that we'd go on as normal, but I haven't been able to stop thinking about it and last night's dinner ended up in the lavatory. And I woke up in the night and felt sick at the breakfast table as well. Mum and Dad heard me being sick and you can guess what that looked like.'

'What it looked like? You've not known the lad five minutes.'

'Long enough, but don't you worry. We've not been up to the things that you lot did at our age. Anyway they got it wrong, whether they thought it or not. But I couldn't bring myself to say what the matter was, and then I went and chucked up again. I feel terrible. I still feel sick. And I can hardly remember getting on or off the bus to get here.'

'It's shock Patsy love, pure and simple. Proper shock coming out. And best that it does, darling. You've had a shock. You've found out for yourself, which is what I always dreaded, but who listens to me . . .'

'But I don't really mind about it, Nan, so why do I keep being sick?'

'I just told you. Shock. It can kill, you know. Oh yes, I've known people to drop down dead with shock.'

'Cheers for that. I feel a lot better now and I don't think so.' Then, without realising it, Patsy smiled. 'You're like a mad woman at times you are. Fancy saying that to me.' Unable to stop herself smiling properly, Patsy started a chuckle which turned into laughter. Real laughter. 'I don't know if you do it on purpose or not,' she said.

'I don't know what you're talking about,' said Molly, pleased that her method had worked. 'And I never heard that chain go by the way. You didn't pull it did yer. How many times have I told since you were knee high to a grasshopper? Pull the chain even if you've only done a wee!' She then strode out of the room to do the job for her, calling out as she went. 'Two mothers? You've bloody well had three, including me!'

Coming back into the room she smiled warmly at her beloved Patsy. 'Think of it like that sweetheart, and it won't all seem bad. And think of why it was done.' Bracing herself she sat in her chair knowing how close to a flood of tears her granddaughter was – never mind herself.

'Now . . .' said Molly, softly. 'Start at the beginning and tell me how you found out.'

'Pardon? You mean you're not even gonna ask if I want a nice cup of tea?'

'No. Not this time. Would you 'ave said yes had I of asked?'

'No.'

'Well there you are then. I can still read you like a book. Blow your nose and wipe your face. Now then . . . I think that what you need is a little drop of brandy sweetheart. Brandy with a little warm milk.'

'Go on then. If you think that that can undo everything that you lot have done. Fancy not telling me? What were you thinking?'

Hearing her granddaughter talking as if their roles had suddenly reversed, Molly shrugged and got up again to make a medicinal drink for Patsy, and one for herself. She needed it. She needed a straight brandy never mind the milk.

With tears hovering again, Patsy stared down at the floor. 'I can't believe that anyone would give their baby away and then never let it be mentioned again. I thought I could come to terms with it all when Auntie Eileen told me the truth. But . . .' stopping in her stride Patsy couldn't stop the bottled-up-emotions from pouring out of her, before she went on talking.

'What were Mum and Dad *thinking*? And Aunt Eileen – how must she have felt having to do a thing like that? I wasn't a doll to be given away to someone who didn't have one. And all this time everyone knew except me.'

'No, they never. Your cousins never knew they had a sister.'

'No, Nan. Not my cousins. My *brothers*!'

'Oh whatever. It's all in the same bloody family so what difference does it make. Cousins, brothers – who gives a toss. You've probably spent more time with them than you would have done if they'd been living with you, all under the same roof and rowing probably. But there you go – if that's what's upsetting you . . . the fact that you'd like to have been brought up by Eileen instead of Alice . . .'

'No! Of course not! I love Mum and Dad of course I do! I'm all mixed up! Bloody hell Nan! Wouldn't you be?'

'Of course I would. Especially finding out the way you did.'

'Danny thought that I already knew so just don't start sounding off about him. He's not to blame. He just happened to mention it. And I've been bottling it in for weeks on end.'

'Oh dear . . . that's a real shame, Patsy love. I wouldn't be too pleased if I were to suddenly find out I had brothers from a stranger. But then, they do say that you choose your friends but you can't choose your family.'

'Oh, that's a nice thing to say, Nan. Very nice. And he's not a stranger! He's my boyfriend!'

'Nice or not, it's the honest to goodness truth sweetheart. Like it or lump it. So it's come out then, and if you want my opinion, I'm glad . . . except to say that your mum and dad will be beside themselves with grief. And before you say anything else, they didn't tell *you*, because they were protecting your feelings. And as for your Auntie Eileen, she was only too pleased that you were in a good loving home. At the time when you were born she and your uncle were working around the clock to pay the bills as it was. They hadn't planned to have another child but it happened. And unlike a lot of women in those difficult times she wouldn't even consider having an abortion.'

'Well maybe she should have done, then none of this would have happened. I don't know what to do or where I'm supposed to go. I feel like climbing into a hole and staying there. I thought I was fine but I'm not. I feel as if I want to be away from my family for lying to me for all this time. And especially *cousin* Ritchie. We've always been able to talk about anything so why couldn't *he* have told me that he was my brother? Why?'

'Because he didn't know! That's why. He's not that much older than you are Patsy, don't forget. Use your common sense girl!' Then, drawing breath and very close to spilling tears that she was determined to hold back, Molly spoke in a whisper as she laid a hand against her forehead. 'Have you asked your mother to explain why she didn't bear children herself?'

'No, I can't bring myself to, and anyway I *know* why – about Dad and everything – because Eileen told me. I can't help the way I feel. If Mum had of told me I would have understood, whatever the reasons were. I love Auntie Eileen, you know I do. It's just been a bit of a shock that's all. I feel as if I want to run away from it all. Far away. That's why I came to see you now. In case I pack my bags and leave in the night or at the crack of dawn.' With that Patsy stood up and burst into tears, then turned around and ran from the flat.

Hearing the door slam shut, Molly stared out the window and whispered, 'That's all right. She'll be back. Probably just wants a moment to calm down.' Then, sighing heavily, she slowly shook her head. 'You didn't handle that very well, Molly old girl, but there we are.' She then leaned back in her chair and shed private tears. It was all a bit much to take and quite shocking one way and another. And if truth be told, she wasn't feeling too good herself. She, just like her granddaughter, also needed a bit of time to adjust. She could be a good actress when needs be and she had covered her feelings well . . . but it was as if her heart had been gripped with a clamp when Patsy had fired those invisible bullets at her. Now all that she wanted was to be by herself. 'I don't know if I can take any more family upset,' she muttered to herself. She looked across to the photographs of her family and one of herself with Bill, the man she had loved more than life itself. 'Sometimes I wish I had gone with you sweetheart. Honest to God I do.' Then, as if the man she had loved so deeply was in the room with her she could almost hear his voice and what he would say to her: *You're bound to feel like this, old girl, but it will pass. Once you've had time by yourself to think sensibly. Of course Patsy's gonna react this way. Who wouldn't? But given time, just like you, she'll see things differently. There's not been one bit of wickedness done. Only kindness within a close-knit family. She'll see that . . . in time.*

'I'm not so sure,' Molly murmured, as if talking to Bill. All choked up. 'I'm not so sure. I don't know if she will be better or worse off for it. It's true that she's got three brothers that she didn't think she had and she's got two sets of parents who dote on her. So maybe you're right, sweetheart . . . it's not all bad is it? And she'll see that. In time. She is a sensitive girl . . . but I don't think that this will destroy her. Will it?'

Sighing heavily, she looked at the picture of Bill smiling out at her and said, 'Don't take offence sweetheart, but I think I would like to be by myself for a while. I think I shall go for a little walk. And then I can come back here to you and Gwen. She's only a brick wall away after all. I promise you that when I get back, if I feel lonely and sorry for myself, I'll go in to see my old chum.' She then kissed the tip of her finger and placed it on his photograph with a sad and a loving smile.

Then, just as she was about to collect her coat, there was a tapping on the window. It was Gwen. Opening the door to her, Molly smiled and said, 'I might have guessed you'd come back to see if I was all right. Well I am. And our Patsy has found out the truth for herself, don't ask me how or when or why. She knows that Eileen is her birth mother. I'm gonna go for a nice long walk to clear my head now.'

'All right Molly . . . but don't you walk too far and not know how to get back. Don't you do anything silly like that.'

'I've had it with silliness, Gwen.' Molly smiled sadly and shrugged. 'I should have insisted that my son tell Patsy that she was adopted. I never did feel right about it, and now it's too late. I just need to be by myself, my dear.'

'Of course you do. But you know where I am.'

'Yes I do. I'm more upset by my granddaughter's

tears than I have ever been in my life. And that's the truth.'

Alone again, Molly looked around the room at her familiar things. She wondered if she had been selfish in moving away from her roots and her family. She was the eldest and she was on the top branch when it came to the pecking order and now she believed that she had let everyone down. Suddenly feeling that she was in the wrong place at the wrong time, a surge of urgency swept through her. She needed to go back home. She started to ask herself what she was doing in Wanstead. Why she had left her roots.

She went into her bedroom and took out her light summer coat and then collected her handbag. She knew that in a small zipped compartment of the bag she had the key to the front door of her little two up, two down house. She was now assailed by doubt, thinking that she should never have left, that she should have stayed to watch over Patsy. But perhaps she could turn back the clock before it was too late. Yes. That's what she would do. Go back to the old street. She didn't know, nor did she care, whether Joe would still be living there or whether he had moved in with his tart, Glenda. Just to look at the outside of the place again would be enough, she didn't need to go inside. And of course it was possible that another family might have moved in, or that it had been boarded up by the council. There had been talk for long enough that the row of ancient houses was going to be pulled down to make room for modern maisonettes. Whatever the case, she knew that she just had to go there before she headed over to Alice and Andy to see how the land lay where her beloved granddaughter was concerned.

So, in a strange, almost trance-like mood, she left the basement flat and slowly climbed the stone steps that led up to her small black iron gate. After closing it she glanced back at the house and wondered what the hell she had done. How could she have left the home where she had been born and bred and where her family needed her. Patsy needed her. Alice and Andy needed her. And then, of course, poor Eileen, who had never wanted to give her baby away, would also need comforting. Misfortune, circumstance and kindness were at the bottom of the trouble that had now surfaced. Her son Andy hadn't been able to father his own children and Tom hadn't been able to afford to rear a fourth one – Patsy.

Looking along the pavement to her right, a habit of old, she knew that she was behaving as if she was back in old Bethnal Green and watching to see if Joe was staggering back home the worse for drink. But it didn't matter. She told herself that she couldn't expect old habits to die that easily, and walked slowly towards the bus stop to catch a red double-decker that would take her to the Mile End Gate. From there, she would meander along the Waste and Whitechapel market just so as to be back in her familiar surroundings, and perhaps even go into Joe Lyons for a nice cup of tea. She smiled sadly at the memory of how she and her first husband would go to the market every Saturday, come rain or shine, and buy fruit and vegetables from the same man who had been running his stall for years. She could so easily picture the pair of them, her and Bill, arm in arm and smiling while shopping at the stall where the red-faced old boy could always be found, wearing the same old cap, always on the slant.

With other wistful memories floating in and out of her mind, Molly was seated on the bus before she fully realised it and was gazing out of the window at the shops and the people in and around Stratford East. And when she passed the old-fashioned building that was the Forest Gate skating rink she felt a lump in her throat. This was where she had met her Bill all those years ago. She could see it all as if it was happening now. The little skirts and the long white boots attached to the skates that she and her mates hired at the place for fivepence a day, and she could hear the music that used to drift out of the public address system. Music to skate to . . .

Caught up in her recollections as if the years hadn't passed by, Molly almost missed her stop, where the conductor was dinging his bell and calling out, '*White-chapel! Off here for Whitechapel!*'

Quietly thanking him and the driver, Molly followed a few others who were getting off at this stop and, once back on the old pavement that she knew so well, she felt as if she had come home. It would never change – apart from the people. This part of London was the first port of call for those coming from abroad to what they believed to be the Promised Land. And while they were on one ship coming over here, men and women from Britain had been sailing past them on another, crossing the seas to look for a sunnier place in which to live. She had loved living in this area with all of its different kinds of people coming and going. She loved it even as a child when it was quite a different scene, with motor cars driven through the area by the wealthy folk and the poor riding on the penny-a-ticket trams.

Back in the hub of it now, she couldn't help but think about her mother and father and the way of life back in the old days. She hadn't shopped in White-chapel for some while because her old house was closer to the Bethnal Green market. Bill always used to say that Whitechapel was much nicer and livelier than Bethnal Green and Roman Road markets, and today she had to agree. It *was* lively – and possibly a bit too much for her right at that moment.

Making her way over a zebra crossing so as to be on the stall-trading side of the wide road, Molly smiled to herself because there, within spitting distance, was the London Hospital where she had been in the maternity ward on two occasions to deliver her sons. She could see the café close by where she and Bill had sometimes treated themselves to egg and chips and a mug of tea soon after they were married. Strolling along, she approached a little old-fashioned snack bar, thinking that she might go in for a cup of tea. She glanced once, and then twice, into the slightly steamed up window of the café because she thought she saw someone she recognised. At first she thought that it might be a poor old neighbour from way back when, who now looked a sad and sorry sight, a poor vagrant who had to rely on a drop of something to get him from one day to the next.

The old man was sitting at a small round table, gazing into his tea cup and looking lonesome, while at the same time brushing the shoulder of a jacket that had seen better days – it looked as though he probably slept in it.

Then, almost as if he could feel Molly's eyes on him, the man raised his head and stared at her through the misty glass. She wasn't sure if he was looking at her or not for a moment, but then the penny dropped. There was the man she had once thought she could grow to love but had grown almost to hate. Joe – the man who had caused her to run from all she knew and loved. And the curious thing was that all she felt at that moment was pity for him, as she would for any lonely person down on their luck. She didn't know whether to go into the café or walk away, but then he glanced up again, this time staring at her, and she knew for certain who he was and that he had now recognised her. She watched as he clumsily pushed his chair back, scraping the legs on the floor as he hauled himself to his feet. Once in the open doorway he drew breath and narrowed his eyes again in that way that was so familiar to her. He then pushed his head forward a little and did his best to focus as he peered at Molly. And now that she saw him in the daylight, swaying and squinting, she knew from the filthy looks he was giving her that this was quite definitely Joe Spinks. He stumbled forward, then steadied himself and, once he was in spitting distance, he noisily drew phlegm from the back of his throat and gobbed at her feet – just missing her shoe. Molly looked from the pavement that Joe had so disgustingly soiled to his face to see that he was now sneering at her with a look of contempt in his bloodshot eyes, as if she was the scum of the earth. She felt like spitting back at him but wasn't about to lower herself to his level.

With everything else that was going wrong in her world, Molly found it impossible to stop the tears that were now cascading down her cheeks and her neck. She could hardly believe that things had come to this. Joe then turned and staggered away and, before she could stop herself, she called his name. Glancing back over his shoulder, he curled his lip in a contemptuous smile and, without fear or thought, Molly strode over to him. Once close enough, as if driven by a force beyond her control, she drew back her right arm and with every bit of strength in her body, she punched her closed fist into his face. He cried out in pain and staggered backwards, losing his footing and crumpling to the ground like a sack of old clothes. Surprised by her own strength, Molly didn't move but simply stood looking at him while two other men, who clearly slept rough, struggled to get him up and onto his feet. Other passers-by simply looked away. They had no doubt seen this kind of thing many times before in this part of London. The two down-and-outs then walked him across the road towards the London hospital, where they could be guaranteed a cup of tea and a biscuit as a reward for bringing in another down-and-out who had fallen and was bleeding from the head.

Watching the three of them stumble away, Molly guessed that once Joe's head was cleaned and bandaged the three old boys would then make their way along to the Salvation Army hostel for homeless men. Staring after him in a state of shock, she looked around and could hardly remember getting to this part of London, or why she was back in Whitechapel. She told herself that she had moved away and then tried to remember where . . . Wanstead. Yes, that was it. She had moved out of her old house to a nice little basement flat in Wanstead, and she had come back to look at her old house again. She couldn't quite remember how she had arrived, but it didn't matter because she knew where she was going and she knew that she was in Whitechapel.

But she did need a fresh cup of tea and a sit-down because she was trembling. Her entire body was trembling. She needed a little pause. Once inside Joe Lyons she sat at a small table for two by the window. Her throat was dry and she needed a glass of water, followed by a freshly poured cup of tea. And this she managed to tell the young waitress, who wore a little black dress with a pretty white lace-trimmed apron, and who was smiling all friendly as she wrote her order down on a little notepad.

Molly knew that she was probably in shock after Patsy's news and then the confrontation with Joe. She had always thought that, left to himself, he could end up in the gutter, and told herself that it shouldn't have been that much of a surprise to her. Even so, she was very grateful for the sanctuary of this tea room. She needed to just sit quietly by herself and wait until she remembered why exactly she was there and what she was meant to be doing. There was a purpose to it she knew – but she had no clue right then what that purpose was beyond seeing her old house.

Fifteen minutes later, having enjoyed her hot tea and thought about all that had happened, Molly paid the waitress and gave her a threepenny tip for being so kind. She left the tea rooms and made her way slowly along Whitechapel Waste and through the backstreets until she arrived at the little turning that backed onto the park. When she reached the front door of her old house she wasn't surprised to see that the windows had been boarded up. They were probably still waiting for a new tenant. She had her key in her bag and that was the most important thing. She could go inside without the fear of anybody being in the house because she had just seen Joe going into the London hospital.

Fumbling in her bag for her key, she was so concentrated on what she had to do to get inside the house that she hadn't noticed Patsy's young friend, Rita, who had been cleaning the inside of her front window and had come out to see what Molly was up to. If Molly could have seen her own reflection in Rita's gleaming window she would have noticed how awful she looked, much paler than usual, and much slower. And Rita was worried, wondering why she had come back to the now empty house. Not wishing to startle her, she waited until she was inside the house and then, from her open doorway, quietly called Molly's name in a calm, cheerful voice as if nothing was wrong.

In the once cosy sitting room Molly, who hadn't heard her young friend calling to her, was shocked to see the mess and dirt everywhere. Empty baked bean cans lying here and there, dirty cups and plates littered the floor, and a pile of dog ends lay in the filthy grate – the grate that she had so carefully swept and wiped over before she left the house. There were also several screwed-up fish-and-chip wrappers all over the place. It was clear that Joe had shacked up in the house for a while until his laziness had made him see fit to move on. She had little doubt that the girlfriend called Glenda didn't want anything to do with him once she saw the side of the man that Molly had known all too well.

And Molly was right in her assumptions. Glenda had asked Joe to leave after only a couple of weeks or so of him staying in her immaculately clean home. The smartly dressed man who she drank with, laughed with and slept with had soon shown the other side of his character when familiarity began to breed contempt. He had then gone back to what was once Molly's lovely home and shacked up by himself. It hadn't taken long before the place was a filthy mess and his clothes dishevelled, and he had been deemed unfit for work by the company who had been employing him. From that day onwards he had slipped further and further into the gutter, on the dole and sleeping in shop doorways, drunk and out for the count. Eventually he was taken into the men's hostel in Whitechapel to live amidst others of his ilk. Men who, for one reason or another, had lost their way in life.

Ignoring the filthy mess, Molly went into the kitchen to try the cold water tap but, as she had suspected, the water board had turned off the mains supply. This must have been why Joe had gone, she thought. There was no water and no electricity. And of course no-one to clear up after him.

Dropping into an old painted kitchen chair that she had left behind, Molly cupped her face and cried softly into her hands. She had never felt so alone in all of her life. She looked around and wondered how and why things had come to this. Here she was in the house, where she and Bill Lamb had been so happy, and it was cold and dirty and derelict. Her first husband was dead, the second was a down-and-out, and her lovely home that she had kept like a little palace smelled horrible and was littered like a bombed-out ruin where tramps set up for a night's sleep.

With the tears trickling down her cheeks, Molly was just about to haul herself up from the chair and go out into the back garden for some fresh air when she heard soft footsteps in the passage and all but froze with fear. Had Joe followed her? Was she about to receive the worst hiding from him ever? Her hands began to tremble and she was about to cry out for him to leave her alone when the sweet lovely voice of Rita gently floated through from the passage.

'Is it all right if I come in Molly?' she called. And then she appeared in the doorway like an angel of mercy. 'The door was open,' she murmured, 'so I took the liberty.' She knew that Molly was far from her normal self, and she could see she was deeply upset. 'I wondered if you wanted to come into mine for a nice fresh cup of tea.'

'Oh, what a sight for sorry eyes you are. I came back

for a last look . . . I think . . . I'm not sure. I caught the bus to Whitechapel and then made my way here. I think I went in Joe Lyons for a cup of tea although it might not have been Joe Lyons. It might have just been a café.'

Placing an arm around Molly's shoulder Rita swallowed against the lump in her throat. 'Come on sweetheart. You don't want to be in here any more. Your lovely furniture's in your little flat in Wanstead, where I'll be coming in the morning to visit you.' Rita then held Molly close with one arm and walked her slowly out of the now airless unpleasant house. The house that had always been spotless and smelled of Persil and wax polish when there wasn't a cake or a pie in the oven to override the lot.

'Are you? Coming to visit me? That would be nice. My Patsy would like that. Maybe you could come together?' She then stopped in her tracks as if she was trying to remember something and said, 'She's upset. My granddaughter is upset.'

'Well, you can tell me all about it over a cup of tea. Errol's playing cricket today for his club. At Leytonstone. So I've got all the time in the world.'

'All the time in the world', Molly smiled. 'That was my first husband's favourite saying, you know. If ever I was rushing because I was late for something or the other, he would say, 'Molly sweetheart . . . we've got all the time in the world.' She smiled warmly. 'And so Errol's a cricket player now. Good luck to him.' Then with Rita's arm in hers she left the old house for the very last time, slamming the door firmly shut behind her and leaving the key inside. She no longer needed it — or wanted it.

Arriving at her front door, Rita said, 'You should have knocked for me, Molly. I would have made you a drink and then gone into your old house with you. It's understandable that you would want to come back to say farewell. Natural. Anyone would want to do that. You lived there for a long time and you were very happy once.'

Once seated at Rita's kitchen table with everything familiar to her, Molly said, 'I am glad to see you Rita. You are a little light in the dark. Did you know that Patsy has been told, sweetheart?'

'Told what?'

'That she was adopted at birth?'

'Yes, I do know; and I knew about it years ago.'

Molly then peered into Rita's face. 'How come you found out about it?'

'I've always known. Mum was working in the Hackney hospital when Patsy's aunt Eileen was there on a check-up while pregnant. They were mates and Eileen told her what was going to happen. It was a lovely family thing to do. And I'm sure that Patsy will see that.'

'No, Rita. No, I don't think so sweetheart. She came to my little apartment and was all upset and crying. It's the shock of it. It's bound to upset her. I don't really know what to do about it, or what to say for the best.'

'Don't you worry, because I *do* know what to say. But it's you I'm more concerned about. You coming back to see your house in that state.'

'I should have expected it really. I don't know what I was thinking, or what I was doing for that matter.' Molly smiled ruefully. 'My Patsy would say that I was going round the bend.'

'I don't think she would. Joe shacked down for a while and shouted the odds in the street because you'd taken your furniture and then went on about you having hidden your money. It was hilarious Molly. I wish you had been here to see it. I felt so proud of you, and of what you'd done.'

'Did you sweetheart?' Molly grinned. 'Yes, it was brave wasn't it? But I did it. I bloody well did it.'

'That's it. That's more like the Molly I know. The old man was as pissed as a newt as usual.' She smiled. 'The old bastard had a bed and clean linen that you left him and a chair and a table. He should have been grateful for that.'

'Never mind,' said Molly patting her hand. 'It's over now. I saw him you know, in Whitechapel. I think he's lodging in the men's home. He'll enjoy it more there than he did living with me. I suppose his tart thought differently when he turned up on her doorstep to shack up with her. I imagine he would have done that. But who in their right mind would want an old drunk to move in with them?'

'No one. He might have looked all right when he was all spruced up for work, but you can't fool all of the people for all of the time. That's what you used to tell me. Remember?'

'Spruced up for work. Yes, you're right. He was. That's where he met his girlfriend Glenda. She must have seen the side of him that I never saw, but there you go . . . What will be will be.'

'So why did you come back then?' asked Rita, a gentle smile on her face.

'I don't really know. And to be honest with you I don't even remember thinking that I would. Or even leaving my little basement flat to come here. I don't think that I'm quite myself. But I'll be all right. I'll be fine.'

'Of course you will. Errol will be home soon and after a nice cup of tea we'll drive you back to Wanstead and you can show us your new place. If you're up to it, that is.'

'I'll be fine. I've just had a bit of a shock, that's all.'

'You've had a lot on your plate Molly. What with being in hospital and then that bastard going off at you. And moving home is no small thing. And then of course there's Patsy and all of that.'

'Patsy?' Molly spoke in a whisper. 'Patsy . . . yes . . . I think it was something to do with her. And wanting to turn the clock back. But I can't think for the life of me what it was.'

'Something to do with her childhood?' Rita gently pressed a button that might jog her memory again.'

'Yes . . . it was. Oh yes! That was it. But I already told you that, didn't I?' She narrowed her eyes and looked into Rita's face. Her lovely warm face. 'Do you know about it then?'

'That she was adopted by Alice and Andy? Yes Molly, I just said so. She came round here to me, crying her eyes out. And I'm sorry . . . but when she told me why and she was sobbing I couldn't stop myself from laughing at her.'

'Oh Rita – surely not darling? You wouldn't have done that?'

'I bloody well would. She was going right over the top. So what if an aunt is really your mum and your mum is really your aunt? The family is close and the adoption was done with love. Lots of love.'

'And you spoke to her the way you're speaking to me about it now?'

'Yes I did. And I told her that if she didn't perk up I'd kick her up the arse. I was annoyed. She should be hugging and thanking both those women. And the men. What they did was wonderful!'

'Well . . . put like that I suppose you're right.'

'I am. I'm sorry Molly, but it really did get my goat up. When you think of all the children that are in homes because no-one wants them – and Patsy got two lots of parents all to herself. Well, almost. She's got three brothers to share one pair with. But even that should have her opening a bottle of champagne. She's got brothers that she never knew she had.'

'Oh Rita . . . you are so wise for your age sweet-heart. Thank goodness I came here today and you saw me. I think I was in a bit of shock over it all you know.'

'Well, you couldn't bloody well remember why you came so I think you must have been in shock. But never mind. And to repeat what I have heard *you* say in the past: Always look on the bright side of life. You've got rid of the old bastard, you've moved into a lovely flat next door to your best friend. And Patsy has found out that she's got two sets of parents.'

Molly smiled. 'You're right. There's really no more to be said is there?'

'No. Except that you have had to adjust to change, and then this Patsy thing, and you're not getting any younger . . . it's *you* who's in shock. *You* who should be looked after. Now, do you want me to drive you back home or do you want me to take you to your Andy's house? We don't have to wait for Errol to get back.'

Smiling warmly, Molly squeezed her young friend's hand. 'Take me back to my little flat. My home. I don't know what I was thinking coming back – I don't belong here any more. Let the mice and ants have a field day.'

'That's more like the Molly I know.' Rita leaned over and gave her a hug, and said, 'I must go and close my front door. I don't want to get burgled.'

Molly was beginning to feel more like her old self. 'We never used to have to shut our doors in the old days did we? We could keep it ajar, couldn't we? The East End's not what it used to be though. It was all right in the old days, you could leave your front door open, but not now. Not any more.'

When Rita was back in the kitchen, Molly said, 'What a topsy turvy life we lead these days. Everything seems to change from one week to another. It never used to be like that, but then we used to sometimes complain that life was dull – so there we are. It's all or nothing.'

'Well, from where I'm sitting Molly, I would say that I view your life as having changed for the better in *all* ways. You're happy in Wanstead and that secret that's been kept under wraps for all these years is out in the open. Can you imagine what Patsy's three cousins are gonna feel like when they know they've got a sister. They'll love it!'

'Well, I suppose you've got a point there.' Molly leaned back and gave long sigh of relief. 'Fancy me coming back here Rita . . .' 'I suppose I just had to come back and see it to know how lucky I am now. I love living in that house you know. It's fun. You'll love my new friend, Grace. She's posh but a real card. She makes me die at times. Do you know . . . thinking about that house is bringing it all back to me? Patsy came . . . but I told you that bit. Oh yes, that's what it was. That's what I was happy about. Grace who owns the house will soon have a flat to let. A lovely one at that. I think that Patsy might like to live in it. What do you think?'

'Oh Molly . . .' Rita smiled, 'You are funny. You're still trying to run the family. Of course Patsy won't want to live in a house with people old enough to be her gran. No matter how lovely the flat is.'

This took the wind out of Molly's sails. 'Of course she would want to. She'll be spitting distance from me.'

Again Rita laughed at her. 'Exactly. And you're her nan. Come on Molly, wake up! Would you have wanted to move in with *your* nan when *you* were eighteen and in love?'

'No I wouldn't, but that's different. I'm young for my age. I've heard you say that so you can't deny it.'

'Well, first things first.' Rita knew that she wasn't

going to get far. 'Leave her alone until she's got used to the idea of family stuff and everyone's done their crying and laughing and all of that. Then ask her.' Again Rita laughed. 'I'll say this and then I'll leave it be. I love you to bits but I wouldn't want to live under the same roof as you. You'd drive me round the bend.'

'Would I?'

'Yeah, In the nicest possible way, but you would. How many times did you used to tell me how much the price of flour has risen by? And butter. And jam.'

'So I repeat myself. How bad's that?'

'Bad. You'd be a right pain in the neck I reckon. And you know it. And you'd love every minute of driving Patsy mad without knowing you were doing it.'

Molly sniffed a touch haughtily. 'I do like to torment and tease as it happens but I didn't think it showed. So how am I gonna get back home to Wanstead then? By bus again?'

'No. Like I said, we'll go in Errol's van.'

'A van?' said Molly. 'You drive a van?'

'Yeah. Why? Nothing wrong with that is there?'

'I don't know. I don't know anything any more. The world's changing too bloody fast for me.'

'Exactly. And you expect Patsy to live under the same roof as you? Pigs might fly.' Gazing into the face of the sad old woman whom she had known for most of her life it dawned on Rita what the pair of them should do next. Where they should go.

'Well, maybe pigs did once fly – way back when dinosaurs reigned over our planet. Who knows?' Molly smiled as she gazed down at the floor. 'Anyway . . . I suppose I had best get back to Wanstead then?'

'Yes, but not straightaway. I've just had an idea. Why don't we go in the van first to Alice's house and then perhaps to Eileen and Tom's?'

'Why? Why would we want to do that?'

'To bring every thing out into the open. Hopefully your Patsy will be home by now. In fact, I'll give her a call. I've got her home number somewhere.'

'You don't have to worry about that, I know it off by heart.'

'Well, let's give it a try. I'll say that I'll pop in while I'm over there paying a visit to my mum and dad who live a few turnings away from—'

'I know where they live sweetheart.'

'Of course you do. So what do you say then? Shall I give her a call?'

'Go on then. You seem to know what you're talking about, Rita, and I'm not sure that left to myself I know what is what any more.'

'Good. Now we're getting somewhere.'

Having made the call and finding Patsy at home, Rita didn't mention that she would have her gran on board. She checked to see if her parents were there too and with a telltale sigh Patsy had said yes, then whispered down the line that she needed her and Rita to be by themselves. That she needed advice. Giving nothing away once she had replaced the receiver Rita smiled at the old woman. 'She can't wait to see me again and she sounded all right. Not in a two-and-eight or anything.'

'Well, that's a relief. The waters are calm. But not for long. Come on, you're bang onto rights. Let's go and bring the whole darn lot out into the open. Let's clean up the mess before the maggots start to hatch.'

'Oh God . . .' said Rita, cringing. 'You do come out with some things sometimes Molly.' With that she told her to get herself outside and into her van. 'And I'll be watching you. So don't go and lose your temper. Stay calm. Be a sweet old grandmother for a change.'

'To be honest with you sweetheart, all I want is a quiet life now. I'm only too happy to let those younger than me get on with things. It's worse than being in the centre of a wrangle over nothing in *Coronation Street*.'

'And which character would you be I wonder? Ena Sharples or one of her two mates?'

'The dozy one I should think.'

'Yeah? I doubt that!'

The ride through the back streets took no more than ten minutes and Rita parked her van around the corner from where Patsy's family lived. Then, walking along with Molly, she slipped her arm through the older woman's and squeezed her hand. She was pleased that the old girl wasn't trembling in the least and that her worried look had been replaced by one of calm acceptance.

Once on the doorstep Rita pushed her finger on the bell and winked at Molly while they waited for someone to answer. Having been told by Patsy that Rita was on her way, Alice was surprised to see her mother-in-law. 'Well I never . . . how did you two get together today?

Well, come in, don't just stand there.' She waved them both into the wide passage.

As they walked into the house, Molly said, 'I went back to have a last look at my house – and Rita found me.'

Alice laughed. 'Well, that *is* a surprise. Go through to the living room, Patsy and Andy are in there. He's reading the *Daily Mirror* and she's staring into space. She's in a right old mood, *and* she's been crying on the quiet. I can always tell.'

Once in the room, both of them were instantly greeted by the man of the house who was up from his chair with a welcoming smile, 'I suppose it's me who's got to make the tea and coffee while you lot have a mother's meeting?'

'Mother's meeting?' said Patsy, more than a touch sensitive than was good for her. 'Why would we want to do that?'

'Because you're women, that's why.' He winked at his daughter.

'Oh really?' said Patsy, getting up from her armchair. 'How cosy. Well, I can't say that I'm in the mood for miles of smiles all round. I'm going to my room!' Passing Rita on her way she indicated by a look that she wanted her to go upstairs with her.

Turning to the others Rita smiled and said to Andy, 'I'd love a cup of coffee, Andy. Two sugars please.' She then followed her friend upstairs and into her bedroom. Closing the door behind her she whispered loudly, 'For God's sake Patsy, act your age!'

Dropping down onto her bed Patsy lay back and

placed her hands behind her head. 'Oh thanks. You're all I need.'

'Actually . . . you're bang on right,' said Rita as she sat on the edge of the bed. 'You need me to tell you to stop acting like a spoiled brat. What do you think you're playing at? That's your family down there. The family who have all doted on you one way or another from the day you were born. How dare you think that you can behave like this?'

'I dare to because I'm upset and angry. And so would you be! How would you like to find out from a stranger that you'd been adopted?'

'I would hate it, but it's done. And it can't be undone. And you have to forget about that bit. And I've got blame on my shoulders too. I heard it from my parents years ago but was told not to ever tell you or anyone. And I kept to my promise.'

Patsy was only half listening to her now, not really taking anything in. She looked at Rita and said, 'What bit do you expect me to forget?'

'*Hearing it from a stranger*! That *was* unfortunate. But look what's come out of that chance remark. At last the family secret is gonna be talked about where it *should* be talked about. Here, in *this* house where you were lovingly brought up. And let's spare a thought for your cousins who don't know that they have a sister. How do you think they're gonna feel?'

Lowering her eyes Patsy drew a trembling breath and then quietly said, 'You make me sound like a right cow. A spoiled brat.'

'I'm only trying to shock you into seeing things

another way Pats. You know I don't really think you are a spoiled brat – I just want you to see what you've had, rather than just noticing what you haven't had. You've been lucky enough to have a lot of loving attention all round from this family.'

After a quiet pause, Patsy pinched her lips together, then looked sheepishly back at her friend. 'I suppose we should go back downstairs?'

'I think so. But only when you're ready. Just remember what your mum and dad must be going through. Never mind your nan.'

Patsy sighed. 'You're right. As always.'

'No. Not always. We often had arguments and who was right and who was wrong was fifty-fifty. At least we never had a cat fight.' Rita smiled warmly at her friend.

'That's true,' said Patsy, wiping a tear from her cheek with the back of her hand.

After a brief pause Rita spoke in a whisper, 'So . . . are you ready?'

'To discuss it?'

'That's why I brought your nan over. She's upset, she's low in spirit . . . and she thinks that everything is going pear-shaped. And she's an old lady Patsy. She might not be acting like one now that she's in that flat of hers but she's a pensioner after all. And she thinks the world of you and her family means everything to her. She's so worried about all of this that she's starting to feel guilty about leaving Whitechapel. You don't want that now, do you?'

Patsy slowly nodded. 'You're right. We'd best go down hadn't we?'

'All in your own good time.'

'I'm okay now. Come on.' Once the friends were on their feet Rita held out her arms and they hugged.

'It'll all be fine you'll see.'

Back in the sitting room, Alice looked from one to the other and said, 'Sit yourselves down. And tell me what this is all about before Andy comes back in with the tray of tea and coffee. I'm not daft. Something must be up.' She then looked across to her mother-in-law. 'Are you okay now? The colour's coming back into your face.'

'Not really, but the nausea has passed,' said Molly, comfortable enough in her chair and now easing her shoes off. 'Patsy has something to say to you. Now then, Patsy . . . tell your mother what you've found out.' She looked across to her granddaughter and smiled with a wink. 'She's not gonna bite sweetheart.'

'No,' said Patsy. 'I want to wait for Dad.'

'Wait for me for what?' said Andy, coming back into the room with a full tray of hot drinks and some biscuits. 'So what's this all about then, Mum?'

'Don't ask me, son, ask Patsy.'

Patsy looked from one parent to the other and then to her gran. And she could see by the look on Molly's face that she was giving her a silent message. A message to say that now was the time to be calm, quiet and understanding. Taking a deep breath she then quietly said. 'Can we give Aunt Eileen and Uncle Tom a call? See if they're in and if so tell them to come round.'

Alice immediately felt her back go up. 'Why, Patsy?'

'Because I want them to be here, Mum. There's something I want to say to them and to you. They're only five minutes away after all.'

'I realise that darling. But why? What's this all about?'

'Oh for heaven's sake do what she asks, Alice, or I'll pick up the phone myself and tell them to get round 'ere,' said Molly. She moved closer to her daughter-in-law and squeezed her arm as she whispered, 'It's for the best sweetheart. Trust me on this one. I promise you won't be sorry.'

'Sorry? Why would I be?'

'Precisely. Now calm down and go with the flow. We'll have a quiet chat later when we're by ourselves.'

Alice, looking into Molly's face, felt the same bond she had always felt when it came to her mother-in-law. 'All right,' she said. 'You usually know best, so whatever it is I'm okay about it.' She then whispered in Molly's ear, 'Am I going to need my handkerchief?'

'Possibly darling, possibly,' Molly whispered back. 'But they will be easy tears so you let them flow. You've been a brick all round for a very long time. So you cry if you feel like it when the moment comes.'

Deep down Alice knew what this might be about and the knot of worry that had been in her guts on and off just lately seemed to dissolve. 'I'm in your hands,' she whispered. 'We all are – as usual.'

Andy, his instincts prickling, left the room to use the phone in the passage and was back in less time than it took for there to be a long awkward silence. He knew by his gut feeling what this was all about. 'Eileen and Tom are on their way,' he said.

'Didn't they want to know what the rush was, Dad?'

'No, Patsy. I told them that you were here with your gran and your best mate Rita and that we all have something important to say.'

'And did Auntie Eileen ask what it was about?'

'No sweetheart, but I've got a feeling she knew. Am I right?'

'I think so,' said Patsy, gentle tears now trickling from her eyes.

'Well, it would be nice if one of you filled me in,' said Alice, her voice and expression giving her away. They all knew that she knew too that the time had come for the family secret to come out and be aired and celebrated.

'Let's wait for Eileen and Tom, Alice,' said Andy, choked and close to tears himself. He pinched his lips together as he glanced at his wife. 'Don't look so worried babe. This is what we both wanted but couldn't do. And guess who's at the helm as ever.'

Alice glanced at Molly, who was also clearly choked up with emotion. She drew a breath and waved a hand as if to say, *'Don't say another word or I'll fall apart.'*

Cutting through the emotional silence Rita, with a touching expression in her eyes and a soft smile on her face said, 'We wouldn't all be here together like this if it wasn't for madam here. Can you imagine how taken aback I was when I saw Molly strolling past my window along the turning, as calm as you like, and then using her key to go into the old house? I thought she was a ghost at first. She scared the life out of me. So I followed her. And I'm glad that I did. She wasn't quite her old self to say the least, but she's all right now.'

'I went back to have a last look. That's all. And I think that it might have been God's will. I'm glad I came back. If I hadn't of done we wouldn't be here now with this lovely girl. Rita's long been a friend to me as well as to Patsy. And not only since I ran away from Joe but long before it. She's been a light in the dark for has me has Rita . . . and more than once.'

Molly knew exactly what she was doing by bringing the attention to herself as well as her young friend. She had to keep things going until her other son and his wife arrived. Her instincts were telling her that this was bound to go so much better if they were all in the same room at the same time. And she hadn't to wait long because the sound of the doorbell pierced through the house.

'I'll get it,' said Patsy. 'You sit yourself down, Dad. There's something I need to say to all of you.' With that she left the room to answer the street door.

'Jesus Christ . . .' said Andy, 'If this is what I think it is . . .'

'Hold your tongue 'til you know what's what – for once in your life!' said Molly.

Andy looked from Molly to Alice and shrugged. But Alice's maternal instincts were kicking in. There could be only one reason why Patsy wanted Eileen and Tom. One reason and one reason only. She had found out about the adoption herself. They *had* left it too late in telling her. Catching Andy's eye, Alice slowly shook her head giving him a silent warning to keep his mouth shut. This was the time of reckoning which they had both been dreading. Picking up her silent message, Andy sat back in his chair and as he did so Eileen walked into the room, looking a touch sheepish, with her husband, Tom, following.

Once they were all in the room Patsy immediately broke the hushed silence. 'Okay . . .' she said. 'Now I'm gonna ask Dad to open the best bottle of port he keeps for special occasions. Because this is a special occasion. A celebration.' She looked at Andy, to see that he was chewing the inside of his cheek. 'It's all right, Dad. I'm not gonna say I'm pregnant or anything like that.'

She then gave Rita the eye and nodded towards the small cocktail cabinet, and with the help of her friend she took out the glasses and the port and set about pouring them each a drink. She handed them round while everyone waited in silence for what she had to say. Taking a deep breath she began. 'Now . . . I'm glad that we're all here together as a family and I couldn't have asked for a better and closer friend to have brought Nan round, but we'll drink a toast to Rita *and* Nan later on. First I want to raise my glass to my mum and dad and my *other* mum and dad. And how lucky am I to be able to say that? Nobody that I know can boast of having two sets of adoring parents, never mind three brothers who I thought were cousins.' She showed the flat of her hand and continued.

'Please . . . no words . . . no tears. Not right now. Just let's raise our glasses to mums and dads. Even though my brothers are not here to join in, let's toast the most generous, understanding, warmest family in the world. Ours. To our family!'

Speechless, Alice, Andy, Eileen and Tom did as Patsy asked. She then looked at them and said, 'Thank you all from the bottom of my heart for what you did. If it hadn't been for the four of you I wouldn't have had the most fantastic upbringing. You've each loved me in your own way. And of course we mustn't dare forget the very special person in this room who is and always has been at the top of the tree. Because without my gran – *none* of us would be here!'

'I'll drink to that,' said Eileen, and raised her glass again. 'To Molly!'

The toast done, the room went quiet as each of them tried not to shed tears. Emotions were all over the place. But the most poignant thing was that no questions were being asked as to how and when Patsy had found out about the family arrangement. And no excuses were being put forward as to why the adoption had come about. And this was because Patsy in her wisdom had left no space for such sentiments. They were there to celebrate, not to commiserate. And it was of course Molly who cut through the heartrending mood in the room.

'Jesus Christ,' she said. 'It's taken the youngest of the lot of us to know how to go about this. Rita and Patsy. So do you know what? I think it's *they* who we should be toasting. Not us. We all cocked up by keeping something special a secret and these two youngsters have got every right to laugh us out of the room for doing so. But no. Not our Patsy. She's just said that she's got not one set of parents but two. And not just three cousins but three brothers. We've got a lot to thank these two youngsters for.'

Then, cutting through the moving scene came the sound of the doorbell. Patsy guessed who this would be because Danny had said he would be popping in during the afternoon. 'Well, go on then – give me and Rita a toast so that I can open the door to Danny.'

'Here's to Patsy and Rita!' said Molly, getting it all over and done with. She had had more than enough of having to keep her emotions in check today. The door bell sounded again. 'Go and let him in Patsy. We can all relax now. Thank Christ.'

Leaving them to it Patsy went to open the front door and after a brief hug and a peck on Danny's cheek she led him into the room where the family were now quietly sipping their drinks. It was over. The secret was out. All boded well.

'Now then you lot,' said Patsy, 'Danny's got something to tell the mums and dads so can we pay attention please.' She smiled cheekily and then looked at her boyfriend. 'Go on then. Tell them.'

Blushing a touch, Danny said, 'But Patsy how did you know? I was keeping it a surprise. Who told you?'

'Told me what?' said Patsy.

'About the car.'

'Danny . . . what are you talking about?'

'My light blue Anglia parked outside. It's done two years but it looks brand new.' He turned to Andy. 'I wanted it to be a surprise.'

Andy, unable to contain a chuckle, said, 'So what were you expecting him to say then, Patsy?'

Patsy looked at Danny and raised an eyebrow. 'My nan's here, Danny. Does that ring a bell? My nan. You having to find yourself a flat for when you project-manage the demolition and rebuild of the store?'

Danny smiled and then laughed. 'Sorry everyone. I forgot all about that because of my car. It's not brand new but it's beautiful. It rides like a baby and the chrome has hardly got a pit mark on it.' He then looked at each of them as they looked at him, waiting for what it was that Patsy wanted him to say. Then the penny dropped.

'Oh right, yeah. I thought that I might rent that flat above yours Molly? In that lovely big house.'

'Well I never. I'd never thought of that,' said Molly. 'But it would kill two birds with one stone – I'd get to see you and Patsy.'

Andy then chipped in his pennyworth. 'But won't you be working in Whitechapel on the new super-market project? I thought your dad was gonna fix up one of them back-street houses for you. Or was that all pie in the sky?'

'No, but I just fancied the idea of Wanstead, that's all. It's only a bus ride away. It's practically in the East End. I wouldn't be any trouble and I don't play my records too loudly. And the family company would pay the rent so I wouldn't be a cheapskate having to penny pinch.'

'And I thought you was gonna ask if you could slip a diamond ring on her finger. Typical man.'

'Nan!' exclaimed Patsy, embarrassed. 'We've not known each other that long!'

'Er . . . hang on a sec,' said Danny. 'Can we slow down a bit here?' He then turned to Molly and gave her a mock scolding look. 'As it just so happens I did want to talk to Andy – privately. But since you've put me on the spot I'll say what I planned to say now.'

'Whoa . . . slow down, son. Slow down. If you *were* gonna ask if you can get engaged to my Patsy we'll need a little chat in private, you and me. And apart from me, you're gonna have to ask my brother as well.' Andy glanced at Tom and then winked. 'Do you agree?'

'Absolutely,' said Tom, clearly as pleased as punch by what his brother was doing. 'The three of us'll go for a pint in the week. That way me and Andy can get to know you better, son. And apart from diamond rings and all that, I've got something to thank you for. We all have. I believe it was you who brought the skeleton out of the cupboard – even though you didn't know that one was in there.'

'Yeah, all right. Enough said.' Molly gave Andy a sly wink and then did the same to her other son, Tom. 'I'll have a word with Grace about the flat, but I'm telling you now . . . there'll be no hanky panky. No funny business. My granddaughter might have two sets of parents Danny boy, but I've only got one grand-daughter. So be warned,' she said with a mischievous smile. In her own sweet and artful way she had got what she wanted.

*

There really was no more to be said. The head of the family had had the last word and as she looked about at them all, she felt proud. They'd had their secrets, but everything had turned out for the best. Patsy was happy and so were both sets of her parents. All boded well, she thought. It felt like a new era — the times were changing, and they would get through it as a family. And right now, it seemed there was lots to look forward to — a wedding on the cards for her darling grand-daughter, and the cruise of a lifetime for Molly and her chums. Who knew what was around the corner, but for this moment, life was good. She was, after all was said and done, the oldest bird in the tree, and she deserved to be on the topmost branch. At least she thought so.